ADVANCE PRAISE FOR
FLASHPOINT:
Book One of the Underground

Flashpoint is jam-packed with spiritual truths, and with Creed's unique style of writing, combined with his geeky knowledge of techno-babble, and incredible kung-fu style fight scenes, the story will certainly keep your head spinning. I highly recommend this book for anyone interested in end-times speculative fiction.
—M.L. Tyndall, author of *The Redemption* and *The Reliance*: Legacy of the King's Pirates series

Move over, *Matrix*, here comes the Underground. An explosive futuristic thriller infused with humor and spirituality, FLASHPOINT delivers the goods. Set in a dark future where technology has nearly usurped faith, FLASHPOINT grabs hold and launches the reader into a mind-bending race for survival, never letting go until the final breath-taking moments.
—Daniel I Weaver, author of *When Nightmares Walk*; Christian fiction reviewer

Creed is a gutsy writer who gets you into the story at light speed, builds a believable futuristic world that keeps you wanting to find out more.
—Steve Macon Y30 Sci-Fi staff, yellow30scifi.com

Bursting with vivid neon colours and the sounds of the future, Flashpoint will take you places in your soul you've never been before. A treat not just for your mind and spirit, but for eyes and ears as well.
—Grace Bridges, author of *Faith Awakened*

Creed provides a thrilling tour through dingy city scenes with a snappy Film Noir dialogue style that permeates the book. The novel twists like a pretzel through multiple dead ends, blind leads, and unexpected turns to make for an enjoyable and satisfying whirl through Creed's dark Chicago of 2036.
—Adam Graham, author; host of the Adam Graham Program

Frank Creed pushes the boundaries of Christian fiction with Biblical cyberpunk—when he talks about "God in the machine," he's quite literal. He's been thinking and playing in the genre since long before William Gibson made it popular—and Creed can give Gibson a run for his money.
—Karina Fabian, author; reviewer for Virtual Tour de Net

Imagine a book that combines the super-cool action of *The Matrix* with a big portion of *Left Behind,* and then mix in a few tablespoons of Frank Peretti's *This Present Darkness* and the powers of all the superheroes you know. This only begins to give you an idea of what to expect in Frank Creed's futuristic Speculative Fiction book, *Flashpoint*.
—Catherine Hassan, reviewer TeenAge Magazine

Flashpoint is an excellent fast-paced read. Even non-Christians will enjoy the action in this novel. Kudos (and plenty of Winterfresh gum) to Frank Creed for a job well done.
—Heidi Hecht, sci-fi author

Most importantly, Creed manages to balance techno-punk sci-fi and Christianity to near perfection. I would highly recommend this book to anyone who likes biblical fiction or science fiction.
—Stoney M. Setzer, teacher; author

Matrix, move over! Frank Creed delivers non-stop action and pulse-pounding suspense in the best book I've read this year! Frank's dry wit laces the story with humor, breathing life into unforgettable characters, in a future you won't wish to see. Frank Creed's style is pure genius, and you'll delight in the unique language he brings to this novel. Flashpoint, this first book in Mr. Creed's series, is sure to leave you clamoring for more!
—Deb Cullins-Smith, author and poet

In a world where Sci-Fi rules the shelves and the box office it's about time that Christians established a place among them. Flashpoint delivers the Gospel in a style that will have everyone wanting more. Frank's writing is a colossal step towards delivering the Gospel to a new generation and an inspiration to future writers that Science Fiction and God are not mutually exclusive.
—Jonathan O'Hearn, Pastor

A thriller that touches the soul, Flashpoint by Frank Creed hits the ground running. A run-for-your-life adventure riddled with action, suspense, and what it means to serve the Lord in times of severe persecution.
—Donna Sundblad, author of *Windwalkers* and *Pumping Your Muse*; fantasy columnist at inspiredauthor.com

This is a fun read with adrenaline-pumped moments and lots of attitude, refreshingly creative and artistic.
—Rachel Starr Thomson, author of *Heart to Heart*

Tight plotting, convincing setting, and intriguing technology work together with believable and sympathetic characters to draw the reader in and refuse to let go.
—Karen McSpadden, author; reviewer for *Christian Sci-Fi Journal*

I find that the characters were believable and it was very difficult not to want to cheer on Calamity Kid as he fought against the uber bad guy in the last few chapters of the book. I was highly mad that the book even had to end. I wanted to see more stories based in this world. It was hard to leave. This is destined to become a cyberpunk classic.
—Joseph Ficor, author of *Rocketships, Cherry Blossoms, and Epiphanies*

I'm near tears. This story is just pure dynamite. Whatever I try to say about the climax would not encompass even a fraction of the nerve-racking, breath-taking, heart-leaping action and emotional attack of it. Humour. Suspension. Originality. Mystery. Emotion. And something to tell the world. Something about values long ignored. Something an agnostic like me embraces as vigorously as any Christian. Something about caring and helping. Something about love.
—Malin Solstraud, fantasy author

FLASHPOINT

Book One of
THE UNDERGROUND

FRANK CREED

A Lost Genre Guild Book

A Publication of The Writers' Café Press
Indiana

This is a work of fiction. All the characters and events portrayed in the stories in this anthology are either fictitious or are used fictitiously.

FLASHPOINT: Book One of the UNDERGROUND

by FRANK CREED

Scripture taken from the HOLY BIBLE, NEW INTERNATIONAL VERSION®. NIV®. Copyright© 1973, 1978, 1984 by International Bible Society. Used by permission of Zondervan. All rights reserved.

Cover Art by Cynthia MacKinnon

A Lost Genre Guild Book
Published by The Writers' Café Press
Lafayette, IN 47905
www.thewriterscafe.com

ISBN:978-1-934284-01-8
LIBRARY OF CONGRESS 2007928666
Creed, Frank.
        Flashpoint / Frank Creed. -- 1st ed.
        p. cm. -- (Book one of the underground)
        LCCN 2007928666
        ISBN-13: 978-1-934284-01-8
        ISBN-10: 1-934284-01-7

        1. Fundamentalists--Fiction. 2. Persecution--
Illinois--Chicago--Fiction. 3. Chicago (Ill.)--Fiction.
4. Science fiction. 5. Christian fiction.   I. Title.
II. Series: Creed, Frank. Book ... of the underground; bk. 1.

        PS3603.R442F53 2007   813'.6
                                QBI07-600152

First Edition: SEPTEMBER 2007
Printed in the United States of America

This book is dedicated to . . .

The Boss. Capital He gets top billing, and all the props. And I don't mean Springsteen.

Second only to Him, is my editor and wife, Cyn. From a continent away, He introduced destined soulmates, who'd never have met unless we were in exactly the same unlikely place in exactly the right unpredictable time. Cyn, my love, there is absolutely no way I'd have gotten to this place without you, and my undying gratitude is yours. No, you.

My family. Mariah, Sean Richard, Lydia, Martin, Little Grandma. Joe and Amber too. So many hours have been sacrificed on the alter of fiction. I pray I don't regret the loss. His will.

With nothing to gain, M.L. Tyndall, author of the Legacy of the King's Pirates series (Barbour), and Stephen L. Rice, author of the League of Superheros series (The Writer's Cafe Press), offered literary and theological criticism. Readers who enjoy Flashpoint—blame these talented authors. Look for their books at lostgenreguild.com.

Christa Mullen, Deborah Cullins-Smith, Karri Compton, Karen McSpadden, Audrey Hebbert, Karri Compton, Donna Sundblad, Malin Solstroud, Daniel I Weaver, Andrea Graham, and A.P. Fuchs. Some of you know what you've done, and the rest are all Jimmy Stewart Wonderful Life how much you've contributed. Virtual pizza all-around. If we're ever in the same place at the same time, I'm buying. Your friend got published and all you got was this stupid dedication.

Everyone at Elfwood.com, Particularly Larry N, J Schroeder, Christina Deanne, Mandy "Mandymouse" Burnham, A.P. Reckert, Heidi Hecht, Kim Schoonover, Naomi E. Thrower, James Bowers, founder of the Herscher Project, Eugene Erno, and Chris Jackson, winner of the USA Booknews Bestbooks 2005 award in Fantasy and Science Fiction. For your inspiration, literary criticism, and encouragement, you have my gratitude.

Sharron E, and Marsha Stewart, my Kaneland High School creative-writing teacher. You two laid tracks. Without you, I'd never have arrived at this station.

And to the folks who plunked down hard earned cash? This is for you.

Now, into the Underground!

THE UNDERGROUND

Timeline . . .

TIME LINE

1980s

- news media refers to Islamic terrorists as "Fundamentalist" terrorists

- Christian Fundamentalists only substantial psychographic left who believe right/ wrong to be as real as laws of physics--not just man-made rules

1990s

- group of politicans in the old US government want to legalize concepts Bible calls wrong
- Fundamentalists only group to speak up

- many of the same politicians lose election
- powerful coalition assembles to seek downfall of Christian Fundamentalism
- later this year Supreme Court rules religious speech not protected freedom under First Amendment

early 2000s

- after 9/11 G.W. Bush creates Office of Homeland Security in response to terrorist threats
- attacks on other US cities over next decade prove government can't guarantee safety

- 3-day period in August known as "Clinic Crisis." Bombs rip over 100 abortion clinics nationwide
- Ebola outbreak scourges population of Austin, NV
- news reports blame *National Right to Life* movement
- though no arrests made, "Clinic Crisis" forever marks Fundamentalists of any religion as "terrorists"
- US enters into state of emergency
- OHS creates Federal Bureau of Terrorism to place Fundamentalists ("terrorists") into mental institutions

late 2000s

- medical experts recognize Fundamentalism as mental illness
- report in Journal of AMA declares people dangerous when they think they're part of God's plan and begin to think they are superior to non-believers
- report states, historically, Fundamentalism has claimed lives of millions and because of this, people are not safe

2012

2016
- revolution in Nigeria sparks Global Oil Embargo; 2nd Great Depression begins
- international peacekeepers patrol U.S.
- OHS hires millions of unemployed, forces workers to sign citizenship papers denying the Koran and Bible
- ID chips with police, medical, credit records injected into every worker's left hand
- OHS laborers mount cameras on every streetlight; build razor-wire topped fences
- cities divided into wards; rural areas into counties
- government maintains fences will control terrorism, rioting, killer-virus outbreaks

- •Federal government orders cities to re-zone wards according to usage
- •economic wards, industrial wards and residential wards are policed
- •"Lost wards," where rioting has destroyed whole city blocks, erupt into peacekeeper/ gang wars
- •OHS empties jails and mental hospitals into Rehabilitation Wards
- •rehab patients lose rights, freedoms, and US citizenship

2023

2026

- •BOC webcast exposes U.S. government ceded national sovereignty to global government as far back as 2008
- •for first time in history, representatives of the One State address citizens of the world
- •One State claims united world government necessary to protect humankind from Fundamentalist terrorists

2029

2033

- •Saints underground in Chicago Metroplex's "Lost Wards" post classified documents on Web
- •government denies "Clinic Crisis" in 2008 was first-strike-- counter-strike operation of OHS
- •government claims documents forgeries

- •Saints of Chicago underground, now called "Body of Christ," strike again
- •new documents reveal policy of peacekeeper service in a different culture not based on theories of multiculturalism, but studies performed by Soviet Union in 20th century
- •translated text reads: *it is easier for soldiers to shoot people who are very different from themselves*
- •again, government denies charges

**2036
Present Day**

Flashpoint [Function: noun] 1: the lowest temperature at which vapors above a volatile combustible substance ignite in air when exposed to flame 2: a point at which someone or something bursts suddenly into action or being 3: TINDERBOX: a potentially explosive place or situation

—merriamwebster.com

CHAPTER ONE

THIS IS IT, WE'RE HERE. Climb the slope on the right shoulder. Hide in the beams as best as you can. Whatever you do, stay under the bridge. If you come out, the cameras will spot you and all this will be pointless."

The highway overpass loomed ahead. My father continued, "The car can't be hidden under the bridge too long or they'll figure out where you went. You're gonna have to jump out while we're moving."

It was time.

"Sometime, someplace, I know we'll see each other again. Use your freedom well. Now!"

That single word launched me out the door. As it swung shut behind me, Dad screamed at Jen, "Go!" I stumbled into a run watching her bail-out. The Geo Aphid sped off.

* * *

Jen had sprawled on the street. I helped my kid-sister to her feet. She'd hurt herself, but the bleeding amounted to pink smears on the palms of her hands.

"C'mon, let's hide."

"Dave!" She whimpered my name, but followed.

We clambered over the rough, fist-sized stones that covered the slope. At the top, the slope met the girders that supported the road above us. I pulled off my t-shirt and cleared the I-beams of spider webs and bird droppings. We slumped on opposite girders, facing each other.

Jen's wide eyes glinted shell-shocked madness. "We'll save them! Whoever comes for us, if they'll help us, we could get them out!"

"We don't even know where they'll be taken," I grumbled.

"I'll hack that off the Web!" She reached for anything to pull herself from calamity's quicksand.

I was in no mood to do this. "You don't have a com-vision, Sis."

Tears welled-up in her eyes again. I didn't want to start an argument, and I definitely didn't want to shatter the kid's hopes. "I want our family back too, Sis, but Rehabs are usually guarded."

We'd do well just to avoid the peacekeepers that had to be looking for us. Who could Dad trust to help us? How would they get us out from under the bridge without anyone seeing? Where could they hide us from searching peacekeeping units? How would we even get food? The hum of a motor grew near and we both shrank back against cold steel. A car passed beneath.

I tried to turn the conversation to something else. "I hope Mom and Jeff are okay."

Jen buried her face in her hands, her shoulders rocking with sobs.

Real smooth. Nice going, fool. "I'm sorry Sis. Like Dad said, we gotta have faith—" I kicked myself.

When her tears ran out, Jen scowled and whispered, "If we're His children, why's He doing this to us?"

I left her in silence. Like I could answer that. How could He even allow a world where belief in the Bible made one a terrorist? Ripping apart our family would teach, what? What kind of lesson was this? I finally thought about how parents treat children. "I think it's like when we're kids. Mom or Dad punished us, and made us try things we didn't want to. Having fun or being happy all the time isn't the most important thing. I guess God's like that, too. Dad said we're being taught something, remember?"

"Yeah. How to miss your mom, and worry if you'll ever see her again," she pouted.

Little sisters out there, I speak for big brothers everywhere when I ask, please don't stick us with hard questions that you've already answered. Very annoying.

I dug my pack of Winterfresh Extra out of my jeans' pocket and let the conversation die. We moped into a sullen silence, our hopes shredded by our thoughts.

Spattering raindrops came and went. So did tears. Minutes piled into hours. Tracking time became impossible. That made me think of my e-wallet with the broken watch function. I powered it up and clicked past the com-vision white and yellow homepages. I selected the picture frame feature. Jen and I passed it back and forth, watching our party vids. Jen's driver's license and Jeff's twenty-first birthday last month. My high-school graduation party two years ago. Jeff and I moving into our first apartment . . .

Bad idea. I pocketed the e-wallet. Our thoughts spiraled into deep gloom, leaving Jen to weep her way out, and again we sat in silence.

My gum had lost its Extra-long-time flavor for what must have been hours before I realized the building I'd been staring at was a church. The bridge cut off its steepled roof. The One State allowed only one kind of church. Dad told me about people who called themselves Christians, but believed the Bible to be myth, and equal to the Koran, Upanishads and Bhagavad-Gita. With no truth to argue over, 500 years of church splits healed overnight. They called themselves the One Church. No points for creativity, but I guess it represented their unity.

Dad said when he'd once asked a One Churcher how he knew that love was any better than hate. The man had said the answer's in our heart. Dad then asked what was wrong with the hearts of criminals. There, next to the bridge, out in the open, people were being taught to find love in a broken heart. Here, forced to hide under the bridge, were children of the Heart Surgeon.

If I leaned down I could see a sliver of eastern sky. I began watching for dawn's brush to paint the clouds. Pigeons roosting under the bridge started their morning cooing. Cool dampness raised goose bumps on the backs of my arms. Finally, my shivering grew worse than my t-shirt's filth. I shook it out and put it back on.

Then the end came.

CHAPTER TWO

POWERFUL BIOFUEL ENGINES SOUNDED, and grew loud—fast.

In as much time as it took me to sit up straight, four peacekeeper Humvees jerked to a stop under the bridge. Jen's tear-tracked face twisted in panic's horror. Hugging our knees, we flattened ourselves against the girders trying to become part of them. A door squeaked open to eject a uniformed man, his face glued to a flip-com screen. He paused for a moment before looking right up at us. My stomach did ugly things as he pointed, yelling in German. Green uniformed peacekeepers poured from the vehicles to line up on our side of the road. Captain Flip-com barked an order and six of them started up the stony slope.

Save Jen! Defeated, I stood. "You found me." I started toward them, hoping they'd somehow miss her.

Then movement, from the very corner that Dad had turned. A figure in an oilskin duster and thick-soled boots strolled down the sidewalk toward the scene. The rain fell in a light mist, but his hood was down. A black Samurai-style ponytail swung with his every stride. His face betrayed oriental blood even though mirrorshades hid his eyes. Walkin' in the rain. Wearin' sunglasses. You know—just in case the sun rose in this overcast pre-dawn sky.

A few peacekeepers turned rifles in his direction. Waving their free hands, they ordered him away.

To my disbelief he actually smiled and continued right toward them.

I decided this was either the first time he'd left the desert island he'd been raised on, or he'd lost his mind and was out looking for it.

More peacekeepers noticed him and fanned out to face the newcomer. Captain Flip-com shouted orders, and the soldiers coming toward us stopped. One close to the stranger yelled an English word known by all peacekeepers: "Freeze!"

Lured by sounds and my surprise, Jen slid from her perch.

Still smiling, the stranger stopped, folded his arms, and said something in their own language. They looked to each other, muttering in angry tones. Three started toward him. All held their rifles more seriously.

The stranger touched the fingertips of both hands to his forehead, then spread his arms. Air between the stranger and the soldiers shimmered—heat off a July blacktop. Peacekeepers flew backward as though a truck had plowed through them. They tumbled to a stop and lay still. Whatever he'd done had downed nearly half of them, including the six on the slope.

Captain Flip-com barked an order and rifles cracked, but bullets passed through empty space. The stranger leapt as though he'd been launched from a trampoline. Turning somersaults in the air, he landed on his feet near the top of the slope between them and us. He'd just jumped more than ten meters. Uphill.

Again, he touched his forehead and swept his arms wide, cartwheeling more soldiers into another time zone. Only a handful remained. By the time the survivors swung their rifles, he was dive rolling down the slope, a human cyclone, his duster and ponytail whipping behind him.

Peacekeeper rifles tracked him, but without warning the stranger came up in a crouch, a pistol in each hand. Twin guns gave off quick dull thumps and soldiers spun to the ground without getting off a single shot.

He stood and the guns were gone from his hands as though they were never there. "Call off the heat 'cause you guys are done," he announced, polishing fingernails on his coat's lapel. Wit died on the deaf ears of senseless opponents. It looked as though some giant child had left his green army men strewn across the driveway.

The stranger stared at one of the empty Humvees they'd left running. It drove out from under the bridge to park sideways in the street just beyond the fallen peacekeepers. Then the next one did the same. One at a time, the other two vehicles blocked off the street on the other side of the bridge. All at once, their light bars lit up the area in wildly flashing blue. He turned and made straight for us, smiling again.

"We don't want anyone to get runn'ded over," he explained.

The last vehicle had parked just in time. A yellow rental truck pulled up to the intersection, paused a long while, then turned away.

The stranger stopped before us, and bowed deeply at the waist and neck. "David and Jen Williams, you may call me Legacy. I'm sorry, but the closest thing I have to a password is: Your *Flashpoint* was dirt-cheap."

CHAPTER THREE

H-HOW'D YOU D-DO ALL THAT?"

"I was reformed when I joined the Body." He said it as though it answered everything.

"Huh?" came my clever response.

All I got was a scrunched-up look. "I know you've got questions, but the PKs have backup units rolling, so we gotta move fast. For now, do what I say and give your tongues a rest." He jerked his thumb over his shoulder. "That yellow truck driving away behind me is gonna circle the block once. Next time it pulls up to the stoplight, we're gonna jump in back. Hold out your left hands."

Jen and I looked at each other and did as ordered. "We can't leave the bridge."

He ignored my objection, unclipped a black object from his belt, flipped a switch and touched it to the backs of our hands. "This'll fry your I.D. chips. Most people don't know it, but there's a tracking signal built into them. That's how they found you. Your dad was smart to hide you under this bridge. It razzed your signals and bought you time. They had to physically retrace his route in order to find you."

"Just a sec, I gotta check somethin'." He angled his head up and away from us, doing a mime impression of a satellite dish, and went stone still.

Jen elbowed me and turned her palms upward as if to say, "huh?" I shrugged, shaking my head. Shivering and hugging herself, she frowned at distant siren screams.

Legacy turned those mirrored shades back at us. "When I say run, we've got one minute to be in the back of the truck with the door closed, but don't leave the bridge 'til I say, 'kay?"

"No! We can't leave the--".

Legacy cut me off. "A Hack friend of mine just recorded the truck at that intersection. She'll feed the image back into the street cams the moment the truck stops. The cameras will be blind."

He looked up the road. "I was almost too late and for that I'm sorry. I left as soon as I could. Even prepped on the fly. Razz, this is gonna be close." The sirens wailed dangerously close when the truck finally rolled up to the light.

"Run!"

He ran away from me like fast-forward. Even in my years on the high school track team, I'd never seen anyone move like that. The guys who'd placed at the state meet were said to have world-class speed, and even they couldn't have kept up. Not even close.

We splashed through puddles and sodden grass in a straight line to the truck. He'd opened its rear door and stood waiting inside when I leapt in. Jen, fast for a high-school com-vision geek, slid in on her belly just steps behind me. Legacy slammed the door, plunging us into darkness.

The truck lurched. Thrown off-balance, my rump found floor the hard way. The truck turned away from the bridge and trundled up the hill. We were still picking up speed when the sirens screamed past us. By Doppler effect, I counted six more PK Hummers, and something I couldn't place, all fly past the truck.

I scooted, shoes squishing rainwater, until I bumped into the truck's inside wall. "What was that weird siren?"

"Federal Bureau of Terrorism ready team," he spat the name as though just saying it tasted bad.

That made no sense to me. "Why would the FBT be called in for a couple of runaways?"

"They're not here for you. There's been no response from four peacekeeper units since they found you. Not to brag, but the only time that happens is when a Sandman dozes the whole patrol."

You could feel ice forming in the black silence. Jen's voice squeaked small and afraid, "Sandman?" From what the com-vision said about terrorists, Sandmen were the venom in the viper.

"That's my job as a Saint. Sandmen are the muscle in the Body of Christ."

"Oh, goody gumdrops," Jen's tone found him guilty, "I can't believe our father left us with a man whose job is killing peacekeepers." A true CV-geek with sister-manners, Jen rubbed people like rough wool on sunburn.

More silence. It reminded me of sand in my swim-trunks: very uncomfortable. It ended when Legacy calmly stated, "He didn't."

"Don't lie!" she cried. "I saw you pull guns and shoot those men back there!"

His tone stayed gentle. "You gotta trust me when I say your father put you in the best hands he knew of. He's a well-mannered man. Pity he hadn't passed that on to his daughter." The last part was a blade over a whetstone in the blind dark.

"The men I shot will wake up in about two hours. The tranquilizer rounds I use affect the nervous system instantly. I'm called a Sandman because I only put people to sleep."

Now it was Jen's turn for awkward silence. If she could rub a genie out of a lamp I knew her first wish would be that she hadn't said that. "I'm . . . I'm sorry."

"Accepted—and thanks. Your family's just been slagged so I'm sure you're not quite yourself. Besides, I know the com-vision makes us sound like monsters. They want folks to fear us so it's not really your fault. Don't believe everything you find on the Web."

I came to her rescue and changed the subject. "How do you know our dad? He'd always said he knew someone who'd help if we were in trouble, but he'd never say any more."

"Mmm . . . I'll just say we go way back and leave it at that. We've got some time, though. Let's hear some a' those questions."

Jen spoke right up. "Did they get Dad? What happened to our family?"

"I did some checking on the way to get you. Nothin' on your dad, but your family and all the others arrested in the raid were headed to Rehab-Nine. That is, Rehabilitation Ward Nine, run by the Ash Corporation. They'll be questioned, uploaded, and forced to work twelve hour days in one of the Ward's factories."

"Uploaded?" she pressed.

"For the last fifteen years, makers of biochips have been using DNA strands in biochips to carry—"

Jen cut him short, "—the binary code used in com-visions. These biochips can even be inserted into living creatures and mesh with their biology more effectively than synthetic chips, I know. I mean, what do they upload?"

"Our father calls her e-girl," I explained.

"Heh, I see why. The chips are loaded with programmes that monitor body chemicals and brain waves. In other words, feelings and thoughts. Prisoners' minds are broken then fixed so they're, um . . . better citizens. It doesn't work on some inmates."

That one rested on us both for a while. Legacy didn't push us. It was worse than we'd thought. If we ever saw them again, they'd be strangers.

New topic time. "What will you do with us?"

"That depends on you. What should I do with you?"

Jen spoke my mind, "Teach us to do what you do."

"Yeah. Make us Sandmen," I added.

"You'd have to become part of the Body of Christ," he warned.

From what I understood, we already were. "Okay."

"I know your father, but I don't know either of you. Why should I do that? What makes you part of the Body of Christ?"

CHAPTER FOUR

I THOUGHT FOR A MOMENT. "We believe in God."

"So does Satan. There's more to it than that."

"Well . . . we trust that God's told us the truth in the Bible. We need Him. Christ's blood covers our failures."

Legacy agreed, "Then yes, your relationship with God is different from when you were born. That's what makes you a member of the Body. If you join the underground Saints known as The Body of Christ, what will your goals be?"

Jen answered almost before he'd finished, "To save our family."

"And?"

"And our church," I added.

"And then?"

I knew where he was going. "Work together to change things so Fundamentalists can live free of the terrorist label."

"And after that?"

I thought my answer was pretty much what the Body worked toward. Our brains churned before Jen blurted out, "End human suffering!"

"There've been people who've attempted this throughout history, but Christians know better. As long as mankind is fallen, humans will suffer until the second coming. How will you succeed where others have failed?"

This time, neither of us had an answer, so he gave us a hint. "Family, country, and even the world are too small; tell me why."

Minutes went by. What could be bigger than helping others and making the world a better place?

Wait a minute . . . that was it. We'd been thinking of ourselves: of humans. "Jen, do you remember what Dad said right before he dropped us off? We'd learn how to serve God in new ways. We've been thinking of people, not God. We help people, because that's how we serve Him."

"Yeah . . . Dad said God's moving us on in order to teach us."

"Well said. I really didn't think you two would be ready, but you're more ready than most who come to us. What should we do with you? You already know the answer to that question.

"Slave is a word you've been taught to hate, but humans were made to be slaves at first to serve God as our master in a beautiful place. But things changed. From birth, everyone's master is emptiness. Slaves to emptiness spend their days giving emptiness different things. Fun, people, work, games, hobbies all seem to do the trick for a while. But in the end, the emptiness is back, hungrier than ever. When you chose Him, you found the only thing big enough to fill emptiness.

"His overall plan for your life is no mystery. We have His book and His talents to use here . . ." he spread his hands ". . . where

He's chosen to place us in space and time. Think about the talents and passions you use every day. A wise guy once said the chief end of man is to glorify God. The meaning of life is being what He made you to be: doing what you're good at. Which brings us back to your question. Tell me, then. What should we do with you?"

For the first time, Jen's tone carried a bit of hope, "Well, I know scads about com-visions—"

"Hardware or software?"

"Both," she beamed, "but I'm way better at processing software."

He nodded. "Very useful. We have a team of Hacks called the Body Surfers, and a Field Hack works with each Muscle Cell."

"I'm not sure what that means, but I'll use stuff I know to help out."

"What about you, Dave?"

I always hated when this came up. My day job at Slider's mini-mart paid my half of the rent. Sixteen-year-old Jen always came off like a brainiac with a twenty-year-old loser of a big brother.

"Well, the only things I've ever really been good at are com-vision games. You know the kind where you see the barrel of your gun and the room around you? They're called first person shooters. I've won a couple of corporate-sponsored Web tournaments."

My tone never topped a mumble. For some reason hobbies didn't seem very important right now. I didn't even try to make it sound good. People never understood my useless skill.

The usual response is oh-that's-nice, so it raised my brows when he said when he said, "You mean like *Peacekeeper*?"

Someone who understood my hobby usually had to listen to me chatter. Not today. "Yeah . . . I played on a *Peacekeeper* champion FBT team, and won the single player terrorist escape for the last couple years."

"I've heard those games are some of the best Sandman training a kid can get."

True, I measured shorter and skinnier than your average convenience store cashier, so I ignored the kid thing. "So how do we get started?"

"Where we're going depended on this conversation, so give me a minute."

We rode on in silence. I wanted to talk to Jen but kept quiet to avoid disturbing Legacy. I broke out my last three sticks of gum.

"'Kay, next time the truck stops will be at a stoplight. We're gonna switch vehicles in traffic. Stay as close to the back of the truck as you can. There'll be a semi-truck in the right lane blocking the street cam. Follow me into its trailer's false floor. The semi'll take us through some Ward checkpoints, so when we stop, stay perfectly quiet. The rest of the ride'll be too noisy to hear each other, so just try 'n rest til we get there."

"Where's there?" I wondered aloud.

"You'll join the Muscle Cell I'm in. We work out of a mission . . . um . . . a secret base. Anyway, when we feel the driver backing up, we're there. He'll kill the engine, restart it, and kill it again as a sign for us to get out. Got all that?"

"Got it," I said.

"Yep," echoed Jen.

"Here's something to think about on the way. The FBT keeps an I.D. chip file on everyone with medical, educational, and financial info. We try'n make it hard for 'em to figure out who you used to be. It helps protect not only you, but family and friends still living in the One State. That's why we take street-names when we join the Body. You must pick new names.

Tonight, the two of you disappear . . . two new Saints are born."

CHAPTER FIVE

THE SWITCH WENT AS PLANNED under a dim clouded morning sky. At three Ward checkpoints, footsteps of Illinois Department of Transportation agents went right over the top of me as the IDOTs checked the trailer's cargo. The whole trip took forever. Time moved slothy, and my thoughts kept slipping back to the last ride in our dad's Aphid . . .

* * *

Rain wet razor wire gleamed under the highway checkpoints' floodlights. Relentlessly steadfast streetlight security cameras swept the bumper-to-bumper twenty-four lane parking lot. The Chicago Metroplex's war on terror. Originally built to be tollbooths, cameras, razor wire, and peacekeepers weren't added to stop toll cheaters. Everyone paid safety's price tag by waiting in lines.

We'd made good time. Five minutes of creeping had us halfway to the booth, and Dad had cleared our shopping trip with IDOT so we could use an express lane. Traffic usually thinned this close to sunset on a weeknight. Nobody wanted to be caught out after curfew.

I cracked a fresh pack of Winterfresh Extra and offered Dad a stick. Because of him, the Wrigley's Corporation had most of my childhood allowance. He'd gotten me hooked on the stuff way back when I was in the second-grade.

Dad, of course, accepted. "Thanks, boy! Maybe you're not as bad as your mom says."

I reached into the back seat to give my sister a stick. Jen peeled it, popped it into her mouth and relaxed against her headrest.

I threw a, "You're welcome" at her silence. She had the manners of a . . . well . . . the manners of a sister.

Racing from the hand-me-down shop through pouring rain had soaked us and stringy wet hair wilted to her shoulders. Bright hair colors were the-stuff and wet or dry, hers screamed hot pink. I'd say she looked cute in her tattered jeans and my old hand-me-down sweatshirt, but hey, she's my sister. That'd be sick.

The beat of Railgun's *Liquid Thunder* rattled the Geo Aphid's plastic windows, but she didn't seem to notice. Black shades hid her eyes. Panasonic Gutenberg reading glasses let her mind wander other worlds. The reading glasses linked her to the Library of North America via satellite, and beamed whatever she wanted right onto her eyeballs. Jen showed off those sister-manners by chewing her gum open-mouthed.

I turned my attention to the small box on my lap, the reason for our trip. I couldn't help stealing another peek. Parting cardboard flaps, I poked through crumpled paper until my fingertips untangled the small cold treasure. I cupped it in both hands.

A one-ounce bottle of perfume.

In the world of perfume, this was the-stuff. It didn't just smell good. The pheromone love-potion affected the brain's scent and pleasure centers. Smelling just a sniff of *Flashpoint* shot Cupid's-arrow chemical reactions on a Romeo-and-Juliet level, which is why it sold for more than $1200 an ounce. A golden glaze coated the skinny crystal pyramid. Its stopper was a tiny exploding sun, fragile spikes set around a center ball. Inside the sun were a dozen micro-prisms. At twelve hundred an ounce, you'd better get some ace packaging. When I uncupped my hands, multicolored lights shafted out in all directions, twinkling like bottled starlight.

"Hey, put that up, I'm drivin' over here!" grouched Dad. I lowered my hands back into the box.

I saw why Mom liked it. She'd taken Jen and to the junk-shop for school clothes, but seeing the little bottle made her face all dreamy. She checked the price, scrunched her eyes and moved on. When we'd finished she went out of her way to pass-by once more. That's when I got the gift idea. Mom was tied-up at the check-out and I went back to check the price. I couldn't guess why it said only one hundred dollars. With her birthday only days away, I'd found a decent present for once. It meant half a week's wages from my job at Slider's Mini-Mart, but we're talking about my mom here.

I carefully re-packed it with a smile.

The blast-techno rock faded out, replaced by a commercial-break. I lowered the volume. "Thanks for takin' me to get this, Dad." His ten-hour workday started well before sun-up and he was usually in bed this by this time.

"Thanks for sayin' thanks. Makes it sound like someone brought you up right."

"Won't happen again."

Silence from the back seat. I pointed over my shoulder. "She just uses those glasses for romance novels."

He snorted, "Anything to get her off the CV! Besides, better than when Jeff used his allowance to get his eyelids pierced." Our big brother could peer at us from behind closed eyes through tiny flesh-colored eye-rings.

"Billy had his done and Jeff thought it was spiff. He said he wanted to gross-out Jen."

"Billy's a rehab waitin' to happen. I wish your brother wouldn't hang with him so much."

Jen whipped-off her glases and leaned forward, "I heard his dad was raggin' on him about drugs. Billy told him to back off or else he'd call the peacekeepers and have him arrested for makin' the family join a secret Fundi church."

I hate that word. The kind of people who called African-Americans the *N* word now called Fundamentalist Christians, Fundis.

Dad just shook his head, so I said "I don't think you shoulda' voted to let them into the church. Mom's afraid Billy's gonna rat us all out."

There were seven families in our home church. If we were found out, we'd all be arrested and sent to Rehabilitation Wards for a hi-tech brainwashing.

"Naw, he's just hangin' that over his Dad's head so that he'll get his way," said Jen.

"Shhh!" The DJ was talking and Dad turned the sound back up.

". . . rest slack tonight, Chicago's a safer place! Another buncha Fundi terrorists have been busted in the 'burbs, and those peacekeepers are busy as a teenager's flip-com. The Federal Bureau of Terrorism's throwin' a press party in thirty minutes and we'll play it live. So open your ol' pal DJ Ray a cold one, and kick it up! 'Til then, here's more noise to rock your block off!" Music pounded and Dad turned it back down.

Jen thumped the back of my seat with her fist, "Why do they arrest people for believin' in the Bible? I'm so sick of teachers sayin' to stay away from Fundis because we're crazy and dangerous! I'm no terrorist, and nobody in the church is a terrorist!"

We reached the checkpoint gate. An IDOT agent with a flip-com scanned Dad's license plate chip. The have-a-safe-day sign lit up, tire spikes dropped into pavement slots, and a peacekeeper swung his assault-rifle's barrel and waved us through.

The Aphid's tiny electric motor hummed us up to speed, slower than usual. We hadn't been able to use any electric gadgets around the house so there would be enough juice to recharge the car for this trip. I hated it when we burned our power ration before the day was over. Cold showers in the dark were right up there with sweet potatoes on my least-favorite-things list. "Hey Dad, don't forget to recharge the car tonight."

"Uh-huh," came his deep grunt. That always meant he wasn't really listening. I caught him frowning at Jen in the rear view mirror.

Then he launched into the why-the-One-State-makes-people-fear-Fundamentalists speech. I'd heard this one a dozen times. Even with practice, it didn't get any better. Good old Jen made it longer by asking questions. My mind wandered into tomorrow's delivery at Slider's. Just when I thought Dad was done, Jen began another question and I rolled my eyes.

"Why didn't you and Mom . . .?"

I don't remember if Jen stopped in mid-sentence, or if I just stopped hearing her. My eyes got big. A hundred flashing lights split the dusk out my window. The road we traveled ran atop a ridge. We were almost home and our street stretched out below. The rows of town-homes flashed red from police strobes, and blue from peacekeeper Humvee light-bars. The picnic table with its faded green umbrella marked our tiny back yard. Our house sat right in the middle of the scene.

"What happened?" I wondered aloud.

"There must have been some kind of accident." Jen answered. "I hope Mom 'n Jeff are okay!"

Dad boomed, "Shut-up, both of you! Just be quiet! Let me think."

He stabbed a finger, killing the stereo, which made the humming motor and whining tires suddenly seem loud. Now I worried. It took something big to shake Dad like this. Jen's face lit up red and blue with eyes as round as her O-shaped lips. I realized that my mouth hung open as well, and closed it. Jen shot me a look that said something bad was going down.

The road ran down the ridge, sinking below rooftop level, hiding the scene. Dad passed our neighborhood's entrance.

Then my shock frozen brain thawed enough that it hit me. The news about the Fundi terrorist bust—it was our church!

Dad always said if the wrong person found out about our Sunday morning worship, we'd be arrested, split up, and Rehabbed. I wrote off his ranting as drama, although deep down I knew he was right.

Rehabs broke minds down and rebuilt them. Some found insanity before rehabilitation. Those who resisted were classified as "SERVICE TO SOCIETY." Nobody knew what this really meant, but urban-legend held that when the rehab Wards opened, organ donor lists shrank big-time. My track coach, Mr. Robert, had survived a Rehab. He was creepy. We'd called him Robert-robot.

Jen's eyes fixed on Dad. Her lower lip quivered.

Dad's face statued, a faraway look set into his eyes. My breath came in gulps and the tuna-noodle-casserole we'd eaten for supper sat in my gut like a ball of ice.

Dad's voice cracked, "Both of you take off your seatbelts and stay as low as you can."

We crouched on the floor. I tossed the box with Mom's *Flashpoint* into the back seat. At least the three of us were still free. Not for long though. They'd find us.

"What can we do?" I asked.

He rubbed at his eyes. "Well, rain clouds mean the satellite sky-cams can't see us, so we only have to worry about the streetlight cams. You bought the *Flashpoint* with your own ID chip, and my plate was scanned at the checkpoint. That means they have times and places to begin tracking you. We have to get you hidden as . . ."

Jen cut in, "You? What do you mean, you?"

"There's only one thing I can do," he said softly.

She launched into full panic, "Dad, you meant *search for us*, not *you*, right?"

"They'll find me. The car's processor has a tracking signal. I can't just make it disappear."

Terror lifted her tone, "You can't give yourself up! You've gotta come with us!"

His whisper could barely be heard over the Aphid's motor, "Jen, slow down. You'll never be alone."

He rubbed his eyes again, and announced in a new bold voice, "Mom and I decided what to do if anything like this ever happened. It's what we should've done a long time ago. I know a place where the cameras have a blind spot or at least they used to. It's under a bridge. You'll both hide there until someone comes for you."

I tried to argue, "Dad. It . . ."

"Dave, you're an adult, but . . ."

"Dad!"

"No! I know you're both scared, that's why it's time to zip lips and use your ears. Trust those who come for you. They'll show you things that Mom and I never could, so do whatever they tell you. When one lesson is over, He moves you on to the next thing.

That's what He's doing now, so be ready for whatever He shows you. And don't forget who's in charge. We're always in His hands; never forget that. Always have faith that His will is being done! If He's with you, who can be against you?"

The entire One State could be against us, that's who.

Was His will being done to our family?

What kind of lesson outranked our church's brainwashing? As if we could make a difference in this rotten world anyway!

Jen sobbed, and Dad reached between the seats to hold her hand. His steel gaze had softened, becoming, well, calm. He looked so just-another-day that I wondered how he did it.

I considered Dad's advice and peeked at my sister, "Jen, He doesn't want us in a Rehab. We're being put somewhere else." That seemed to help. She blinked at me from between the seats before resting her cheek on the back of Dad's hand. We drove on in silence. I kept finding myself watching Dad. This could be the last time I ever saw him. What Billy'd done set my temper to doin' the slow burn.

* * *

The semi brought me back to reality when it stopped, backed up, and the diesel engine died twice.

Legacy whispered, "Follow me."

CHAPTER SIX

WE SLID OUT ONTO A PUDDLED concrete pad littered with fast food garbage and cigarette butts. Our driver had chosen a bay in the middle of the loading dock. Any possible camera views were blocked. Alone among the trucks, we followed Legacy to the trailer's rear, and stopped just short of the building. He took hold of a long narrow iron grate, set into the ground, and pulled. A three-meter section swung up, and he motioned us inside.

"This is the front door to your new home." The dark hole wasn't even a meter wide. It sloped toward a tile drainpipe at its middle. I peeked at Legacy from the corner of my eye. He saw my look and nodded.

Whatever happened to ladies-first? I lowered myself into that narrow pipe with my arms and discovered chiseled footholds. My knees couldn't bend very far without knocking the the pipe's sides, but the rough ladder's steps were close together. I hadn't climbed very far before my foot kicked air, searching for a toe-hold. I lowered myself with my arms to splash down in the storm sewer that ran beneath. A moldy smell polluted the air. I squatted and moved down the new pipe.

Jen joined me. The grate clunked shut above. As my eyes adjusted to the gloom, a weak circle of morning light filtered in. The pipe held a trickle of rainwater that glistened the slimy floor dark green.

Legacy joined us, and with a, "This way," we scurried after him.

Past the skylight, my eyes worked just as well open as they did closed. With every step I slipped and slid on the rounded floor. My shoes and socks, nearly dry from the long drafty ride, squished anew as I splashed along. To keep from going on all fours and touching the slick scum I bent into a right angle at the waist. Even with my arms propped on my thighs, burning back muscles made me squat and try the duck trot. But it was slow going. I heard them moving farther ahead of me and resumed the oh-my-aching-back walk.

We went on like that for too long, until we came to a pipe like the one we'd climbed down. It led up to a steel manhole cover. Legacy tossed it aside with one hand as though it were cardboard. A bad fluorescent tube on the high ceiling flickered. The room cluttered with metal equipment and machinery. Oil soaked dust and corrosion covered everything. Pipes and ductwork all but hid the walls. A huge square duct came out of one wall and dropped straight into the floor.

Legacy walked to it and unlatched a small maintenance hatch set into its side. "Almost there."

We climbed down a ladder and blinked in the harsh light. Where the storm sewer had been damp, slimy, cool and dark, this air shaft was dry, dusty, warm and well lit. Hundreds of copper, stainless steel, and PVC runs crowded the shaft. A string of caged sixty-watt light-bulbs hung from a ceiling conduit, bound by those black plastic twist-ties that secure toys to cardboard packaging.

Legacy must have seen my concern. "Chemicals and solvents run through these lines to everywhere in the factory. This is an exhaust run as well as a supply corridor. If there's a leak in the building, it can be blown out through this air shaft and filtered with emergency exhaust filters."

"Nice," I grunted. *These people live in a dangerous hole.*

"Don't worry, it's just for emergencies. Anyway, we're here."

He stooped beneath a series of copper pipes, and opened a hinged ventilation grate. In we crawled. He followed, and parted a woven wire curtain. On hands and knees, we entered a wide concrete room, and stood.

I could touch the low concrete ceiling, shrouded with wire mesh identical to the entry curtain. I'd used an electric blanket before. In *Peacekeeper.* It could gather electricity from outside power leaks while hiding the electric signals of anything beneath.

Large colorful rugs covered the floor. Heavy forest green curtains hid walls, tied back where feature-lights lit art hanging on bare concrete. Shelving units lined the walls. I'd never seen so many books.

The wall to our right featured com-vision workstations. The largest CV angled toward a corner sofa pit.

Behind me, a microwave beeped. Next to the hole through which we'd crawled, a young man in a nylon t-shirt fetched a steaming Campbell's soup-cup. He rattled ice from a freezer tray and dropped three cubes into his soup while studying Jen and I. He pointed toward the room's center, where armchairs and PlastiWood end tables clustered. A silver-haired man rose gracefully from a chair and approached. "Hymn to Him." His accent belonged in a London lecture-hall, not the Chicago underground.

"Glory," Legacy replied, then he addressed Jen and I. "This is Grandpa. He's our Elder. Elders run cells. Be nice to the old guy, 'cause believe it or not, he's 72."

I didn't. His fit frame moved smooth, and his weathered skin hardly showed a wrinkle. I'd have put him in his fifties, tops.

Then I noticed Grandpa's eyes. They gleamed so intensely gold that a jeweler must have fashioned them. Well, his contacts at least. Legacy made for the kitchen area. "Hey, someone left some coffee in the pot!"

Grandpa turned his odd eyes on us. "Legacy's legacy is that of a coffee drinker. I'm sorry to have heard about your loved ones." With a sad smile, his eyes flashed kindness. A trick of light gave the gold a blue tint. I've never seen anyone able to say so much with a single look. Those two wells of sorrow cried out so clearly, I swore I could *hear* them.

Grandpa motioned for us to follow, and led the way to a plain concrete hall that had not been there when we came in. "I'm afraid we were not quite ready to receive you. Please take a moment to freshen-up."

* * *

"Freshen-up" meant using the crudest bathroom I'd ever seen. Five toilet stalls consisted of Plasti-Wood boxes with holes cut in their tops. They sat over a waste-water pipe.

Legacy followed us with his steaming cup, and chuckled as we looked around. "It's not as bad as it looks."

One of those stainless steel flash washer/ dryer units gleamed in the corner—the room's only upside. Three curtained shower stalls had been fashioned from sections of huge PVC drainage-pipe. Legacy introduced us to the room's single five-liter-pail soap-dispenser that spigoted a vomit-colored liquid into plastic cups. Do-not-drink pictogram stickers decorated the wall near every tap.

"When you shower, keep the water off your face. Wash-up and brush your teeth with this." He nodded at cartons of bottled water. "Toss out your clothes, and I'll clean 'em." He flipped towels over our curtain rods.

We got in, stripped down, and did as instructed. Now, how to work the plumbing without getting scalded. I saw no handle. A single corroded pipe protruded from the wall, elbowed ninety degrees up, and ended in a rusted shower head. Ah, there it was, a ball-valve lever behind the corroded pipe.

"Hey, Legacy, this lever obviously turns-on the water, but how do I adjust the water temperature?"

He chuckled. That was my first clue. "Just grit your teeth, and crank the handle."

A cold shower—my favorite.

Ninety seconds later, I didn't care if all the soap was off. Chattering teeth and shivering anatomy had had enough.

As I toweled-off Legacy flipped flashed clothes over our rods.

I dressed and opened the curtain, rubbing my upper arms. Legacy was cleaning the dryer's lint trap. "After you're re-formed, the cold water doesn't bother you."

"Re-formed?" I asked.

Jen's curtain opened, and Legacy said, "Let's go."

The two men in the common-room exchanged nods. One tall wearing a gray turtleneck and a beard neatly pointed. Both his close-cropped black hair and his beard flecked with gray. He carried a battered aluminum briefcase. That face . . . I knew him from somewhere.

A dark East-Indian man with a matching briefcase and blue shirt smiled. The irises of both men's eyes glinted gold.

The tall one rumbled a voice that could ripple water. "You two have impressed your rescuer. From what he's told me, you two will fit well into our family of saints. I am Lightfast." He nodded again. "And this is Sensei. If you've chosen those street-names, how may we address you?"

Legacy had been with us. When had Legacy told him anything? How'd he know we were supposed to choose new names? That thought sparked dimly because the FBT's most-wanted man stood right there. Lightfast. I now recognized him from the Terrorist Webwire's Ten Most Wanted reports.

A few years ago, nobody knew the One State government that had been rumored by conspiracy theorists, really ran most of the world. Saints hiding in Lost Wards posted data on the Web that proved the United States government had been a puppet show for years. Lightfast was one of these saints.

After they'd been outed, One State spin-doctors said a united world government made it easier to protect everyone from Fundi terrorists. The public bought it. Fundis were still blamed for checkpoints, bombings, curfews, and peace- keepers.

As one of the founders of the Body of Christ, Lightfast was notorious. His exploits made him the number-one bad-guy of children's pretend-games. My brain still frazzled shock-numb when Jen answered, "My mom and dad call . . . called me e-girl and I kind of liked it."

They looked to me. "Uh, there was a name I used when I played CV games. After what's happened to our family, it fits: Calamity Kid."

Lightfast bowed. "Well Calamity Kid and e-girl, it's my pleasure."

"Sir, you said Legacy told you about us, yet he was with us the whole time. You two haven't even spoken."

He headed for the sofa pit and spoke over his shoulder. "The answers will come once you're re-formed."

Jen and I looked at each other. "What's reformed?" I asked.

Legacy answered while stirring his java, "You asked me to teach you how to do what I do. I've brought you to the man who taught me. You're about to be schooled, cubbies."

CHAPTER SEVEN

SAINTS IN ARMCHAIRS SMILED AS we crossed the room, all of them greeting us with gold irises. Some tinted with blue, orange, and yellow. *What are we getting into, here?* But at the same time, I could somehow feel those stares welcoming me to this place. These saints didn't need to use words. Even so, Jen walked with her eyes glued to the carpets, and her shoulders tensed. Neither of us had ever been comfortable in big groups of strangers, but next to CV-geek-loner Jen, I was a public speaker.

Jen and I sank into cushions. From the corner behind the sofa, five arms of a floor lamp arched over the pit group. A sturdy man in tan coveralls sat in the corner. Every kind of tool I could think of, and a few that Craftsman's design-engineers had yet to invent, poked out of his many pockets. He looked like he'd given up shaving for Lent—about three years ago. From the way he glared at us, someone must have run over his dog and blamed a short guy and his kid-sister.

He grumbled to his feet, "Rotten oozin' scobs! Hey Tinker, what's your cell's job? Oh, we do childcare. God's babysitters we are. Teach 'em how to play good guys and bad guys . . ." He moped away through the armchairs.

A blonde woman in an olive zippered-jumpsuit gave us both bottled water and smiles before sitting next to Jen. e-girl, I mean. Whatever. "Ignore Tinker. Only thing worse than his pranks is his charm. You two hungry?" Even though we hadn't eaten in hours, we both shook our heads. In the acid tornado of my stomach, food had no place.

Lightfast rolled up one of the workstation chairs and sat facing us. "I must admit that I have a concern. We've never re-formed anyone as young as e-girl." He took her hands in his. "Everyone entering the underground must adapt, but I fear things will be even more difficult for you. Your whole life has been spent in suburbia. Your home was heated in winter and cooled in summer. You could eat and drink even if you weren't hungry or thirsty. Clothes were worn for reasons other than to keep your bodies warm and covered. Much of your time was spent having fun. We spend no time here entertaining ourselves. In this mission we're far enough underground that the temperature remains constant. But few saints live in such comfort. Most of the time, we're cold in winter and hot in summer. Most of our clothes come from people who've grown tired of them, and have given them away. Sometimes we've nothing to eat. Even clean water can be hard to find. Sometimes we must go days without eating."

No food? Heck with Jen, I had concerns about me. I examined the saints in the room and noticed none were overweight. I'd seen pictures of starving people in third-world countries. I'd wondered what it was like to go hungry. Didn't mean I wanted to find out.

"What do you do here?" asked Jen.

"Work. There's much to do and we all have our parts to play," he answered flatly.

"What about on the weekends?" She wasn't getting the picture. Their idea of fun hovered somewhere between washing dishes and stocking shelves.

"This is what I mean. Our lives are so different from what you've known . . . you'd have to learn a whole different way of thinking. Things would be hard for awhile."

"No weekends?" Jen sounded horrified.

"Our weekends are just two more days we hope to have food; two more days to serve Him. We do look forward to Sunday worship though."

e-girl paled. She hated home church worship. She knew it to be wrong, but she'd much rather have been allowed to sleep-in, or play on the CV. She shook her head. "We have no choice."

"Yes, you do. We could place you with people who'd care for you . . ."

My sister then cut off the FBT's most wanted man. "No, I mean no matter how rough it might be, this is something I have to do."

Lightfast looked at me. "And you both feel this way?"

I nodded.

"Why, as your sister says, is it something you have to do?"

My heart said we had to help our family, but my mind made my lips say, "To serve Him."

Lightfast sat back in his chair, looking at Legacy, "You're right. They are quite ready." There it was again. They still hadn't spoken, yet somehow they knew each other's thoughts!

It was time for Jen to show off those sister-manners. "Hey, Flashlight," she blurted, "why does everyone down here wear those colored contacts?"

He chuckled deeply at the murdering of his name, "No one's wearing contacts. What you see is a side effect of our re-formation. They're always gold, but take on shades according to our moods. Blue for sadness, red for strong feelings, yellow for happiness, and so on."

As long as she'd begun a question and answer session, I shook my head and asked again, "What does reform mean? You keep using the word, but we don't understand."

His eyes took on a golden glow that drilled holes in me. I got the sense of a wide-eyed twitching-tailed cat watching a mouse.

I swallowed hard.

"Re-form is how you saw Legacy take a spinning ten meter leap and land on his feet. It's how he dozed four peacekeeper units without breaking a sweat. Because we're both re-formed, we'd been communicating long before you'd arrived. Everyone here uses the process called re-formation to serve Him. It helps us live every moment in the place where our talents and passions cross paths.

"I know the meaning of life. I know I'll live forever . . . that I'm immortal. I know what love really is. The things that I know, plus my wanting to serve Him, equal the things He allows me to do. That is re-formation. You'll have all of this after your re-formation. You've both asked to be taught our ways. To train and work as a Hack and a Sandman, correct?"

We nodded.

"Then let us begin," he said.

CHAPTER EIGHT

LIGHTFAST MOTIONED AT THE East-Indian man in the blue shirt seated on an office chair across from e-girl. "Sensei has re-formed the body's youngest member to date, and I've asked him here to re-form you. This won't take long, so just relax."

It always makes me tense when people say *just relax*. This began to remind me of a dentist visit. On my favorite-things-list, dentist visits were right up there with cleaning public restrooms . . . and bumping my head really hard.

"Will it hurt?" asked my sister.

"Everyone asks that. You'll feel different things, but pain won't be among them. Before we can get started, we must prepare. Please answer the following questions either yes or no. Are the Father, Son and Holy Spirit all God?"

e-girl and I answered at the same time, "Yes."

"Did Jesus Christ physically rise from the dead?"

"Yes."

"Did His body physically rise into Heaven?"

"Yes."

He asked us things to which only Fundamentalist Christians would answer yes. I did relax a bit, but only a bit.

Other saints gathered in the pit, kneeling around us on the floor. With folded hands and bowed heads each prayed silently.

Least we can't see those weird eyes.

"Do you admit that you've been wrong both in things you've done and in things you should have done, but didn't?"

"Yep."

"Are you sorry for these wrongs?"

"Yes."

"Have you been baptized?"

"Yep."

"Good."

Sensei readied a small silver cup and tray.

Lightfast knelt and gave us communion, then said, "Father, we come to you in the name of the Son. We thank you for all things, and ask wisdom to use these things to serve you. May Calamity Kid, e-girl, and all saints, act as lightning rods for the power of the Holy Spirit. Amen."

Lightfast and Sensei retook their seats.

Our teacher continued, "Now we're going to focus your minds. Stare into our eyes. You can blink, but try not to look away." After he sucked in a deep breath, his strange gold eyes pulsed and throbbed.

Just as I wondered if we were making a big mistake, they broke off the staring contest. After stretching arms and necks, they opened their briefcases on the floor next to their chairs. Both tangled with colored wires and circuit boards. Thick fiber optic cables ran from each briefcase to, of all things, baseball caps.

Each man put on his cap and then Lightfast put on a smile. "We call these our thinking caps. They're extra memory for data storage. During this next part, you'll feel hot. We're going to be working in the area of your minds that has to do with instincts. You know, like putting your hands out when you fall. We'll also tweak involuntary muscle controls, like breathing and heartbeat. Your bodies' temperature will rise enough to open sweat glands, but sit as still as you can. An alarm will go off if your temperature nears the danger level. Ready?"

We nodded, but shared a nervous glance. Their eyes went gray. Seconds into it, pores opened. Every pore on my skin. Sweat ran down my forehead. After only minutes, my shirt stuck to me like a second skin. Someone gave us towels to wipe our faces. By the time their eyes flashed gold again we both sat dripping.

I felt no different than before.

Lightfast said, "Very good. Now we're going to adjust your long-term memory. You'll feel tingling and twitching on your scalp. It will tickle and even itch, but what's going on is happening inside your skull. The wrinkles on everyone's brains are caused by learning. The more you know, the more wrinkles you have, and the deeper they become. You're about to learn a lot, so your wrinkles will get much deeper, and new ones will form. Scratching your scalp won't help, so as before, just stay as still as you can."

I smiled weakly, but he looked to e-girl, "Don't worry, you're doing just fine."

"Goody gumdrops," she muttered.

The moment their eyes went gray again, an itchy-wiggle-tickle swallowed up my head. The sudden craving to rasp my scalp with fingernails consumed me. I squirmed. Fingers knotted. I sat on my hands and digits fidgeted, and managed to stay pretty much in the same spot for the whole thing. Well, most of me did.

Finally, Lightfast leaned back. "That's it. Done."

"Errr!" I scratched at my head, but the itchiness was gone.

He took off his ball-cap and smiled at us from beneath arched brows.

"How do you feel?"

CHAPTER NINE

"FINE." I SHRUGGED, BUT THEN it hit me. I'd been crazy tense and worried ever since the horrible scene at Mom and Dad's place. That was gone. In its place, calm and peace filled me as water fills a glass. I found new parts . . .

Meaning-of-life parts.

Knowledge, yes, but so much more. A mushroom cloud of spirituality blossomed above, and I laughed, in awe. e-girl and I laughed—her hot pink hair now clashed with gold irises—but eye-color had nothing to do with our laughter.

I sucked deep breaths, and enjoyed the warm relaxed glow that centered deep in my gut. Not until this moment was I able to measure how few hours of my twenty years had been spent truly living and loving. So much wasted time. On the meaningless. But all forgiven. Sin no more.

Meaning-of-life magnitude-nine-plus.

Oh, my God, yes. Such live energy filled me that I wanted to run, yell, laugh and cry all at the same time.

e-girl grinned like she'd just found Planet Dream Works tickets, in her Christmas stocking. "Kid, I can hear your heart!"

Sensory perception on steroids.

I could hear hers, too. Our hearts weren't beating any louder. Our hearing was that much better. Colors, sounds, smells . . . even the movements of air across my skin all painted such details in my brain. And then there was . . . without turning my head . . . Whoa.

I sensed changes in the electric and magnetic fields. I closed my eyes, yet I could see the room around me. A whole new sensory perception.

And new confidence—at one with the world around me, yet a master of it. In sync with creation. So in-charge, yet so responsible to Shepherd all of Eden.

e-girl's voice foamed rabid excitement, "Everything feels so different . . . I feel so different. Like I'm not even human anymore! I'm a whole new somebody!"

"Sis. You realize how spiritually nuclear we just went?"

"Yes, I am." She jumped to her feet, "Oh this is epic—I'm not afraid anymore! Of anything!"

I had to disagree. "We must fear Him."

"Well, He also loves us, so—" She gave me a raspberry. "We were so weak and helpless before. Whinin' l'il puppies. Now I'm so . . . so complete!"

I shivered with excitement and from a new feeling I could only explain as a force—some kind of power. Then I sensed the buzzing. From beyond the electro-magnetic. All around me.

The Power's source.

Holy—

I fell to the floor, flat on my belly. There were sudden "Ohhhs" and "Ahhhs" from the saints. Their murmurs changed to laughter. Not a ha-ha-look-at-the-idiot laugh but a good sound that spoke, saying Isn't it fantastic? They knew what I'd seen.

He was in the walls and floor, in the air and the saints. Everywhere at once. I just lay there, thanking Him for making and keeping me.

Pure love touched my soul. I knew joy. I finally got up wearing the biggest smile ever to split a tear-slick face. My sister lay ragdoll-face-down-on-the-floor, giggling in shock.

Lightfast handed me my water bottle. "Drink all of it. You've lost a lot of fluid. Sweat, tears—let's quit before you add blood to the list."

I emptied the bottle, not even stopping to breathe. I'd never thought of water having taste, but it tasted incredible. The world was so plainly perfect—because it was exactly how it had to be. The end of our family wasn't good or right. It was as it must be under His watchful eye. I panted gulps of air and wiped my lips. "What I feel can't be put into words . . . what's happened to us?"

Again, Lightfast drilled me with his golden glow, but this time familial love passed like voltage through copper wire.

He leaned close. "It's something that's always been around, but never understood. You've heard of people walking on beds of hot coals without being burned?"

"I'd always figured those things were faked."

He pointed up and crooked his head, "Nope. Supernatural plus human will. God willed everything into being and we're made in his image. It's really no surprise then, that using our will, we can do things as well.

"Re-formation is the study of the mind, quantum physics, comvisions, and Biblical theology all rolled into a single science. We just uploaded decades of study and synthetic experiences. You now have a basic college level education, a few dozen languages, new skills, abilities, and a small library in your head. You've been given, all at once, what most people need a lifetime to learn. You have, for example, memorized the entire Bible."

I shook my head. "But it's more than just knowing things . . . my senses . . . I even sense Him!"

He chuckled in his rich bottomless tone. "Human beings are part animal and part spirit. Re-formation re-forms the spiritual you with the physical you. Everyone knows about his or her animal self, but few know anything of their spiritual selves. Re-formation opens your senses to both sides. Someone once said that faith is the distance between the heart and mind. Re-formation overlaps the heart and mind. If you ask me, God's giving us back a little of what it was like to be human before the fall. Maybe even a tiny peek at heaven.

"Legacy can answer more of your questions. Sensei and I have some business in another mission. But this mission is my home, so we can talk more when I return. Welcome to the Body of Christ, little brother!"

Tinker, who'd joined the others in prayer, rose from his knees and grouched his way toward the other side of the room. Again, he muttered to himself as he went. This time I could hear his every word; including the part about not changing our diapers.

e-girl threw her arms around Sensei just like she'd do with Dad. "Th . . . I was gonna say thanks, but, it's Him I thank. Keep doin' this stuff for Him though!"

"That is my hope, babe e-girl." He picked up his briefcase. "His will be done . . ."

". . . on Earth as it is in Heaven." she beamed.

The blonde woman who'd given us water put her hand on e-girl's shoulder. "I'm Serene. While Legacy tricks out your brother, I'll be helpin' ya learn your way round a com-vision."

My sister puffed up like infected bee-sting. "Oh, I already know scads 'bout CVs. I write procedures in C-plus-cubed. Is that the language you use?"

Serene smiled, "We're gonna ride fiber optics bareback on mindware afterburners. You know all about that, L'il Sis?"

e-girl's eyes saucered. Her words thrilled in a whisper, "Mindware? That's brain wave technology! Epic!" She danced.

Grandpa seated himself in the sofa pit and called out in his Queen's English, "First things first, pup. We've much to do if the two of you are going to assist in tonight's rescue."

"Resc-rescue our family?" she stammered.

CHAPTER TEN

GRANDPA SHOOK HIS HEAD with a frown. "No, no, no." The corners of his mouth bent up in a smile. "Your entire church."

Drama lingered a moment before he continued in a leader's voice. "Serene will now play Web-hostess and tour guide as we visit Rehabilitation Ward Nine." Then to e-girl, "It is necessary that you verify your church's presence." Other saints joined him in the sofa pit, slipping into wraparound virtual goggles.

My sister spun, swinging her hand at me. I slapped my palm into hers, hooked our thumbs, and we grinned. A red-yellow-orange wildfire burnished her joy-wet golden eyes. "He's answering hard-'n-fast."

"Can you believe this? We've gone from Nero-prey to Nero-nightmares."

"So spiff. Enjoy what you're about to see. Gotta work." e-girl made an iron-to-magnet line toward Serene.

A balding middle-aged man handed me virtual goggles. I wedged into the crowded cushions next to Legacy. "Whose call was it to rescue our church?"

He winked, "I pushed for it. Your dad's important. I told you he and I go way back. We're half-brothers."

My poor overloaded brain. "That makes you . . . you're our uncle?"

He nodded, bobbing his Samurai ponytail. "Your grandfather married a Japanese woman before he married your grandmother. They had one child together."

"Dad told us. You were that child?"

He nodded once. "I've been trying to get your father to bring you down here for years. It's nice to finally meet my niece and nephew."

I dug out my e-wallet, and keyed up the picture frame. "There's some family history in here."

Serene had settled into one of the workstation chairs still facing the sofa pit. "Um, if Legacy and Kid-cubby could quit their little party over there, we can get started?"

Legacy whispered, "You're my long lost nephew and I do want to see that, but here's a sandman tip. Never cross your field hack." He winked and pulled on his goggles.

Serene patted the chair next to her. "Mount up e-girl. We gotta get your feet wet." My smiley sister bounced into the seat. "You'll feel everyone piggybacking you. You're their eyes and ears to the Web. Let's ride."

Their chairs leaned back and leg-rests came up so they lay flat. Eyelids fluttered over white orbs as their eyes rolled back in their heads.

I slid into the virtual goggles and gulped a deep breath. Swirling clouds of spectrum skimmed past so fast they almost blurred.

Then something really weird crossed my senses: I heard Serene's voice, but not with my ears. The sound shortcut into my brain. She said, *Ladies and gentlemen, please fasten your seatbelts 'cause your driver's a rabid Hack puppy whose just itchin' to get live on some Fundi hatin' Neros! Let's play plug-'n-hack.*

I had to smile at her slang. Nero, the first century Roman emperor, had been reborn in the One State. Nero payback time.

Colors took on shapes and I found myself in a small, neon red room with blank walls. The only other person in the room was easily the most beautiful woman I'd ever seen. She wore a close fitting, silky jumpsuit the color of pearls. Sleeves ended in lace gloves to cover her perfect hands, leggings became boots that laced knee high. Her white-blonde hair gathered in a gleaming silver ring atop her head and fell like a fountain to frame her face. The woman looked at me. I blushed so hard and fast that the blast of blood rushing through my ears sounded like an erupting volcano. On a scale of one to ten, she rated in scientific notation.

e-girl gasped, *Are you an angel?*

The angel smiled pure goodness and I melted like s'Mores chocolate. *It's me. Serene. We're not sure why people using mindware appear the way we do, but Lightfast says these are the natural icons for our souls. So, I'm dressed in His glory. Heh, wait 'til ya see a Nero. Talk about the living dead.*

His glory cleans you up pretty spiff too, girl. Serene put her hands together in front of her. When she pulled them apart, a mirror stretched out in mid-cyberspace. e-girl sighed out a *Whoahhhh!* There were two angels in the red room.

e-girl looked down at herself. *I don't get it. How are we here? Our soul leaves our body?*

It's like gropin' a hole; your soul reaches and feels around.

Mmm. So, how do we write procedures?

Using mindware's nothing like using com-vision languages. The mindware Sensei loaded into your head writes CV procedures a thousand times faster than the slickest CV-geek ever could. You tell the mindware what you want and it does it. Let's say you wanted to pick up a pencil that's sitting on a table in front of you. Writing the procedures in a CV language is like telling each muscle, one at a time, to act with so much force, for so long. Using virtual input hardware's like reaching out and picking up the pencil. But with mindware, you just want the pencil in your hand, and it's there.

Fingers wiggled in the air as e-girl made like a magician. *We're magic!*

Serene fluffed her fountain of hair. *We're e-nchantresses. Ride time. Chase Rehab Nine's CV system.*

e-girl turned to face one of the red walls. It flickered and liquefied. Like a bullet from a gun, we quaked down a silver tube that stretched forever.

With my reformed senses, the adrenaline hit me like leaning back too far on a chair's back legs. The hopeless moment you realize there's nothing you can do to keep from falling backward, your whole body twigits. My fingers dug into sofa cushions as every muscle hardened in fight-or-flight panic.

We raced at forever's dead end, another red wall, at a speed suitable for interstellar travel. I put my arms out to brace for the crash. A dinner-plate sized hole opened and we were through it. Rocketing through a twisting copper tube stopped my breathing. At this speed, old-fashioned human control would have left us smudged on the wall.

I closed my eyes, but couldn't help opening them again. Couldn't miss a second.

This tube ended in a silver sphere. Just as I thought we'd splatter against the wall of the metallic globe, we made an impossible 90-degree dragonfly right turn.

Then the trip changed.

We glided smooth down a clear-walled tunnel that stretched several football fields wide. Shooting-star streaks of light flared toward us, while comets dazzled alongside, alien 360 turn-signals blinking safely through head-on traffic. Cyberspace's stellar highway.

Running lights reflected in the curved clear walls. Beyond, lie websites. We'd just entered Fairyland.

It was like seeing through the ground directly into basements or dungeons. Most websites had something alike on each of their pages. Colors, patterns or shapes made it easy to see where one site ended and its neighbor began. Some sites huddled small, their rooms tight. Others rambled huge. Some rooms towered so high, ceilings couldn't be seen. Other sites twisted around neighboring pages.

All sites filled with activity. A society of software robots slaved for human masters. Connecting the whole beautiful world were gem, metallic, and prismatic tubes, with textures and shapes that stretched perception. It was as though a team of genius-mad artist-engineer-plumbers had been at work for a thousand years.

Uncle Legacy spoke up, *For Calamity's sake, you two could have eased up a bit on that connection.*

Hey, I warned you, then Serene pretended to whisper to e-girl, *is that Legacy a mope or what?*

e-girl giggled.

You've got to address that mean streak, Legacy sounded wounded, but it was too forced to be real.

Serene@chauffeur4freeloaders.hack

That drew a snicker from Legacy. *Um, not quite what I meant. Amazing, huh Kid?*

Uh-huh . . . was the best I could do.

e-girl looked at Serene, e-streaking cyberspace. From the waist down she faded into hot pearlescent glitter, trailing vapor like an e-mermaid-comet.

We ricocheted up, right, then down through a series of silver spheres.

New tunnel.

It was a bright yellowish-bronze and echoed empty.

A blue wall came into view ahead. We slowed; squeezed through the hole that appeared, and landed on e-girl's feet. The hacks stood inside a small neon blue room, but they weren't alone.

A man with pallid sunken eyes and cheeks crouched in a corner. Filthy clothes hung loose on his thin frame like an ate-up flag on a battlefield pole. In places, his clothing had come apart. Through these holes paper-thin skin stretched tight over bones. He reeked of rotting flesh.

Virtual scent?

A curse rasped from the man's thin dry throat, and then he was gone.

My sister sounded freaked. *Who was that?*

Serene crossed her eyes. *FBT hack. Like I said, the living dead. That's what our souls look like without Christ.*

Before my reformation he'd have scared me to death! But now I just feel sad for him. Will he try to stop us?

He wishes. They can't slag us in a Web fight . . . so these days they just spytap.

Then they'll know we're gonna try a rescue!

Naw, we're in and outta these places all day long. Just chase their security controls.

The far wall of the blue room opened and we tore through their system of steel blue pipes.

I gasped and grasped cushions . . .

CHAPTER ELEVEN

WE ENDED UP IN A LOZENGE-shaped room. Its curved walls showed hundreds of security camera views.

Serene continued her lesson. *Spiff. Now, the people seen on the cams are listed in the database. Scan the feeds for people from your church.*

e-girl pressed her hand to the wall, and the room began to spin. No, the camera views skimmed along the wall—we stood still. It stopped on a row of feeds, slid downward and stopped again. She took her finger off the wall, and that camera view enlarged, ceiling to floor.

Ace—you got it. Let's count heads. According to the Terrorism Webwire, your whole church is being held here. Except the boy-hero who snitched, of course.

So Billy had ratted us out. Good to know.

Our camera's fisheye view showed a ten story stackhouse—what the Japanese called a coffin hotel--centered in a cubical room. According to the side-bar menu, the prisoners could be subjected to a variety of gasses and chemicals at a button's touch.

Only half of the coffins were lit. Inside those, prisoners used flip-coms, or lay stretched out, staring at the ceilings of their tiny homes. I searched every lit cubbyhole, and it looked wrong.

e-girl voiced my concern, *I don't get it. No one from our church is here.*

Serene frowned, and poked her gloved finger through cyberspace. Web-imagry warped to her eyes and she looked around. *This is the right place . . . can you see the person in C-4?*

The stackhouses were clearly labeled. And e-girl replied, *Umm, nope, that one's dark—but C-5's lit.*

Kay, their records say C-5 is one Adam Davis.

No, it isn't. Adam was the father of the family two doors down from us, but the man sitting in C-5 was not Mr. Davis.

Razz . . . Serene stared into her Web hole, then asked, *Are you sure?*

Legacy joined-in, *Naw, Sensei nuked e-girl's head while reforming the pup. She said it ain't him!*

Shut up, Sandman.

His tone said he was enjoying himself, *Heh. You da ma'am. Excuse her, kids, she's been underground too long, and . . . well . . . she's a Hack.*

Pompous blippin' slag, Serene fired back.

See? he gloated.

She ignored him and verified three more stackhouses, but each time faces belonged to strangers. Our neighbors and family listed in their data-banks were imposters.

We've been pranked, girl. Dump your riders and breakneck for the homepage to unplug, kay?

Kay.

My goggles went black, and I slid them off. Well, we weren't completely skunked. At least we knew where our family hadn't been stashed. My hopes fell like an October leaf.

Grandpa stood and faced the saints. "If my judgment is correct, we've just seen a trap. Had we not confirmed our data, we'd have attempted to rescue a roomful of FBT agents. The Hacks will do what they do best. Everyone else remain alert and rested. Assuming these people are in a Rehab, we must act before the church concludes orientation, otherwise they'll be assigned to twelve-hour shift work-stations throughout the Ward. Legacy, render your sandman cubby armed and dangerous. Have him assist you with Junkman, then see to it that he collects some down-time."

Tinker the grouch raised his hand, an index finger pointing at the ceiling. "Question. Anyone else get razzed at the idea of kids havin' your back when things go hot-'n-heavy, or is it just me?"

Silence filled the room. No one agreed with him, but neither did anyone jump to defend us.

Tinker continued. "What happens when the team needs somethin' an' they drop the ball?" His honesty hurt, but he had a point. We'd do our best, but the freedom-of-religion game was played for keeps. What if our best wasn't good enough?

Grandpa answered immediately, "That's a risk we take with any saint. Whether a cubby-pup is eight or 80, he—" he nodded at e-girl, "—or she, is a novice. We require the services of a Sandman and a field-hack. The Deacons' wisdom has placed these young people in our Cell. Should they meet with failure, it's His will. They're as much a part of our family as you are, Tinker. I'll have no more discussion on the matter. To work everyone, and His will be done."

Saints rose and scattered. My uncle headed to where the CV and kitchen walls cornered. I followed. The green curtains had been drawn back here to accent a painting. It portrayed a bird's eye view of Christ on the cross, looking down at thousands of people in modern dress. We were two steps away when a crack showed in the wall, and a hidden door swung silently open.

I sensed e-girl stirring and looked back as she sat up in her recliner. I wasn't worried that we were being split up. I had no concern for her safety. He was everywhere, and we couldn't be in better hands.

Spin the Web, Sis, I thought to her.

Onward, Christian soldier, she said in my mind. I gave her a wink and followed Legacy into the secret passage.

CHAPTER TWELVE

FLUORESCENTS FLICKERED ON, AND the door closed behind us. Steel shelves and cabinets cluttered with tools, equipment, and supplies surrounded us.

"Welcome to the armed-and-dangerous room." Legacy moved down the first aisle, grabbing items from shelves and piling them on my outstretched arms.

"How you feelin'?" he asked.

"For workin' on an all-nighter, I feel great. It's unbelievable. I feel driven. I have a purpose."

"When other things must come first, your mindware puts off needs like sleep or food. You'll sleep later. I know what you mean, though. I think this is how we're all supposed to feel."

"Why?"

"God made us for Himself. No matter what we try, we can't find rest until we choose Him over emptiness. When we finally give in to Him, it's like we're recharged."

". . . or reformed," I added. "Hey, question. Lightfast made it sound like reformation only works for Fundamentalists, but Neros—" I made a spitting sound. "—have BW tech. What's the difference?"

"Whoa, horse. No answers before we deal with your hatred. What did Christ say about your enemies?"

"Love them, but c'mon."

"These people you hate so bad are on their way to Hell, got that? Permanent forever-'n-ever darkness. Tell me Ephesians 6:12."

"Unk. I get the idea . . ."

My load got lighter as he began taking things off my arms and stacking them back on the shelves.

My mindware fed me the words: *For our struggle is not against flesh and blood, but against the rulers, against the authorities, against the powers of this dark world and against the spiritual forces of evil in the heavenly realms.*

"These Neros have bought the lies told them by expert liars with an immortality of practice, otherwise known as fallen angels. Now tell me Matthew 6:46, 47."

If you love those who love you, what reward will you get? Are not even the tax collectors doing that? And if you greet only your brothers, what are you doing more than others? Do not even pagans do that?

Legacy replaced the stack on my arms, and vice-gripped my shoulders. "These folks need us to live His love, not cause and effect knee-jerk emotions. Every time your finger strokes the trigger of a non-lethal weapon, you've given an unbeliever a wake-up call rather than a death sentence. Hatred has no place in the Body."

He was rough but he was right. "Sorry, won't happen again."

"Bet it does." Legacy pointed up, "And when it does, apologize to Him, not me." He selected more items from the shelves.

"To answer your question, interfacing the brain and the computer dates back to the 1990s. The US military was the first to research brain wave technology, for use in aviation. A pilot could think *fire guns,* a computer would read that thought, and obey.

"After that, special brain wave suits were created to make soldiers stronger and faster. Lightfast was one of the scientists who invented the suits. When he realized what the One State could do with even those frogman-lookin' wetsuits, he destroyed the project and went underground. But all the One State lost was time. Other scientists pieced the suit together and puzzled out the gaps."

"He destroyed the whole project?"

"Please don't ask him. He said it keeps him awake some nights. He told me his virus crashed the DHS ultra-net. Once underground Lightfast designed the second-generation brain wave suit—a belt-pack of hardware replaced those clumsy bodysuits. The One State arrived at a similar model soon after. Their gen-three design went back to a suit. Each one's several million dollars worth of bio-mechanical tech.

"Lightfast's gen-three went the other direction. When he discovered brain wave technology was achievable without hardware, he began loading a kind of software right into the brain. And so we have mindware. You were reformed with gen-three BW tech. So brain wave technology, or BW tech, is a tool for the will in the same way a hammer is a tool for the hand. The difference is that Neros use their own willpower. Whatever they do comes only from themselves. We use His willpower, and His communication to mankind. That gives us a Divine edge. Anyone can use BW tech, but only Fundamentalists can be reformed."

"So what happens if I want ten million dollars?"

I was serious, but my uncle grinned. "Creating something from nothing is still His department. So far, that's way out of our league."

"This is all so unreal—I'm having trouble wrappin' my mind around everything that's happened. Just meeting someone like Lightfast is such a shocker. The guy's a legend. Why isn't he a big boss Deacon, or at least an Elder?"

Legacy bonked me lightly on the head. "This ain't a trade union. A Body part's job is decided by what we were made to be, not our length of service. Lightfast was made to be a Metaphysician."

Meta-fuzz—easy for you to say.

We'd reached the end of the last row and headed back through the secret door. Following the kitchen wall to the next corner, another hidden door opened. A short hallway led to an L-shaped room. It was the bedroom—a small stackhouse. A dome light blinked on in one of the cubbyholes.

"That's your bunk. Dump your gear in there, and take off your shirt and shoes. Put these on." He handed me a pair of brown ankle-high sport-boots with five centimeter soles.

They fit well, and felt like clouds. Then came a body harness. Black nylon straps looped around my thighs and shoulders to cross in an X over my chest and back.

"Now strap these on your forearms." He handed me two rubber-coated metal tubes. Each had a belt that he clipped onto my body harness at the shoulders.

"They're grappling hooks. Through molecular bonding, they can fasten to and release from any surface. High speed motors will reel in the line as fast as you like."

I didn't see any buttons. "How do I make 'em work?"

He tapped his head. "Just want them to."

"And now the QuickDraw holsters. They work the same way. Want a gun and you're holdin' a gun." The twin holsters slung round my neck, and Velcro-ed around my upper arms.

"Okay, try 'em out." Like he said, all I had to do was want them to work. Black automatic pistols sprang down my arms and stopped at my palms. All I had to do was slide my fingers onto triggers and squeeze.

"Israeli Military Industries nine mill. Baby Eagles . . ." He pointed to the last eight fat centimeters of the barrel, ". . . with built-in flash suppressors and silencers. Their smart clips can be loaded with different types of ammo. The round you want is the round that loads."

With a thought, the pistol slid home. There was a problem though. Holding a real pistol was a wakeup call from my dream-come-true. "Having guns is against the law."

"So's believing in the Bible. When a government does that, it makes itself a false god. Give unto Caesar what is Caesar's, and to God what is God's. We must obey God rather than men. We're ordered to stand against false gods, with any tools we have. A gun is our delivery system for second-chance projectiles. Besides, the One State is no more legit than were the Philistines in Judges 15:11. Slide these on."

I pushed into a pair of gauntlets that fit skin tight from fingers to wrists.

"Electrocutioner shock gloves, with built in pepper sprayer. It squirts from the index finger with a seven-meter range."

"Nice touch."

"More right than you know. They're made from a smart material that lets you feel things as though you weren't wearing gloves at all. The soles of your boots and the gloves are made from the same stuff as the grapples. Whenever you wish, they'll bond molecularly with anything they touch. You can crawl up windows like a fly. Which reminds me, the soles of your boots also change to whatever traction you need. They even have spikes for ice."

"Man, where'd you get all this stuff?"

"Body of Christ gift-shop, don't ask again. This is your tool belt. It has a knife, flashlight, folding tool, chip-fryer, extra ammo clips, grenades, and a taser-net gun." I fastened it round my waist.

"Then there's these." Legacy held up a pair of short swords in canvas scabbards, secured with Velcro closures. He walked around behind me and clipped them to my harness and belt so they'd draw upside-down.

"Naw, I ain't stabbin' nobody."

"That's not what they're for. You're a sandman, remember? It's technical and we'll get to it."

He drew a sword of his own and hacked the sleeves off my t-shirt. "So they won't get in the way of your holsters," he explained. "Put that back on." I did, then, with his help, slid into a full-length army overcoat. Too big. The sleeves swallowed my hands. When I looked in the Stackhouse's full-length mirror, the coat hid all my gear. I seemed bigger. Or maybe gold eyes just made me look wiser.

"Put this in your pocket." He held up a hard glasses case. "A pair of com-shades. They show images, maps, a timer, status display, whatever you need. And they hide your gold eyes when you don't want to be noticed. Pocket this, too." He flipped me a pack of Winterfresh Extra.

"Aw, you da man, Unk!"

"You're welcome. Just so happens we got three cases of the

stuff last week. It's my favorite."

I just grinned, zipped it open, and offered him a stick.

While peeling foil-paper, he said, "One last thing. When Light-fast reformed you, he changed your biochip ID to be a kind of relay. Whenever it's scanned, it'll read whatever you want it to. You become whoever you need to be."

"Right now I need to be gone. Who's this Junkman?"

He grinned. "I'm so glad you asked that. Let's take a walk."

CHAPTER THIRTEEN

WE LEFT THE FACTORY THROUGH more slimy storm sewers. Now my eyes gathered in reflected light, making the tunnel twi-light dim rather than inky black. I tuned-out my nose to the mold-smell that had mugged me earlier. That made me blink. Then I tuned-out the sound of my gum as well. You wouldn't believe how ugly-sloppy gum chewing sounds with reformed hearing.

We traveled farther than our first sewer trip, and now walking bent-over wasn't a problem. This time, our secret passage came out through the concrete basement stairwell of an abandoned building, and into drizzle.

We crossed a six-lane street and cut through an apartment complex. The place was slagged. Where outside walls were miss-ing we could see right into rooms. Rainwater poured in through roof holes. Faint voices came from inside. "People live in that?"

Legacy's reply sounded in my mind. *Practice thought speech. Folks live wherever rent is cheap in the Lost Wards. These living condi-tions are worse than a Rehab, but at least people are free.*

A wave of pity washed through me. I knew Lost Wards were for the poor, but I'd never heard of anything like this. *This shouldn't be legal. It's not safe.*

You had it good, Cubby. That's why your mom and dad raised you where they did.

The parking lot held what used to be cars. Illegal gasoline burners from before the big energy crises. Scraps of plastic or metal covered busted-out windows, hiding the people who used them as homes. But I could hear them. Even smell them. I shivered. Not out of fear, but because their hopelessness ran up my spine.

As we passed something that used to be a mini-van, I noticed patches of glitter hanging in the air around it. Whatever-it-was swirled like a small snowstorm rather than falling to the ground.

Hey, what's that sparkling from?

His thought rose in surprise. *By the van?*

Yeah.

You mean you can see that?

Uh . . . yeah.

He laid his arm across my shoulders, threw his head back, and laughed like a madman. *Most saints can't see angels for months after their reformation, if ever!*

I spoke out loud, "Angels!"

He nodded. *Like Lightfast said, reformation opens your senses to the spiritual as well as the physical.*

I suppose if I could sense the Spirit, then why not angels as well? I wondered if we could see angels through the streetlight cameras, then noticed there were none. *Why don't they use cams here?*

They do. They're stolen faster than new ones are put up.

But that's a huge crime! I'd never even heard of anyone taking the risk.

Class three felony.

The cameras aren't worth that much, why risk it?

He swept an arm back at the abandoned cars. *These people have nothing. Look how they live. To fill emptiness, they give the Junkman everything they have. He gets them food, fake ID chips, weapons, and enough crax to make them forget how skunked their lives are.*

We'd puddled along a townhome-lined street. These buildings were missing some shingles and siding in places, but at least their walls were whole.

Groups of shirtless tattooed men sat on porches and leaned against bio-fuel beaters, some of which looked like they might actually run. They went silent and stared flatly as we passed. *What's with the Xs painted everywhere?*

Legacy waved to a group. They snorted and jerked thumbs over their shoulders at us. *These guys are a street gang who work for*

Junkman. They call themselves Tough Times; the Xs means times as in math. Tough-x is why we're here. Helping the poor's dangerous work, so it's up to us Sandmen to work with local street gangs. Our Muscle Cell's brand new and I've only begun making contact with these guys. We're not on good terms yet.

Patches of smoke drifted around the gangers, and few had cigarettes. *What's with the smoke?*

Figures you'd see them too. Fallen angels.

You mean like demons?

Demons, devils, whatever. They're the angels that rose up and were thrown from Heaven's walls.

Razz—An hour ago demons and gangers would have cramped my jaw muscles from fast-forward gum-chewing. I nearly decided Lost Wards were a creation of Hell before I remembered that fallen angels can't create, they only pollute. Seeing such misery, my stomach felt as though I'd just watched a ten-hour docu-drama on crippled starving orphans forced into slavery at leper colonies.

Get ready to go live, Calamity Kid, my uncle warned.

As he spoke, I sensed why. From all down the street, Tough Times splintered, and puddle-strutted toward us. They kept their hands where we couldn't see them. The only one not advancing stood in our path down the sidewalk.

"Tommy's that you?" Legacy called out to him. "Don't you remember what happened the last time you rolled out this welcome mat? Rover's fur growin' back yet, man?"

They kept coming, followed by the smoky smudges. My uncle prayed, *Father, we come to you in the name of your Son. You control all things, so we look to your leadership as we face fallen men and angels. Please protect and guide us. Let the Spirit's power burn through us and the glory be yours. Amen.*

I'd never seen prayer answered so fast. Glittering clouds swirled at the smoky patches. Both disappeared, leaving only the two dozen gangers to deal with—piece-uh-cake.

They closed on us.

"You guys are real slow learners," observed my uncle, shaking his head.

That's when my internal clock blew a battery. The men moved in slow motion. In fact the whole world lagged into slow motion. It was like one of those running in mud nightmares. Panic slammed open my body's adrenaline valves as Legacy explained,

What you're sensing now isn't everything else slowing down, it's you speeding up. Out of nowhere, you'll use skills you didn't even know you had. When your body goes into cruise control, sit back and enjoy the ride. Oh, and no gunplay. We'll get to that later. Then he announced out loud, "Well boys, I guess I beat you too quickly last time, so we're gonna have to do this the hard way."

One of the men behind me on my right swung a chain at my face. I was so wired that it took forever for the chain to get close enough. When it did I reached out, caught the end between my thumb and forefinger, and triggered my shock-glove. His body jerked and collapsed in a pile of meat.

He hadn't even hit the ground before I reacted to the next closest threat—a baseball bat swinging from my right. I sidestepped its slow arc and squirted a shot of pepper spray at the batter's face. Yelling, he dropped the bat to claw at his face with both hands. I brushed the tip of a metal pipe and discharged my other glove: barbequed-bad-guy.

Spinning to my blind side, I found no more challengers. Screams and the smell of burnt hair seemed to buy us some respect, because Tough Times took a step back.

Four gangers littered the ground around Legacy. Tough-x cleared the sidewalk. Nobody stood between the one called Tommy and us, and I saw why.

Tommy had planted his feet in a wide stance and had a two-handed grip on a pistol. His finger tensed around his trigger—

CHAPTER FOURTEEN

AS LEGACY WARNED, MY BODY shifted into overdrive, my com-shades showed a red line from Tommy's pistol to Legacy's chest. My brain crunched all the stats on his Freedom Arms .38 automatic. My eyes worked out distances and angles. My skin factored in wind speed. I was literally seeing the bullet's path. My body lurched, putting my left shoulder in harm's way.

On a more human level, I think my heart rate matched the year

Columbus sailed the ocean-blue, and adrenaline's panic parked a Buick on my chest. I instinctively threw my hands up to shield myself, as though it would do any good. While stuffing overdrive away into that favorite's corner of my brain right between getting soap in eyes and stubbing toes, a shoulder muscle tweaked where the red line had touched me.

That was all. There wasn't even force from the bullet hitting me. The flattened slug tap-tapped as it dropped onto wet sidewalk. My eyes zoomed in for a close up of Tommy's body language. He was shooting again. The red line ended at my belly. I stood my ground, shielding my uncle. Again, the bullet fell to the concrete. He shot again, and again, and again. Another round bounced off my thigh, but the rest went wide as he lost his aim. He emptied his clip at us.

Legacy marched toward him, Samurai braid wagging. "Put that thing away before you hurt yourself."

The punk struggled to load another clip when Unk slapped the pistol away. Twenty gangers still surrounded us yet not one of them moved. I folded my arms across my chest and strolled toward the action.

Tommy beefed just under two meters, so the uppercut he aimed at Legacy's jaw could have split a cinder block. To make it look good, my uncle moved his head with the punch. If I could flatten bullets, I figured Tommy's fist was gonna do time melting ice packs. His yelp said I was right. Legacy tilted his head the other way, tapping his opposite cheek. Demonstrating the kind of judgment that led to street gang membership, Tommy drew back and tried to crush the knuckles of his other hand.

"Finished?" my uncle asked. Tommy whimpered, doubled over and dropped to his knees, swelling meat-hooks held limply to his chest. Legacy stood next to him, knotted the injured man's hair in his fingers, and jerked back. Stiffening the fingers of his other hand into a blade, he drew back to crush Tommy's throat. Freezing there, he looked to the watching gangers.

"This is what Tough Times respects? Might makes right? Your leader's at my mercy. Lucky for ol' Tom here, there's a new game in town." He pulled back on Tommy's hair until he splashed on soggy sod. "We're just on our way to pay Junkman a little visit. Your boss-man needs to know that *he's* got a new boss. He's gonna play by new rules, or find a new game. The new king of the hill is Liberator, and Liberator says treat everyone how you'd like them to treat you. You're gonna be livin' by that. Next time we pass through, we'll see who's followin' the rule, and who needs another lesson." We turned our backs and ambled down the wet sidewalk.

I liked these boots. My socks were still dry. *Why did you call God, Liberator?*

Some of Tough-x are in the One Church. They've been taught the Bible's a myth. If I said Jesus or God, they'd have been thinking Easter Bunny or Tooth Fairy. They've got to see that people can live as though He's as real as Junkman.

A voice spoke in my mind. It was familiar yet strange at the same time—like someone I knew from my childhood. *1 Corinthians 9:19-22*, it said. I knew the verses. They showed that Paul spoke with Jews differently than with Greeks. He met people where they were at in life. That was how Legacy spoke with the gangers. In their own terms.

But who sent me the verse? Was a Hack helping me? I ran mindware check on my com-shades. It came up normal. It also showed my uncle to be the only one thought-speeching me. I could tell him I was hearing voices. *Not!* I answered myself. *So, we're bulletproof, yes?*

Mostly. Ever heard of people in the far-east sleeping on a bed of nails?

Yeah.

Same kind of thing. We call it the flinch response. A metaphysician's got more degrees than a thermometer so Lightfast uses lots of really big words to explain it. My mindware didn't come with a PhD in physics. From what I understand, our senses judge the bullet's path, and that spot on our body changes at the molecular level. Somehow the bullet's stopped, and its force is absorbed. But it only works if we know the shot's coming. If you hadn't seen Tommy shooting, your mindware wouldn't have helped. Most Sandmen fall to snipers.

I eyed the rooftops. *So you've tangled with these guys before. What was that thing about Rover's fur?*

That brought a smile to his face. *Do you remember when I found you under the bridge, how the peacekeepers were thrown backward after I touched my forehead?*

Yep.

I scorched 'em. Hit 'em with a brain wave attack that overloaded their nervous system. I make the same gesture—touch my forehead—every time I scorch, to focus. You'll have to find a focus-motion you're comfortable with. Anyway, I scorched Tough Times when we first met. Tommy told his pit-bull I was a chicken-flavored chew toy. Brain waves from a scorch travel in a cone shape, affecting everything in their path, so Tommy and his pals went down with the puppy. I'd never used the attack on an animal before. I thought I'd killed the poor beast. It stood long enough to mess all over Tommy's shoes before they both took turf naps. I checked Rover and he still had a heartbeat, but when I ran my hand over his coat, fur came out in clumps.

Hey, we could open one of those doggie barber shops. A little yellow flip-com blinked on the left corner of my com-shades. I answered it.

Cut the chatter you two, it's glory time.

Instinct triggered teasing mode. *e-girl's got new toys.*

Sandboys get toys, Hacks get skills. While you two've been playing with the neighbor boys, Serene's been showin' me round Terminal.

Terminal? You at the airport or bus station?

Legacy answered, *Junkman runs things out of a dance club called Terminal. That's where we're headed. Brief your brother, e-girl. I haven't told him a thing.*

Well for starters, the rocket surgeons have the com-vision that's running their security, wired to the Web! The Body Surfers have been spy-tappin' the place for over a week now. Oh, and they know you're coming. Tough-x just warned Junkman.

I winced. *Razz. Woulda been nice to have had surprise on our side. Tell me about Terminal, Sis.*

Look for yourself. A blueprint appeared on my drizzle-dotted lenses. Features on the map lit up as she named them. *Outside, it's a plain gray pole-barn. Inside, there's three main parts. The warehouse area is the dance club, the upstairs half loft overlooking the dance floor is Junkman's office, and below the loft are some private rooms. A set of stairs goes from the warehouse up to the loft, and another goes down into the private rooms. There're three outer doors: a loading dock/ front entrance, an emergency back door, and an overhead side door. Their security cameras record both audio and video. There are two outside on opposite corners of the building doin' a slow sweep of the whole area. You've got four more inside scannin' the whole place with no blind spots.*

Our uncle elbowed me and winked as he spoke. *Hey, ask Serene if you ladies can kill the cams while we're in there. No need to give away pictures of ourselves . . .*

Hold, please. e-girl returned a moment later, *She says she's hurt 'cause you think so little of her.*

Legacy chuckled. *Awww. Tell her I'm sorry.*

She says you're real sorry.

Legacy laughed. *Okay, okay, give Calamity a head count on Junkman's bad guys.*

We can see 'em on Terminal's cams, but a static generator frazzles the sound every time we try to get audio in the loft.

Video from inside the place replaced the blueprint on my comshades. The camera angle panned around the club as she named the players. *You've got two muscle-heads working the front door. Junkman's up in the loft with his bodyguards, and these two stick to him like Band-Aids. Five gunslingers have joined them up there since Tough Times called. Add four bartenders, and that makes fourteen bullies. Since we can't get sound, Serene's been readin' lips off the video feed. She ran the bodyguards' streetnames through the peacekeeper database.*

The view zoomed in on a thin man in a desk recliner. With slicked back blow-dryer hair and a black button-down shirt, he belonged on the set of a German performance-car commercial. I hoped the news of our visit had something to do with his scowl. *Junkman must be as slick as he looks, because all they've got on him is not payin' taxes. Word on the street: if you can pay for it, he'll find it.*

Bad guy number two calls himself Hacksaw. The peacekeepers have a file on him, complete with vid. A picture of a big ugly nasty floated next to his vid-shot. Lacking Junkman's fashion sense, he was currently wearing the same leather vest from the peacekeeper file. I decided it was a very real possibility that he hadn't changed clothes since his arrest. With a goatee, scar, and a bald tattooed head, there had to be a key in his pocket that started a Harley. What he lacked in hygiene, he made up for in measurements. His arms were easily as big around as my waist. *His hobbies are armed robbery, assault, gun runnin', breakin' bones, teasin' animals, and takin' candy from babies. Nice boy.*

His buddy Dragoon could be a problem. The Terminal footage zoomed in on an average sized man wearing what looked like a black hooded wetsuit with a weird set of thick wire mesh goggles. *Yes, that's a gen-one BW tech suit he's got there. Hacksaw and Dragoon are underworld problem solvers. When their boss wants to make sure something slacks his way, he sends one of them. These two hadn't been* seen in Terminal until after Legacy met Tough Times last week. Since then they've been on Junkman thicker than his dry-look hair gel. He must pay some fat fees to Ward Three's crime lord if they're both here.

Legacy cut in, Thanks, e-girl. Good work, Pup.

Thanks back. Gotta hack. His will be done, guys. The yellow flip-com disappeared.

Rounding the corner of a small factory, Legacy pointed at the plain gray building in front of us. Sounds like you're gonna have some fun. When things go hot 'n heavy, we use our pistols to clear the room. You saw bulletproof clothing in that feed, so aim at foreheads. Nap everyone except Junkman. He needs to see what we can do or else he won't deal. The wildcard is Dragoon. We'll just play him as we go.

That all? I asked.

Nope. Still gotta talk to the Boss. My uncle led our prayer as we slopped across the wet gravel parking lot.

My socks were still dry.

CHAPTER FIFTEEN

WE HAD TO SWEET TALK our way past the bouncers. Electro-cutioner shockgloves helped a bunch. Colored strobes and la-sers sliced through the dark smoky room in sync with an acid rock beat that thumped my innards. My mindware leveled off the room's lighting like a night-vision scope. It muffled the music too, allowing me to pick up other sounds. I adjusted my nose to dam a river of smells. Even with reformed senses it was hard to tell where cigarette smoke left off and demons began. Although it was mid-day, thrill seekers packed the place.

Pleather and silk mixed with dirty cotton and denim. Dancers decked in oils and perfumes swayed alongside others with daily choices between food and soap.

Along the walls, mounds of cushions hid the floor. Those not dancing sprawled out in groups among the pillows. The corner to our right featured a square bar, the stairs to the loft just behind.

My uncle sniffed the air and made for the bar.

"Is that fresh brewed coffee I smell?" he asked the bartender. The man nodded. His sour look said he'd rather suffer an IRS audit than talk to us. He'd seen what we'd done to the bouncers and he stank of fear.

"Well, I'd love a cup. Triple caffeine, please," said my uncle cheerfully.

The bartender filled a plastic mug. As Legacy added enough sugar to trigger diabetic seizures, the bartender checked the stairs and leaned close, "You don't want to go up there."

Legacy gave him the big-innocent-eyed look, "Why on earth not?"

"They're waiting to kill you!" he hissed.

"Goodness!" My uncle sipped his mug. "Well, at least I got a trip-caf java before they send me home, eh? Thanks, pal."

He ran his hand under the ID chip reader. "There's a little something there for you too. Just might cover a down payment on a new place in a new ward, if you know what I mean."

We climbed the stairs staring up the barrels of an Ithaca 12 gauge and two Fabrique National .308 assault rifles that still wore powder-blue peacekeeper globes on their stocks.

A static Sound Barrier muffled the music and kept most of the smoke out of the loft. Furniture of real leather and wood bugged my eyes and gave the loft a Fortune-500-CEO-command-center feel. Our grandmother had an old dining room set made from that stuff. Sitting on dead trees and cows always seemed weird to me.

Hacksaw held two pistol-grip sawed-off streetsweepers in his huge hands, one on each of us. The other bullies had a grab bag of firearms. In fact, the only ones not holding guns on us were Junkman and Dragoon. The Capone still sat behind his desk, and his rubber-suited problem solver sat slack on a leather sofa.

Legacy swept his free hand at the dance floor below, "Quite a setup you've got here, Junkman. This will do nicely."

Junkman ignored the comment. "So, Liberator sends a man and a boy to tell me I gotta start payin' him dues."

My uncle spoke in my head, *He's name-dropping like he knows what's going on to shake us up and see what we do.* Legacy strolled through the loft sipping coffee, cool as absolute-zero, like he didn't care half a dozen guns were ready to make him holey.

"Tommy got it all wrong. Liberator's in the business of freeing people." He grinned and lifted an eyebrow at Junkman. "You wouldn't believe what you're going to get out of this deal. You'll have to give up your free will, of course."

"And do what Liberator wants, right?" Junkman's voice oozed baditude.

"You're sharper than Tommy, that's for sure. May I sit here?"

The bully sitting on the arm of the chair looked to Junkman. His boss gave a tight nod. The bully moved, glaring a curse at my uncle.

Now he's listening. Time to make our pitch. He sat, placing his mug on the floor next to him.

"What the Big Man wants is for you to stop selling crax, guns and fake ID chips. He'd like to use your skills and hustle to run an orphanage-slash-community-center. See, right now you lack a clearly defined goal. You want more money, more power, and more comfort. You won't stop wanting more 'til you're busted, dead, or replaced by someone even greedier than you. Because you never stop wanting, you can never have enough to fill you. If you can't be filled, you're a slave to wanting. Emptiness has mastered you, and Liberator wants to free you.

"All that Liberator demands is that you stop trying to fill your empty little self and serve Him by helping those around you. Say, you wouldn't have any cream?"

Junkman wore a cold smile, "You're dangerously rude." His poisonous tone grew more toxic with every word, "You walk into my place, and tell me what I'm going to do—"

"Junkman, listen to yourself."

Cutting off Junkman, my uncle dropped into the Capone's low growl, ". . . walk into MY place, tell ME what I'M going to do . . . You're so busy trying to have everything that you missed the part where you lost everything. You see, Liberator's turf is wherever we go. And now, we . . ." he spread his hands, ". . . we are here."

The storm in Junkman's eyes broke loose, "Not for long. Boys, make them not-here."

Mindware put the world back into slow motion. I leapt straight up and did the splits to keep my legs above any shots they'd get off.

The Baby Eagles jumped into my hands before my feet left the ground. By sight, sound, smell, and electromagnetic, I'd already locked targets. My eyes flitted from one forehead to another, my limbs followed squeezing pistols. Sandman guns spat silencer soft, lost in their four crude cannon blasts. That was all they managed.

From the main floor below, screams shredded rock-'n-roll, and terror's stink flooded Terminal.

By the time gravity reversed my direction, I'd napped three of the no-names, and plugged the extra-large Hacksaw twice, just to be sure. He looked baffled for half a second before falling over sideways. *Tim-ber.*

e-girl texted us an update, *The bartenders have headed for the hills. Dragoon and Junkman are alone.*

Legacy'd napped the other two bullies and now covered Junkman. I landed with my right hand pistol tracking Dragoon, and swung the second to join.

The guy had street smarts. Rather than going for a gun and making himself a mindware target for my pistols, he rushed me and drew swords.

Legacy laughed, "Take 'im, Calamity!"

CHAPTER SIXTEEN

NOT SURE WHAT UNK HAD found so funny, I let him worry about everything else and focused on Dragoon. Baby Eagles nested, I drew my own blades from beneath my coat. It looked like I was about to figure out what these pointy things were for. Their design was simple, down to the plain stock crossbar style handguards.

Rolling my wrists, the short pale gold blades spun light and well-balanced. My mindware scythed them in interlocking circles and they sang as they cut through the air. Overdrive engaged and my arm placed one sword slightly above my head while angling the other at my knees, perfectly placed to deflect Dragoon's first blows. A shower of red sparks exploded to skip and skitter around our feet.

Legacy's voice filled my head, *The sparks are normal. Pickups built into the swords hilts carry scorching brain wave energy. It's discharged when the blades touch.*

We began to dance. It felt awkward. My arms and legs dragged the rest of me along to do what they needed. After an hour-long minute, I relaxed some. My balance shifted more smoothly as I moved, but that didn't make me feel any less like a ballet class dropout.

My body seemed to have forgotten that I was right-handed. My left flowed fluid as my right. A blade arced down to split my skull. Sparks flew as I blocked the head-shot with my right. His other jabbed in at my stomach, but I angled my left sword to deflect the gut thrust.

After Dragoon's first blade whistled past my nose, I lunged, turning the block into a slash aimed at his chest. Forced back, he beat down my sword with both of his. He countered, driving his swords in upward thrusts, but I wasn't there.

Somersaulting past him, I kept one blade up to guard against his and swept at his legs with my second. Leaping into an airborne roll, he landed on a nearby armchair. A blind backhand sliced at my chest as I sprang to my feet. In a burst of sparks, I parried and swept at his legs again.

I was beginning to feel like a pirate. *I can't get . . . the feel of this . . . Why swords?*

Without looking, the rest of my senses told me Legacy was back in his chair, sipping coffee. *A BW tech brawl is tricky. If one person even touches the other, a scorch flattens him. Swords are used so you don't see little birdies flying laps around your head every time contact is made.*

Dragoon had leapt over my sweep, putting the chair between us. His voice rolled like rocks over gravel. "I thought a Sandman would be bigger, you're more of a Sand-boy. I was gonna go slack on ya, kid, but you're too fast for that. My mistake. Time to finish this business." He edged around the chair with feline grace, rolling his neck and shoulder muscles.

His Sand-boy remark blistered me the wrong way. "This is pleasure, not business. Calamity may force you into early retirement," I warned. We touched sword tips, circling each other in a sparking flood. He flashed into a spin, both swords coming around like fan blades. I stopped both with my left, and thrust with my right, but he'd anticipated and had already reversed his direction for a block. Our blades parried, slashed and countered.

My uncle continued teaching, *The flinch response will stop a blade as well as a bullet. It's nearly impossible to be cut. The scorch does all the damage.*

Spiff! The thought of bloodstains on my only shirt had me worried sick.

I couldn't tell if Dragoon's blows struck harder or if I was tiring, but he patiently forced me back. Either he was doing something right, or I was doing something wrong. Or both. Was he just better than I? He even smelled confident. Maybe his suit made a difference. My inexperienced showed. Another step back would pin me against the loft's railing. I'd be out of the elbowroom needed to swing a sword.

Then I heard a voice. The one I'd heard on the way here: *When you are persecuted in one place, flee to another. Matthew 10:23.* Great, I thought to myself, *I'm getting' waxed, and now I'm hearin' things.* I got the message though. At least it gave good advice. From my perspective time slowed even further and I watched for an opening.

Dragoon slashed from below, I parried, counter-slashing to buy room. He faked at my face while thrusting at my ribs. This was it. I didn't react until his thrust was halfway to me. He put all his weight behind the finishing blow. He guessed that I couldn't dodge the move, and I counted on this reaction.

Twisting sideways at the waist, my upper body fled. A cookie sheet may have fit between his steel and my ribs, but I wouldn't have bet a stick of Winterfresh. To avoid bounce-testing the warehouse dance floor, he wrapped himself around the railing.

My waist-bend became three cartwheels that took me to an open area, and I sucked a deep breath just to blow it out my mouth. Now I had it. Standing sideways, I faced him down my right shoulder, arm and sword. My left blade positioned itself above and behind my head in a scorpion's sting.

Dragoon's powerful attack had distracted me. For the first time since my reformation, I'd met doubt. I had stopped relying on His strength. Lightfast's prayer at our reformation came to me. *Father, I come to you in the name of the Son. My will and my power are my weaknesses. Let me leave these behind and use Your strength. Make me a lightning rod for the power of the Spirit who fills me. By Your will, amen.*

Again the new voice sounded, *But you will receive power when the Holy Spirit comes on you. Acts 1:8*

Dragoon untangled himself from the railing and faced me. Feet shoulder width apart, he slowly arced both swords to meet above his head. His chin almost rested on his chest as he dropped his arms and came at me, a battle cry emptying his lungs. I didn't flinch. I now knew his drama to be aimed at my faith. But my faith no longer focused on me.

Still meters away, Dragoon leapt into a figure skater spin. Bearing his swords straight out, he became a human blender. Sparks exploded from my blades as I turned his furious strokes. Spinning past me, he dive-rolled halfway down the loft, and spun to his feet. To find me on him tighter than his rubber suit. Barely countering my blows, reformed overdrive gave him something to do. I became his new hobby.

Legacy clicked his tongue, shaming me, *You had me worried for a minute there.*

Yeah, tell me 'bout it. You weren't the only one.

What did you learn?

Great. I'm in the middle of my first duel and my uncle pops a quiz.

The mindware worked so much of my brain that, I barely formulated an answer, and finding enough juice for thought-speech was a laugh. *Except for Lightfast's mindware . . . I don't know a thing about . . . sword-play . . . if I start trusting in my skills . . . I'm no better than Dragoon . . . if I trust in Him, I'm just along for the ride . . .*

He sounded pleased, *Indeed! We call it walking in the Spirit. All this comes to you so quickly. You must have great faith, Pup. As long as you're walking in the Spirit, Dragoon can't beat you. Unless He allows it, of course. There's something else I have to show you, so don't beat this guy with your swords.*

I had to laugh, which made Dragoon shoot me a funny look. *Razz! Think he'll . . . surrender . . . if I ask nicely?* My sarcasm smelled bitter.

Now it was Dragoon taking one step forward for every two steps back. Whenever he stormed into a new series of attacks I countered, held my ground, then pressed. The wall drew close behind him. He fought like a cornered animal and his forced retreat came measured in centimeters.

Finally squeezed out of maneuvering room, Dragoon jumped

back to thud hard against the wall. His breath came in gulps, and his arms hung limp at his sides. I could finish him and he knew it. So why did his eyes glint like light off chrome?

"Now . . . I've . . . gotyou . . . rightwhere . . . I . . . want . . . you!" he gasped.

Dragoon snapped his arm out to point at me. Even though he just stood there pointing, I sensed his attack. The air between us shimmered and swam. Energy streamed through my body like sun through glass. Static invaded my nervous system to rip my senses from my brain, from my muscles. Something tried to erase me. I sucked breath and held it. Overdrive engaged instantly, shaping my brain waves into a battering ram that pounded back. We clashed, and muscle reflex stretched my body tight. Back spasms buckled my knees. My forehead slicked with sweat, betraying the intensity that blazed inside my head. A smell like burnt oil tainted the air.

Legacy explained, *Welcome to the land of scorch. When it's used against someone else with BW tech, it's a battle of willpower. You're both trying to overload the other's nervous system.*

Blood throbbed in my ears. The pain stabbing my temples was like eating too much ice cream too quickly—big-time brainfreeze.

Think of it like arm wrestling, but with thoughts instead of arms. For the loser, it's like being touched by a sword, which stamps one way ticket to la-la land.

Ugh . . . was all I managed.

For some reason Legacy found this funny, *Heh, spiff, isn't it? Just remember, He's using you to save your family.*

Yeah . . . my family. . . Mom, Dad, and Jeff rehabbed . . . gutted and remade . . . my sister's tears . . . our neighbors imprisoned. The thought laced me with a ragged wrath. In the deepest dungeon of my soul, I opened the door to anger's cage. The emotion surged free. I harnessed it and held on.

After tragedy swallowed whole lives of good people, after having no choices, I made Dragoon the object of my rage. Wrath rode rampant while I clung to its back. Fists on temples, I pushed back to my feet and counterattacked through my focus action.

I winked at Dragoon.

My wail of grief thickened into a battle cry. I rode wrath's rage to an atomic pinpoint before striking. My own energy heaved against his, and pushing the flow-point back into him. Deep into him. With a scream his back arched against the wall, but in that instant, my anger was spent. Gone. My fission-reaction warhorse flaked to ash.

In a single gulp, emptiness had swallowed my anger. I'd stopped serving Him, and emptiness had laid me bare. Dragoon's scorch crashed back through me and my world came apart . . . blown backward . . . senses stopped . . . except for sight . . . the whole room bounced . . . like watching the feed from a thrown vid cam . . . flat on my back . . . I asked His forgiveness for looking to my own strength . . . once again.

When will I learn? was my last thought.

CHAPTER SEVENTEEN

LEGACY WAS THERE, HELPING ME off the floor. The time that passed could have been seconds or days. At the moment and in my condition, there was no difference between the two. Large church-bells rang my ears, but after counting arms, legs, fingers, toes, and heads, not only did I possess all the body parts that I'd started with, but after counting twice, it appeared that I'd gained a toe and a head.

Dragoon sat slumped against the wall where he'd last stood.

My uncle spoke gently, *His willpower, not yours, Pup. What a Calamity. Sit and rest awhile.*

Uh-huh. I fell back into a chair.

Legacy took the plastic mug in his free hand, his other still covering Junkman with an Eagle. "Now *that* was entertaining. Well lawbreaker, as I see it, you have three choices. You can work for something bigger than money and comfort. Or you can call the peacekeepers and tell 'em Liberator muscled in on your operation. Kay, that's not really a choice. Or you can run. Retire. Get out of the way because with or without you, this is the here and now. Maybe your buddy Tommy can roll with the changes."

Three of the smoky patches had come back to hang in the

air around Junkman. They seemed strong here. "You said that I would profit. What do I get out of this?"

"You weren't listening. You'd be freed from emptiness."

The greasy man looked unhappy. "Someone else will move on my turf if I stop doin' business."

"That's Liberator's problem now. I'd not worry."

Junkman leaned forward, elbows on knees. "Who's gonna pay for all this bleedin' heart do-gooder stuff?"

Legacy held out his coffee cup, extended his index finger and nailed Junkman in the face with pepper spray. While the Capone squirmed in his chair, Legacy walked around behind his desk and kicked it over.

"You know, this is a really unsafe work area." Mounted beneath the desktop was a sawed-off shotgun. My uncle sat on the overturned desk, handed him a box of tissues that had fallen to the floor, and waited for the pepper spray to thin-out before continuing. "To answer your question, Liberator would foot the bill. He knows your money's tied up. For a rich man, you really have nothing."

Grab their guns, Pup, time to fade. Dizzying to my feet, I began by wobbling over and yanking the shotgun from the desk.

Junkman's eyes and nose ran like faucets. "How do I know I can trust you?"

"You don't. I gave my word, now I'll either do what I say, or I won't. Liberator will prove Himself. But I don't have to lecture a businessman on risk."

Junkman forced a miserable smile, "No, you don't. Don't have much choice, do I."

My uncle looked at the sleeping gunmen. "The Movers will be stopping by in a few minutes to clean up this mess and begin remodeling. They'll go over any details and help you however they can. We'll be by later to check on things."

Legacy rose. I followed him to the stairs. He started singing:

> "Ya better watch out,
> ya better not cry,
> ya better not pout,
> I'm tellin' you why . . ."

Reaching the steps, he turned, "Oh, by the way . . . I gotta tell ya, you brew some really ace coffee. Needs cream, though."

We stashed their guns under the dance floor's cushions on the way out. At the front door that little yellow flip-com flashed on my com-shades.

e-girl squealed *That was awesome! Serene wants me to tell you the Movers are on their way in. You guys were spiff! Well, except for when Dragoon knocked Calamity Kid on his butt!* She giggled, laughed, and then fought to breathe.

Choke on it, com-sneak, I thought-mumbled.

Legacy came to my rescue, *That Dragoon turned out to be pretty good. For a pup, Kid did great. Remember when I said you two were more ready than most who come to us? You're proving it.*

Aw, you say that to all the cubbies. Praise makes me squirm, so I've a habit of humor.

No, 1st Peter 4:2 says, he does not live the rest of his earthly life for evil human desires, but rather for the will of God. Slagging your own wishes to make room for His, comes easy to you both. Believe + learn + do = being who He made you to be. Reformation's purpose is acting in love, and you two are action heroes!

He's given us great teachers. Gotta go, boys. Serene says it's my bedtime and my eyelids second the motion.

Our uncle said the magic words, *For Calamity too. We'll be there in a few. Sleep sweet.*

To Him be the glory, and her flip-com disappeared.

I covered a yawn, "Razz, sleep sounds quad-ace."

"Your mindware knows when you need it, and when you have the time for sleep, your body starts to shut down. Sandmen especially. Using reformed abilities takes a lot outta ya, and you're a pup who's just had quite a workout."

That gave me an opening. Muddled as I was, I had to know, "About my abilities . . . I wasn't gonna say anything, but somethin' keeps happenin'. I'm not sure what to make of it. I'm, uh . . . hearin' a voice." I expected raised brows over a you're-not-the-quickest-flash-in-the-pan look.

I didn't expect his knowing smile. "Speaks in Bible verses, right?"

I really really didn't expect an answer. "What is it? It always has somethin' to do with what's goin' on at the time. Like the mindware's alive or somethin'."

He nodded, "That's the Spirit. He speaks through the Word.

Like seeing angels, hearing His voice usually takes awhile. If the Spirit's leadin' ya, you don't need me any longer."

"Hey now, I just got here."

"You think I can teach you more than the Holy Spirit?"

I couldn't argue that one.

"'At's what I thought, nice talkin' to ya'. Look, you've got the tech stuff down. Your mindware learns from experience so the more you use a skill, the better you get. Things replay while you dream, like training tapes. Nothin' left for me to teach ya."

He mussed up my hair, "Time for that stackhouse bunk, nephew."

CHAPTER EIGHTEEN

ARISE AND WALK, CALAMITY KID." Grandpa's voice brought me out of a deep sleep, yet I was suddenly alert, aware, and focused. It was the first time I'd *ever* woke up that way. If I no longer needed two hours to get my head together, reformation was worth that alone.

"Forgive me for disturbing your rest, but a matter has arisen that requires your attention."

I pulled my boots on and sensed mixed news about him. He led the way to the common room while I dug in my pockets for a stick of gum.

e-girl wore a gray zippered-jumpsuit. She sat with Serene in the sofa pit, watching the main CV. I blinked hard to make sure my eyes were working. A Terrorist Webwire field reporter interviewed Jeff. Our brother was on CV!

"... and what made you call the FBT hotline?"

Jeff wore a serious look "I'd been thinkin' 'bout how my parents had raised my brother and I. My sister's still goin' through it. I finally realized it was my duty as a citizen to call the hotline. What my parents have done is wrong. It's against the law and it's not healthy."

Anger slipped my soul's dungeon and attacked my new stick

of Winterfresh.

The reporter clapped a hand on Jeff's shoulder, "You're a brave man who's made the right decision."

Jeff became a freeze frame that shrank to the upper left corner. The pastry-sweet Terrorist Webwire anchorwoman, Delisha Lix, filled center screen, reclaiming her CV-throne on an insane quest to log maximum air-time. More North Americans watched sports news than any other Webwire. Entertainment and terrorism always ran neck-and-neck for the number two and three spots. Anchorwoman Delisha Lix had a lot to do with the Terrorist Webwire's ratings, like blonde curls, sky blue eyes, a velvet voice, and plastic surgery super-curves that made the number 8 look like a lumberyard mascot.

The anchorwoman finished her story draped across an armchair. "Is he too-good-to-be-true or what? I want one of those for *my* room! The Governor's signed that scrumptious snack to the Patriotic Relations Institute. Mr.-nice-in-shining-armor gets paychecks for charming One State schoolgirls on a globetrotter speaking tour. As a bonus, Jeff Williams is the Chicago Apartment Mall's newest tenant. And we ain't talkin' diamond stackhouse. The IRS has him booked in a Celeb Suite! A champagne-ending for the yum-may boy-hero." Delisha examined her nails and a sidebar popped up beside her.

e-girl worked the CV's menu with her brain wave remote. "I've seen this next one already. Scan this drama."

Delisha strutted another story atop five-inch heels, and behind a tsk-tsk expression. "A related terrorist-cell story stars David and Jen Williams. You guessed it, Jeff William's wicked brother and sister. The Illinois State peacekeepers bagged all the terrorists except these two. As of tonight, Dave and Jen are manhunted-at-large by every PK in Northern Illinois." She struck a pose with both her palms a-ceiling, and our newest school photos appeared in the air.

"These two disappeared right from under watching street-cams. Peacekeepers say they must have had help from the terrorist underground. Think they joined Chicago's branch of the national Fundi terrorist movement known as The Body? You ain't alone. Log in and vote now, but the FBT's already moved their case to the Fundi file. The Williams kids now wear the million-dollar terrorist reward. If you've got information that leads to their arrest, well, can you say shop 'til you drop? The PKs suggest caution though. And I echo that, cause they believe the brats to be armed and dangerous. Dollars and danger, what more can a girl ask for?" Delisha lay long on a coffee table, flipping through a fashion catalog as the sidebar reappeared.

I slumped on the sofa, staring at our pictures. It wasn't Billy, after all.

Tinker thundered, "So the pups join the million dollar reward club. You catch all that slag 'bout their brother? He Judases his own family and that strump talks him up like he's Dudley-Blippin'-Do-Right! When this punk opens his real wood front door, he's in the metroplex's top-ritz mall! Rotten oozing scobs!" He headed for the kitchen leaving a trail of grumble.

Grandpa sighed, "Betrayed by one closest to you. That rings a bell."

e-girl's gold eyes tinted blue and she hugged me.

Serene put a hand on my shoulder. "Never be surprised by sin. We're all in it. For what it's worth, I'm sorry."

Grandpa rolled up a workstation chair. "That was the bad news. And now for the good news: Body Surfers hacked the FBT's system. They've found your mother and father."

I ground my teeth and leaned forward, "Where?"

"The FBT's holding your whole church in a safe house. A factory in Ward Thirty-One."

"So why are we sittin' here? Let's get live."

He held up a hand, "Not quite yet. Acquiring your brother is paramount. Security at the Apartment Mall there is top notch, so we must take him while he's at your parents' house packing his belongings."

I didn't follow. "Why do we need Jeff?"

"To authenticate the church's location. Interrogation. Who knows, he may even be sorry for what he's done."

"Well, I hope so. But you said he's alone. Isn't it strange that there's no security detail?"

"Indeed. As this may very well be a trap, caution is our design. You'll be transported inside another tractor-trailer. The driver will block the streetlight-cam that's posted across from your townhome."

"Sky-cams?"

"Cloud cover remains thick." The global warming effect regularly soaked the midwest in permanent drizzle of Seattle proportions.

"You'll be going-in alone, but the local Muscle Cell will provide you with Sandman back-up. They'll be concealed around your neighborhood. e-girl will accompany you and remain in the truck. You've the ability to send what you see and hear in the same manner as thought-speech. She'll relay your sensory feed to the Sandmen. If there's any trouble, it will rapidly be concluded."

I let out a big sigh, "Okay. Where's Legacy?"

"He's inspecting the goings-on at Terminal. He cannot escort you on this one."

I'd have felt better with my uncle along, but He's the boss. "Truck's in the dock?"

"Positively. Everything is prepared. Same signal as earlier; the driver will disengage the engine twice when you're in place."

e-girl stood waiting, and smelled ready.

I stood. "Then let's fade." Without another word, we headed for the grate.

To save our energy, e-girl and I used no thought speech during the trip. We both needed more sleep to be in top form. With thoughts of Jeff richocheting around my skull with the destructive effect of a bullet, the ride took forever. It had been scads easier to blame Billy for everything. My blood went all orange-bubbly-lava at the thought of my own brother Judasing our whole church. To think I'd actually worried about the dirt skunk. He hated sharing our tiny apartment and there was no way he could afford his own place, but Judasing his way to freedom?

The knife in my back showed his fingerprints. I had to know how it could be worth it to him. Confusion free-flowed my soul in flabbergast, and its dungeon cage still sat empty when the bio-diesel's roar died twice.

"We're here. You talk to the Boss?" e-girl whispered.

"Yep. Scads-o-prayer."

"Start sendin' me your sense feed when you get out."

"Kay." I started the backward wiggle.

She touched my shoulder. "Walk in the Spirit."

"Jeff better pray that I do." Out I slid.

The street stretched empty and I sensed no one. Unlit windows of our church families' townhouses reminded me why.

A breeze whisked bio-diesel fumes over my skin. Not from our truck, but from a Ryder rental truck parked in the Eddingtons' drive. *You gotta be kiddin' me.* The One State wasted no time reassigning housing permits. I slid my com-shades on and keyed the yellow flip-com. e-girl connected with me and I started the feed. Then, dodging raindrops, I made for the front door.

The boxes stacked in the entryway made me squeeze in sideways and I eased the door shut, careful not to click the latch. I picked up a soft noise like rubbing cloth, upstairs in Mom and Dad's bedroom.

I stood for a few minutes listening for any other noises in the house. The place was trashed. Papers, coats, CDs, tools, a light bulb--our family's rubble cluttered the living-room floor. On the carpet near the door, a rainbow glimmer caught my eye. The bottle of *Flashpoint*. My eyes squeezed shut. Dad had made it home before they got him. I crouched to pick it up. The outline of the boot that crushed its fancy sun cap still marked carpet fibers. Again lava bubbled hot in my veins. Within my emotional dungeon, cages marked *grief* and *anger* rattled hard, but I'd prepared for such. During the long ride here I'd used my mindware and His Grace to deadbolt all cage doors. Ignoring my feelings, I picked the shards of crystal from the carpet and dropped them into my coat pocket.

The furnace fan had kicked on and a cricket chirped in the garage. We were alone. I whispered up the staircase, skipping the creaky third step. On the right at the top of the stairs, Mom-'n-Dad's bedroom door stood open. Dresser drawers stacked on the bed and clothes rumpled across the floor. A wedge of light spilled from the open walk-in-closet door. I crept to it, peeked into the hinge crack and saw Jeff, but he wasn't alone.

CHAPTER NINETEEN

SMOG FUMED ALONGSIDE HIM. The devil boiled powerfully thick. Seeing the thing in our home made my teeth grind, but its presence did make sense. If the FBT wouldn't protect Jeff, the fallen angels would sure try. Of course, the thing's job may have just been whispering in Jeff's ear.

Father, in the name of your Son, please give me some time alone with my brother. If it's okay with you, I'd like to talk to him, not to them. Amen.

Swarms of golden glitter burst from the closet walls and surged at the demon. For a moment it whirled, battling. Outnumbered, the smog thinned before both kinds of angels dissolved.

Thanks, Father. Jeff finished whatever he was doing and backed out of the closet, the kitchen garbage can in one hand, cardboard box in the other. Crossing my arms, I leaned against the wall and waited. He nudged the door shut with his foot, and almost walked into me. The trash can and box thumped to the floor as he startled out of his body. His happily busy scent drowned in nervous reek.

"You look like you've seen a demon, Jeff."

The stench of guilt tainted his nervous reek. "Dave! You're okay! They've been looking all over for . . ."

He stank like garbage-in-the-sun and nearly gagged me. "Why'd ya do it?"

"Hey, cool shades. What's with the clothes?" He touched the back of my glove.

"Why, Jeff?"

"Razz, you oughta be thankin' me! Mom and Dad weren't supposed to . . ." The rotten smell almost vanished. That told me he was beginning to believe this lie.

"Yeah, yeah, I saw you on the CV. I mean for real."

"I'm serious, they were breakin' the law! Parents don't have the right . . ." Same weak ugly stink.

Time to push hard. "Overnight you get interested in the law, you dope-smokin', double-yellow-line passin' speeder of a hypocrite? Now you catch goody-two-shoes-fever and rat Mom-'n-Dad? That's weak!"

His heart rate had been dropping as he recovered from being startled, but now it hammered. A rabid look that all little brothers know crept into his eyes. He made the mistake of taking a step and reaching for me. I uncrossed my arms long enough to hose him with pepper spray. Cursing and clawing at his eyes, he staggered back to trip over the box. Gravity offered him a seat.

e-girl sounded inside my head. *Revenge is mine sayeth the Lord.*

Aw, c'mon. You saw him go after me. I just got his attention.

When Jeff's sputtering quieted enough for him to hear me, I went off. "You believin' your own excuses already? This is your brother you're talkin' to. It's always been about what you want, not what Mom-'n-Dad did. Billy's threat to squeal on his dad sounded too good to pass up, so you sold us all out for your own place?"

Eyes and nose running wind-sprints, his face twisted into a mask of rage. He lunged. "I'm gonna—"

Slow learner. Uncrossing my arms checked him with a flinch, and I finished his sentence, "—face the truth, even if it hurts, Judas." Pressing lips together, my heavy sigh made motorboat sounds. I fell back on our parents' bed and locked my fingers behind my head. "I have a whole different life because of what you did. I met a Capone today, and you know what? His soul wasn't half as twisted as the one I'm lookin' at right now. You tore apart seven families. Over thirty people went rehab just so you can have your own place? When the Neros are done marching you through every school in the One State, then what? You gonna play PR-man for the FBT to keep your suite at the apartment mall? I need to know why, Bro."

A soft laugh grew loud and raw from where he sat on the floor--the sound of a bully who's just learned where you carry your lunch money. "A terrorist is tellin' me what a bad guy I am for getting thirty religious wackos a little help! If the streetlight cams spot you leavin' this place, you're gonna be up to your eyebrows in peacekeepers! Doesn't that ring any bells in your religious little skull? Anything I do is wrong, but anything you do is what God wants, right?"

I expected him to sound this way with the devil around, but this was just Jeff talking. "Razz, how'd you get this far-gone?" I kicked over his cardboard box.

"Well, let's see, you're yankin' Dad's coin collection and Mom's jewelry. That's not wrong? You get away with this only because the guys that are slaggin' our family made laws sayin' it's okay. Now, these same people wanna lock me up in a Rehab, because I bow to a higher Lawgiver than them. Wake *up*, Jeff."

He cocked his head. "And how does your Lawgiver feel about His people lying about their faith just to have rare coins, jewelry and a nice house?"

"So you're sayin' our whole church actually deserves Rehab time? My Lawgiver says hiding-it-under-a-bushel's wrong. Mom-'n-Dad made some mistakes. . . " I reached into the garbage can to pull out the album size picture frame with all the family vids, and Mom-'n-Dad's Bible. ". . . but at least *they* didn't throw away their family and beliefs. You know a tree by its fruits. Even your new friends will tell you that actions speak louder than words. Mom-'n-Dad's fruit is wanting to give us too much. Yours is wanting to give yourself too much."

e-girl broke in, *You're runnin' short on time Bro. Let's wrap this drama.*

He got back to his feet. "So why'd you come back here?"

As I drew a breath to answer, he dove for the nightstand--the panic button on Mom's bedroom CV remote! Mindware shredded my peaceful plans. Dropping the books, a pistol jumped into my hand, I chambered a tranq round, my eyes chose his neck, and I shot him down in mid-air. He crashed into the night-stand and spilled limp across the carpet.

I clenched my eyes shut, but the image had already branded into my memory.

Yes, he had it coming. I had to stop him. That didn't make me feel any better about gunning down my only brother. I dropped to my knees beside his sleeping form. We used to be best friends, but now . . . what had gone wrong? When I was little, I wanted to *be* him. I liked the music he liked, the football teams, even favorite colors. With plastic guns and swords, we'd fought evil bad guys together. Now I had real weapons, and we were each other's bad guys. He'd been there my whole life. For the first time since my reformation, I wished things could just go back to how they were.

e-girl seemed to read my mind. *He says He came to turn brother against brother, not to bring peace. Remember what Dad said too; He's moving each of us on to different lessons.*

She was right. I'd stopped being His for a moment. Wanting Jeff back meant I was thinking of myself . . . of emptiness. We had different masters now, and there was no coming together through that. *Thanks, Sis.*

I looked to the ceiling, *Father, I speak through the Spirit, in Your Son's name. What You want is absolute, but You've told me to ask for things, so here goes . . . Please let Jeff come to You. Maybe You're just putting us on different paths home. I don't care how or when, but please make him Yours. I don't want to lose him forever. Please keep Your angels around him, and protect him. If I'm able, use me to get to him so we'll both be Yours. And I'm sorry for wanting to go back to a place that You've put behind me. Heaven's perfect, right? Maybe there I won't be such a meathead. Your will be done, not mine. Amen.*

He touched my soul with stillness and security. I'd done the most I could do for Jeff. His case was before the judging Father with the Son as his lawyer. Using the scanner from my belt, I checked him for bugs and fried his ID chip. I put the Williams' family Bible and picture frame into the box, shouldered Jeff in a fireman's carry, and headed for the stairs. *Sis, my arms are full, is the coast clear?*

Crystal. Mount up, we gotta get gone. Flashlight on line two. It took me a second, but it was good to smile after banging heads with Jeff.

I walked down the driveway when the yellow flip-com blinked. Lightfast's tone rumbled deep, *I guess it wasn't a trap.*

We ain't in the truck yet. Something's wrong. This is too slack.

They didn't expect us to move so soon, that's all. Once-in-a-while they drop a freebie and we get to pick it up. Our rescue team's rolling. We've planned a hand-off. The team will getcha on the fly. When you get out just leave Jeff in the belly box. I'll question him when he gets here. e-girl will fill you in on the rest. It's rescue time, Calamity Kid.

CHAPTER TWENTY

THERE WERE ENOUGH SAINTS in the battered '06 Subaru Baja to test its off-road shocks. The five in the pickup bed and the two front seat passengers made-up the entry team. Grandpa, Legacy and I, the back-up unit, rode in the two rear bucket seats. The veterans got the seats, of course. I had to straddle the rear console. The three of us would cover the main loading dock in case any Neros got past the entry team.

Serene had hacked our route into the Illinois Department of Transportation's CV system. We breezed through express lane checkpoints, laughing as IDOT signs kept wishing us a safe day. We exited the highway, and parked at a Slider's mini-mart to wait for word from the mission. Keeping things light, Grandpa walked away with the rock-paper-scissors-dynamite championship. Then came Lightfast's call. I could hardly believe it, but Jeff had talked. He matched details from the FBT file. We got the green light, sending my heart into the drum solo from *Wipe Out*. They'd be free before midnight. Back on the road, we called the Boss.

An *I'm-going-on-vacation and left-the-water-running* nag niggled and prodded my gray matter. I called up the rescue file on my com-shades and found myself at the utility tunnel map re-re-re-checking our escape. Our exit would be past curfew, so driving out would be suicide. We'd make our getaway through the underground utility tunnels on twelve flatbed carts. The Body Surfers would melt the utility grid's security systems. The carts already scanned as *Power Electric*, in the area for a line upgrade. Tunnels ranked clear, construction free, and everything checked out. Again. We'd be dust before the FBT could drop their donuts.

I tagged the niggle as stage fright, and closed the file. The time I'd logged doing stuff like this in CV games measured in years. But games, even great ones like *Peacekeeper*, couldn't prepare me for the first time at the real thing. I was so wired that my thrill measured on the Richter scale. I went for a stick of gum, but thought about the noisy chewing. I'd need my hearing. My thumbs settled for twiddling.

The target loomed ahead of us. Even by moonlight, a smoky haze hung over the building. Metroplex lights lit up the demonic smog as it did the low-hanging clouds. Our prayers must have bounced every busted-down fallen angel from the building. What a Calamity.

The factory occupied a whole city block. I scanned the front office entrance as we eased past. Nothing. But four men squeegeed windows of the office building across the street—our front door team.

The red Dodge Ram pickup with which Tinker had picked-up e-girl, occupied a space under the front visitor-lot's floodlights. The factory's security system wasn't on the Web, so to have CV support we needed a Field Hack on-site. e-girl had to enter the target and access their hardware. To fix any tech stuff, Oscar the Grouch's ill-tempered twin had to be her partner.

I pointed out the Ram to my now-napping uncle. He lifted his head just enough to see it before leaning back on the headrest and re-closing his eyes.

"Yeah, just pray they're in place," he spoke aloud. Using thought-speech would skunk the rescue. Any nearby Neros with BW tech could pick up our brain waves. A Hack focusing into a CV emitted no BW signals, but the rest of us maintained a mind-ware blackout.

e-girl was to hack a communication's maintenance call into the receptionist's CV as she and Tinker stood at her desk. This would get them through the door, and into the utility area. If they failed, we'd be entering an alerted target without Hack support. Under such conditions, Vegas odds-makers would place our prospects at roughly an ice-cube's chance in Egypt.

After passing the factory's south wall, we reached the end of the block and turned right. The solid concrete west wall slid past. Again a niggling shadow of doubt fell across my mind, and I went back to the escape plan. Every time I tried to put my finger on it, thought's spotlight chased the shadow away. The maps still looked fine, which knotted my jaw muscles in frustration. Once again, I wrote it off as butterflies before the big game, and cleared my com-shades.

Another right turn put us at the north wall's small shipping dock. We were close now, and the old Subaru stank so dangerous I thought we'd wake the neighbors. Excitement's fumes and vapors lingered like paint thinner in a poorly ventilated space. The three-Sandman shipping-bay team strolled down the sidewalk, right where they should have been. Half a block further the driver rolled up to the mouth of a wide dead-end alley.

Finally.

The factory's receiving dock formed the alley's right wall, and its three-story parking garage, the left. Our rescue team bailed out and headed into the alley. Grandpa, Legacy and I followed through fine drizzling mist. My senses wired so fine I could hear blinking. And it wasn't mine. I sucked a slow deep breath, forcing myself to relax, and rechecked the twin Arazzi-9 machine pistols my uncle had given me. They swung from shoulder slings, so my hands had only to close around their grips. Their 50 round banana clips each held 40 normal tranq. The rest were high-explosive rounds in case things got ugly. Just like my games except the part where I could bleed.

This part of the plan made me wince. Everyone bunched together. That meant easy targets. The high walls served as good sniper perches and prevented quick escape. It reminded me of my favorite *Peacekeeper* capture the flag base. Sliding my fingers onto triggers, I scanned parked-car windows for reflections and understood why my uncle had said CV games made good Sandman training. I was in my element. My eyes tracked upward to check the roof-line, but the cloud of fallen angels drew my attention. It hung huge. It had spread, and drifted lower.

Oh no.

I figured it out just as the rooftops went live with movement.

My eyes bulged and I stopped dead in my tracks. Leaving the Arazzis to dangle from their slings, I grabbed Legacy and Grandpa by their upper-arms. "Blessme! It's . . ." was all I got out before gunfire spat hot-'n-heavy. My stop spoiled the snipers' aim. Tranqs popped pavement at our feet. The world went slow-mo. I still clutched their arms and dove right, dragging them along. Explosions behind us bounced bits of factory-wall past. We rolled to our feet seven meters from the parking garage and in one clean move, I sprang over the ground floor half-wall. My partners howled in pain as I used their arms like luggage handles. I landed on my feet and let them go. They sprawled across the floor and scrambled to their feet. We ran deeper into the garage.

"Goliaths!" Grandpa called over his shoulder.

Peacekeeper had taught me that when a Goliath showed up, things really couldn't get any worse. "I thought those were just something some game-designer dreamt up. Fer real?"

"Generation 3 BW tech powered-battle-suits! They walked right through the concrete wall!" shouted Legacy.

Metal and glass crashed behind us. My ears tagged it as an automobile accident. On instinct I turned in case someone needed help. My ears were wrong. *Peacekeeper* hadn't prepared me for what my eyeballs collected. Nothing could have. A three-meter robot swung the back of an oversized hand at a car, smashing it into an adjacent pick-up truck. No, it wasn't a robot. I could see human eyes through its clear face shield just before a blanket of blackness fell.

That would be e-girl doing her field hack-thing.

My eyes switched to light intensifying and heat spectrum vision. I brought up the Arazzis and burned through half their clips. The tranq rounds flattened harmlessly against the armored battle suits while they bashed more cars out of their way.

Overdrive kicked-in. Time to clean house.

Three more Goliaths jumped the half wall. In the perfectly still parking garage it seemed like my reformed speed lagged out-of-order. The brain wave battle suits moved as fast as we moved. Goliath gun-mounts swivelled out from shoulder housings, and I dove behind a Buick LoadMaster. Fifty calliber chain-guns shattered glass, whooshed tires flat, and punched through body panels. Judging by their aim, e-girl's darkness hadn't made a difference.

Yellow flip-com icon. e-girl screamed, *We're skunked! Cut-'n run! There's snipers everywhere! You three and one of the back door team are all that's left!*

"Hell-no you don't! Game-on--try-'n keep up!" Backpedaling low, I palmed my Arazzis and loaded their high-explosive rounds. Behind a Ford Contour, I waited until the Goliaths knocked aside the parked cars in the row before me.

I leapt to its roof, ordered my boots to bond with metal, and opened-up on the floor in front of the bots. Didn't want to send anyone to Hell, just break things. Twin bursts struck concrete. Fireballs. Mindware reacted, compensating for explosions that should have left me blind and deaf.

Fireballs flared out and a wave of Goliaths rolled toward me. That was the bad news. The really bad news? They still poured over the half wall. The really really bad news? The few I'd blown over were getting back up. I sensed a giant exclamation point above my head. *Note to self, News is bad. Have no-news-is-good-news tattooed on forehead.*

Real Goliaths were definitely tougher than their *Peacekeeper* twins. Bullets chewed the Ford to scrap metal as I dove through the aisle behind me and made off after Grandpa and Legacy. They waited two rows away to see how I'd get myself killed. Nice.

e-girl had an idea. *In the center of the garage are ramps to the upper levels. Climb up a few floors and buy me some time. That'll put lots of concrete between you and them 'til I find a way to get you outta there!*

We jumped to the ramp slanting up to the second floor, gunfire popping behind. There had to be a way to slow them down. My mindware twirled like a Rolodex. *These things are tanks. Any ideas?*

My uncle gave his absolute-zero shrug. *This is the first time I've ever seen a Goliath. Word on the street is when you meet one get as far away as fast as you can. They do have a weakness though.*

Seconds ticked by as we climbed. *Well? What is it?*

They failed to mention it. Sorry.

Grandpa grunted out loud. *Whatever would we do without you?*

Legacy beamed his best whatever-would-you-do-without-me look. *I often wonder that myself.*

I ordered my com-shades to pull up a diagram of a Goliath, and to my surprise I found at a complete design blueprint. Thanks to *Peacekeeper*, I knew what to look for. *Yeah-right.* And there it was. The million-dollar BW suits were packed with delicate high tech electronics, but had no ElectroMagnetic Pulse shielding. It also showed the suits' sensory protection gizmos to be older technology that ranked too slow for our grenades. I prayed the units behind us hadn't been upgraded.

Got it! Grandpa, drop two flash strobes. Rig 'em on a motion sensor trigger. Legacy set a couple of audio grenades the same way. Drop 'em here and get to the next level! I dumped a pair of EMP grenades and scampered after them.

We'd reached the highest inner-level, and they looked to me. *Now back away from the ledge and stay together. We'll scorch any that make it this far. e-girl, we're runnin' outta room here . . .*

Way past panic, she'd hit gone-to-pieces. *Just stay off the roof and outta the open!*

Copy that. It's bad on this end. When the snipers figure out we're right under them, it's checkmate.

A Goliath grabbed the edge of the ramp and hauled himself up. Grandpa and I put our hands on Legacy's shoulders. He touched his forehead and spread his arms wide. I felt his focus suck energy out of me. Our gush of power boiled in mid-air. The man in the suit tried to beat back our attack but three on one dropped him.

We scorched two more before e-girl got back to us. *Got it! Southwest corner of the garage.*

We were running before she finished. *Take the stairwell there to the ground floor. Oh-no. Incoming frogmen! It's about to get rabid hot-'n-heavy! Oh hurry, hurry, hurry! They got a blippin' army of Dragoons! RUN!*

Just steps away from the door, Neros swung in over the half wall on grapple lines. Sniper rifles fired one-handed from the waist filled the air with tranq rounds, but even I knew that gen-one's targeting system wasn't built for that.

We burst into the stairwell. I fired my own grapple at the ceiling's center. Vaulting over the handrail, I let out titanium cable as fast as I could fall. Legacy and Grandpa followed in second's fractions. I stopped the reel and cut the cable. My body jerked like a puppet, and I dropped the last few meters.

e-girl hung with us. *On your right's a gray steel door. It's a maintenance room with a freight elevator leading to the utility tunnels.*

The door was locked, so I cranked the knob hard until metal snapped.

Elevator's on its way, and a Mover's waiting for you in the tunnel.

I raced to the sliding steel-mesh door and slapped the button on the wall, as if that would make it come faster. The shaft's walls were steel-mesh as well. The lift crept upward.

Oh.

Sis. *We can see the elevator car. The walls of the shaft are expanded metal. We'll be trapped in there like rats.*

More like sitting ducks, corrected Grandpa.

e-girl sounded like she was going to cry, *Goody blippin' gumdrops! That didn't show in my plans!*

My uncle began backing toward the hall door, wearing an I-know-something-you-don't-know smile. *We got it e-girl. You were great. You and Tinker fade, fast. Love ya, Niece.*

Echo, Unk. We're dust. His will be done.

She broke the connection.

Legacy dropped his com-shades to the floor, his gold eyes glinting a wild look. He flashed his blades from their scabbards and slashed a cross in the air. With a swirl of his duster, he was gone, out into the hall, door shut behind him.

My guts went cold and blood drained from my face.

I felt it.

As always, Legacy sounded absolute-zero. *Brothers, if my home-coming's His will, I pray they've got a pot brewing . . . but when things go live, a Sandman's worth a hundred Neros. To God be the glory.*

I hadn't noticed the doors of the lift open, but Grandpa did. He pinned my arms to my sides in a bear hug. He heaved me into the cage and didn't let go until the doors had shut. His accent rolled soft and slow, "You do realize he's not alone out there. Legacy could hold off an entire army if He allows it."

As the car sunk down the shaft, the clatter of clanking blades echoed with Legacy's words. "That all you got for me? Oh, you want som' a this too, huh? Well come getcha some, scrub! Yeah, thought so. How ya like me *now?*"

I hung my head and squeezed my eyes shut until the elevator doors opened again.

An orange electric maintenance cart waited just outside the cage in the utility tunnel. Two glitter-storm angels guarded its driver. A man in slate gray coveralls asked, "Yo. Someone call a cab?" I flopped down on the cart's flatbed giving Grandpa the front passenger seat. Its electric motor buzzed us down the dim tunnel while my stomach tried to twist me in half. Tears traced wet lines down my face. I prayed for my uncle, and the Spirit spoke to me in the Word.

CHAPTER TWENTY-ONE

BACK IN THE COMMON ROOM, I slumped into one of the arm-chairs. Even a fresh stick of gum didn't help. How Legacy got past hating Neros was beyond me. I knew what I felt was wrong, but the world would be a better place without 'em. I hoped one day to become the man that my uncle was.

Tinker and e-girl made it back before we did. Sis lay flat at a work station, while Tinker watched CV from the sofa pit. He saw me glance at him. As if my day wasn't going bad enough, he got up and came toward me. Rings of blue and orange marked his eyes. That meant he was both sad and worked-up.

A few meters away he stopped and mumbled. "Um . . . just wanted to say sorry . . . for your loss and for how I've treated ya. I've been a real scob. Fact is, you pups are here and alota others ain't. That says somethin'."

I nodded stupidly.

He stood there a moment rubbing the back of his hand on his beard. "Hope he's back soon." He turned around and went back to the sofa pit.

Blessme. I'd always been a sucker when it came to forgiveness. He'd just healed everything between us and I hadn't thought that was do-able.

"Thanks," I called after him.

He flapped an arm as he walked away.

I tuned out background noises and sat alone, reflecting on the past twenty-four hours. Tinker's humility and a roof over our heads aside, I've had better days. Our family awaited torture, I gunned down my big brother, the rescue, Legacy . . . I wanted to crawl into the stackhouse and pull a blanket over my head.

But I couldn't. Merciless mindware fought sleep. So I moped.

Grandpa had busied himself brewing a pot of coffee, and I now sensed him coming toward me with two steaming cups. He held one out to me, "Have a mug, Calamity Kid. You've earned it."

Coffee was never my thing, but I took it anyway. The warm bitter-smelling mug comforted me.

"I feel badly about your uncle. I wish there were something we could have done. Living is a row of sorrow interrupted by moments of suffering. Such is life in a broken world." He raised his mug high. "From where I hail, it's tradition to daily toast those we miss. Since we honor Legacy, a more suitable beverage doesn't exist." His mug lifted even higher and he cleared his throat: 'Greater love has no one than this, that he lay down his life for his friends.' May we all serve as well as Legacy."

I raised my mug, poked my gum into my cheek, and we sipped. The strong liquid warmed my throat and belly. I rubbed my eyes, I checked the lock on grief's dungeon door before aiming my thoughts elsewhere.

"How's Jeff?" I asked as Grandpa settled into an armchair.

"All I know is what Lightfast has told me. After being roused with anti-tranq, the lad willingly answered questions. As you know, his knowledge matched the FBT file data. Since then he's been, ah, difficult."

"So he lied for the Neros. I was surprised that he'd helped."

"Lightfast's sent for a specialist to question him."

"Good idea." I turned my brother over in my mind, looking at him from different angles. What he knew could be important. "Where is Jeff?"

"In our holding cells near the stackhouse."

"I wonder if he'd talk to me now. Think I should I visit him?"

Grandpa squirmed like he'd sat in a puddle. "Look, I know you're brothers, but he's here because of what he knows. You really shouldn't drop in for tea and cakes— 'what fellowship can light have with darkness,' and such."

"Believe me, quality time with the Nero hero is *not* what I had in mind. Our last chat got ugly fast. I just thought he might spill something that could help." I looked over at e-girl and shoved Jeff from my mind. She'd unplugged and slumped dejectedly. I zoomed-in my vision. The deep blue tint in her eyes told me she knew about our uncle's sacrifice.

Grandpa said, "I know you've much on your mind, but I'd like your input on a certain matter."

I stared into my coffee and waited for him to continue.

"Every time I'm prepared to push for the Body to begin rescuing more saints from the Rehabs, a disaster like tonight occurs. I wonder if we'll ever be ready. It almost seems to me as though He wants some of us in those places."

I shook my head, "We just have to do our best wherever He puts us. I know you know that New Testament saints and the early Church did a lot of 'time.' We know we're to use the talents He's given us to glorify Him. Not much of an answer. I'm not sure why He'd put me where He has if I weren't supposed to at least *try* to rescue the church."

Grandpa squirmed again, "Regarding that... I'm not sure what else can be done to save your church. Now that we've spoiled the rescue, the FBT will know if an insect enters the place. What if He doesn't want your church rescued?"

I shrugged, "Then we won't be able to rescue them. His will be done whether I like it or not. But our church wasn't there."

Doubt's frown crinkled his brow. "Begging your pardon?"

"On our way to the factory, something bugged me. Ate at me. My track coach used to call it butterflies."

He nodded slowly, "Something was amiss; you felt anxious."

"Yeah."

"Oh, I do wish you'd have said something. That sensation means one's mindware is having a go at a puzzler."

"It sure solved my puzzle, but the answer came too late, as we walked into that alley."

Grandpa slow wagged his head in wonder. "You deduced the church wasn't there and that we'd entered a trap. You've a remarkable gift for strategy. You behaved like a true professional in the parking garage."

"He is." e-girl curled-up cat-like in an armchair, and rested her chin on crossed wrists. "As both a terrorist and a PK, he's done that ten thousand times."

"She's talking about a com-vision game," I explained.

"He'd play for days on end. He was one of the best. I used to tease him 'bout wastin' so much time on those stupid games, but now it looks like I was wrong."

Grandpa sipped coffee, then nodded. "I've seen those contests on the Com-Vision. They certainly prepared Calamity for sainthood. So how did you know? I mean, what alerted you to our peril?"

I set my mug on an end table and rose. Digging hands in coat pockets, I began walking heel to toe along the border of a large cream-colored rug. "It was plain as peanut butter on white bread. Can't believe I missed it."

My fingers found the pieces of Mom's *Flashpoint* bottle and I hissed a sigh through clenched teeth. "Rehab Nine was clearly a trick. If they really wanted to trap us at the Rehab, they could a put a few of our church members in the stackhouse, or even had all the lights off to make it look like everyone was crashed. We'd have walked right into it. They knew our Hacks have free run of the Web. They knew we'd check before we went. They counted on us finding their trap. Where would our Body Surfers look next? The only place left: the FBT database. They planted the information in their own files."

Doubt scrunched Grandpa's face, "But why go to all that bother?"

"So we'd show up where they wanted us. Somewhere better suited for ambush. To watch how we arrived, or where we came from. To see our reaction. Didn't it seem like there were a lot of FBT agents at the factory, though?"

He closed his eyes. "Ugh. I'd wager every agent in the metroplex was on hand. That cloud of fallen angels should have alerted us. But you don't think they were there to guard your church." It wasn't a question.

"Those were soldiers, not guards, and they were positioned for ambush, not defense. For years, I've made a game out of rescues like that. Game or real-life, the strategies are the same. You don't keep bait at the scene of an ambush unless you have to because the mouse can sometimes steal the cheese without springing the trap. The factory was clearly an ambush. A good one. Seventeen saints walked in, two walked out."

His brow furrowed in thought, "But your brother's information matched the Bureau's data--"

"Sure it did. Jeff was part of the setup. Getting him went slack because they wanted us to get him. They told him exactly what they wanted us to know. Whether he knew of the ambush or not, and I'm betting he did, he passed along their lies."

e-girl sat twisting a lock of hair around an ear. "Hey, Sherlock, what about the fish? How'd they know we were runnin' a rescue to begin with? Somethin' in the plex smells fishy."

Grandpa looked expectantly to me.

I shrugged, "Hey, I don't have all the answers. But I'd bet money to macaroni that when this story hits the Terrorist Webwire, it's reported as an FBT hotline tip."

Our Elder sat rigid in his chair wearing a stone-grim face. He blew out a determined sigh. "Well then, where do we go from here?"

"I've got some ideas, but I need to talk to the Body's FBT expert."

He frowned, "The group that runs the Body is called the Deacons. I can ask them if they know of anyone."

"No, no, I just need one of the guys with the FBT playbook. You know, their strategies."

Grandpa cocked his head, "In my two years with the Body, I'm sure I've never heard of anyone like that."

I slumped back into my chair. "You're kidding, right? Who planned the rescue?"

"I did. It wasn't difficult. The Surfers located your church, and retrieved the buildings most current prints. The factory's security systems are on an isolated circuit, making their cameras inaccessible from the Web. Thusly, I dispatched a Field Hack to direct our operation. Our Sandmen are practiced at this sort of thing. They knew what was what."

e-girl looked at the floor. "We *didn't* know what was what. That's how we got slagged so vast. By-the-way, I checked and there's still no word on Legacy."

"Well, no news is good news." My new motto was working already. "Look, I can fix it so this doesn't happen again. Have Lightfast upload all the FBT's handbooks and manuals into my mindware."

Grandpa erupted with laughter, "Surely, that is the reason we're without a Bureau specialist! The FBT has its own library. You haven't the capacity for that quantity of data."

I wasn't smiling, "Then he can leave out their medical and retirement plans. The Body—no—every cell in the Body, needs to have someone who knows our enemy. The FBT's a government agency. Government agencies do things by the book. If we know the book, we'll always be a step ahead. With traps like the one we just fell into, it's a miracle the Body ain't a corpse."

Grandpa rubbed his chin. "We've never seen anything like tonight before. The Surfers have *always* skated in and out of their system with solid data."

e-girl said, "Hey, Serene told me the FBT's head of CV security is what's known as a Symp. Someone sympathetic toward us and—"

"Well that explains everything! Look, Chicago's Body Surfers have been cakewalkin' till now. This false lead proves that somethin's changed in FBT Web-land. Either they caught the Symp, or he's being watched. Razz, they could have a whole new system in place and run the old one just to feed us skunky fatebreakers."

Grandpa said, "Well, Calamity Kid, it seems you're far more to us than just another Sandman. I planned the rescue because that's one of an Elder's duties. You, however, have talents that I'd be wasting unless I turned this work over to you. Perhaps it's why He's brought you here. Best wishes in your role as our new strategist."

"I'm honored!" Were I not sitting, I'd have fallen over. Speechless, I glanced at my smiling sister, then back at Grandpa. "Since we got here yesterday, I've just been adjusting to my reformation. But back in that alley, old skills clicked with new ones. I find myself fitting into the Body like a puzzle piece. But there are just so few of us."

"Martin Luther was a single man, but he changed western civilization." Point made, he slapped his knee, "Well, lad, it's a grand thing indeed to know one's place."

"Yep. And right now my place is bed," I said, rubbing my eyes.

"Not yet it ain't!" yelled Tinker from across the room. "We made the Webwire!" He beckoned us over to the main CV. "We're all WorldWideWeb famous!"

I tuned background noises back in and immediately recognized the purring voice of Delisha Lix. ". . . if that doesn't just crank my hot button to all-wound-up. An anonymous FBT hotline tip fired up agents and peacekeepers from all over the Plex. The plan took down fifteen Sandmen. Yeah I said fifteen Sandmen. The biggest terrorist bust in Illinois hiss-toe-ree! No one officially knows why the Fundis chose Sunshine Chemicals. But since Sunshine's the world's biggest producer of Sominal, the official guess is terrorists need more tranquilizer ammunition. Well, duh!"

I made it to the CV in time to watch her melodramatically roll those long-lashed eyes so hard they'd should have gotten stuck that way. Our grandmother always warned us about that.

I groaned a silent *Razz* to myself at the news. I hadn't known anything about the rescue site. Sunshine Chemicals' Sominal being the tranq in tranq rounds gave this story high-drama spin. I gave someone an A+ at making us terrorists look terrifying.

The Web-strump continued, "The captured Sandmen are REMing in sleep units, en-route to D.C. where they'll be tried as traitors. Two terrorists escaped capture, and authorities have identified them as the venerable Grandpa and a newbie called Calamity Kid."

Delisha snapped fingers on both hands and pointed perfectly manicured fingers at the upper corners of the screen. Footage of our attack came from Goliath-cam viewpoints. A blurry image of Grandpa climbing ramps appeared in one corner, and a fuzzy view of yours truly blazing away with machine pistols from atop a Ford, popped up in the other.

"Like I always say, terrorists are live voltage with rattlesnake baditude, so leave the action to the FBT. Any info leading to their capture will make you a millionaire. Grandpa's worth twelve, and the new-Kid-on-the-block will net ya another cool mill, so make that call!" She paused and looked up at my picture. "Looks like terrorists come in all sizes these days. You'd think a Sandman would be bigger."

My gum chewing froze. I died from an overdose of oh-this-can't-be-happening, and my face heated blood-red blush. Delisha raised a shapely leg to coyly adjust an ankle strap on her stiletto-pump. She wore heels high enough to give any mortal woman vertigo. How she balanced on only one of those shoes was why she made big money living in front of the camera.

Tinker took my hand and pumped our arms, "Let me be the first to congratulate you!"

"Grandpa's worth a dozen of me, go shake his hand!"

"Yeah but you're the first person I've ever known to have two listings in the million dollar reward club!"

It took a couple seconds to hit me. David Williams and Calamity Kid. "I'll be identified from that footage!"

Grandpa smelled my panic and waved it off, "Not to worry. I've been underground nearly two years and they've yet to match my street name with my given name. Besides, the One State never pays out those rewards. FBT CVs match faces long before any-one's mates ever put the make on them."

He headed toward the kitchen area and called over his shoulder, "I'll contact Lightfast concerning the FBT file you'd like uploaded. Rest well, Calamity Kid. You'll have need of it."

CHAPTER TWENTY-TWO

MY HEAD ITCHED SO BADLY, it curled my toes. Lightfast's gold eyes burned the FBT file into my skull. I'd only slept a few hours before he woke me. The download I'd requested had been prepped that quickly. It turned out the Surfers already used an FBT file for reference. As Grandpa guessed, they had to trim it down for use as mindware, but Surfers clearly worked fast.

Lightfast slumped in his chair, rubbing at his eyes. "There. Finished."

As with my reformation download, I now knew a few hundred thousand scads more. Waves of knowledge splashed and foamed inside my head. I closed my eyes and just sat there a minute. Stabbing streaks of light flashed against the inside of my eyelids. My brain raced, sorting things . . . connecting things I'd already known to the new download. I opened my eyes again to find myself flat on my back, Lightfast bent over me with very gold eyes, sporting a surgeon-at-work look.

I tried to sit up. An industrial strength headrush rocked the room like a Kansas tornado. "Whoa . . ."

His deep voice rumbled, "Definitely. Just relax and enjoy. Welcome back. We've been looking at the whites of your eyes for forty minutes now. I triple checked the file's size before we started, but some people have less memory storage than others. Your head's pretty close to full." Lightfast's concern smelled sweet.

"Never been accused of that before."

e-girl cradled my head in her lap. "You've lost gallons of body fluid. Drink." She gave me water.

What would this world be without sisters? I drank. Then I sat up. The room spun, but more like a Tilt-a-Whirl than a tornado. The sofa tried to run away but I grabbed it with both hands.

"Would you just rest awhile!" she nagged.

"Can't, Mom. Get Grandpa." I rested my head against the cushion.

Queen's English came from somewhere behind me. "At your service."

The room turned as I craned my neck to locate him. "We gotta be careful 'bout a couple things. The whole Body does." As I spoke, my neck rolled circles to make him stand still. "FBT's been keeping the pace fast. They wanna keep us runnin' and off-balance. This helps 'em figure out how we get around. And where we could have come from. We need to change things up, else they'll sniff out every crash site we have. Slow things down somehow. Can't let 'em know we caught on, though. I guess we're gonna haveta . . . I dunno . . ."

Grandpa nodded, frowning at me. "Except that you adopt a more leisurely pace, you're going to damage yourself, my boy!"

"Yeah, okay. That's the important stuff. Pass it on to Deacons or Surfers, whoever. Just so all the cells know."

Lightfast put away his thinking cap and closed up his briefcase. "He'll be fine now." It was easy to see how much everyone trusted him. Orange tainted eyes paled gold and lines of concern eased from saints' faces. Tension melted from postures and worry's burning scent faded fast. He turned to me, "You need more rest, but your mindware will keep you up awhile yet."

Sleep would have been nice. "What for?"

"The Optic from New Galilee is waiting to see you."

"The what from where?"

A small white-haired lady hobbled up to spin alongside Lightfast. Her wobbling and shaking wasn't just me—she leaned heavy on a battered brass-knobbed cane. The shriveled parts of her not covered by last century's polyester print showed pink-gray skin-blotches. She looked old enough to be Grandpa's Grandma. Although it came slowly, her voice chimed a lively note. "New Galilee is the largest mission in the metroplex. Many of the Body's Cells work from there. I've come here to see a young Judas named Jeff. You're his brother?"

Mindware switched-on my battery backup. I stood. The room steadied. "Yes, ma'am. You can call me Calamity Kid." This was the interrogator for whom Lightfast had sent. I offered her a stick of gum, but she shook her head and tapped her jaw.

Ah, dentures.

"Nice to meet you, Calamity Kid, my name is Secret. Specialists like myself are called Optics because we can see things that others cannot." She took my arm, "Let's have a look at this brother of yours, shall we?"

After following Lightfast through another of the common room's hidden doors, we walked down a finished dry walled and carpeted hallway. After a right turn, we encountered six Plasti-Wood doors, evenly spaced along the right wall. On the left hung several still-life paintings of fruit, so boring they nearly over-rode my mindware's sleep control. Fluorescent lighting gave the place that warm glow common to Ward-fence floodlights. I thanked Him for my com-shades. It had all the ambience of an FBT command center.

Between her cane and my arm, Secret moved rather quickly. "I hear you're a spiritual wonder."

"How do you mean?"

"You've sensed the spiritual plane ever since your reformation."

"Oh. Yes, ma'am. The Spirit, and angels too. Both kinds of angels."

"It's an ability that grows over time in most reformed saints. A few are never able to see spirits. Even fewer can see them right from the start. You're gifted. Have you seen a human spirit?"

"Well, in the Web. I saw our Hacks. An unbeliever too."

She smiled, "In the Web, His glory turns toads to princes. Those are just icons though. Pictures of souls, not souls themselves. I mean here in creation. Have you seen the part of the soul that touches our dimensions of space-time reality?"

Hmmm, sure. "Oh. No, ma'am. I hadn't really thought about it."

Lightfast opened the second door on the right. "Take a chair, lady and gentleman." Three steel folding chairs were the room's only objects. Good thing too, because deep and skinny, the room's size and shape matched a common bedroom closet. Its two long walls held panes of black glass that ran their lengths. They glass rose from my knees to the ceiling in height. We squeezed in and sat down. Lightfast closed the door, painting the room black.

I sensed his brain waves churning. The glass pane facing us changed. Starting at the bottom and moving up, it went from black to clear as though a shade were being raised. A Picture Window, one of those computerized screens upon which any image can be projected, looked into Jeff's bare concrete cell. We could observe him, but Jeff was treated to a panoramic view of Chicago on his side. The room's dim light seemed to come from the window itself. From the hallway, the doors had all looked normal, but the inside showed heavy gauge riveted steel. In the far corner sat a roll of toilet paper and a five-gallon bucket. Near the w ndow, Jeff lay on a thick foam pad, his back to the door. Gobs of food splattered near the doorway, around a plastic bowl and spoon. My brother had no angels to watch over him here.

Secret leaned close, "I want you to go in and talk with him. I'll see what I need from here, but first I want to show you something. Look at your brother. Now, close your eyes." I did.

"Remember, human beings are part animal and part spirit. You're used to seeing the animal. When you need to see someone, your eyes only look so far. When I tell you to look at him, do so as though it's the first time you're seeing a person. Look as far as you must in order to see all of him. Now open your new eyes."

That was all I needed to know. I expected something like the Nero Hack from the Web, so I nearly swallowed my gum. Two things existed in the same space, and one of Jeff wasn't human. Well, human-shaped anyway. I looked past his creation body and focused on Jeff the spirit. He existed as a long blood-red rod, bent sharply in six or seven places. Endlessly moving, he zigzagged like a poorly folded map trying to right itself. He had to be made from energy because parts of his bent self would pass right through other parts in the unrest of his confused jumble. Fascinated, I watched him move, somehow knowing he'd bent his spirit inside out. He could only see inside himself. Just as his state of non-stop Twister struck me as funny, I sensed his wanting. Something else too. Pain. A thorn had pierced this strange being to the bone, or whatever. He writhed in pain.

I found that by looking farther I could sense even more. His pain came from a terrible thirst. A small child squirms when nature calls. It was like that but backward. Jeff's dry hollow husk paced in a longing to quench his thirst. I reached out to him, but saw more and stopped. His hunt had driven him to such depths that he blurred with anger and hatred. He flared red from a raging infection, a spiritual madness. His thirst owned him. If I came close he'd try to destroy me.

Looking this hard at Jeff made Secret sound a long way off. "You're seeing the part of his soul that touches our space and time. This is how I read moods, emotions and even surface thoughts." Focusing so intently had faded everything around me and her words brought me back. That's when I noticed my muscles tensed rock hard. I panted like a runner. I'd strained almost this hard under Dragoon's scorch. Closing my eyes, I had to break it off.

My knees felt wobbly, even though I sat. I rubbed at my eyes and neck.

"It costs a great deal of energy to see this way. Even more when your eyes are new."

When I looked at Secret, my new eyes hadn't refocused yet. Her other self appeared peacefully pink. Where Jeff had been a rod, she was more barrel-shaped, kind of dented here and there. Her motion was opposite Jeff's. Filled to overflowing, her stretch was that of a well-fed cat enjoying a sunbeam. Ageless, I sensed she existed as He'd made her to be. Once more I felt the drain, and willed it to stop.

"You saw me," she smiled.

My cheeks flush with warmth.

She touched my arm and laughed softly, "It's okay. I see you too. Your spirit is transparent, clear. Focusing on it only makes it harder to see. Like a cut crystal, it has many sides."

"I don't understand why we look so different. Jeff seems empty and you seem filled. What does my shape mean?"

"Shapes and motion reveal some strengths and weaknesses. Yours shows He's added many things to the great trust you have in Him. You've many talents to invest. You fit well with what's around you. You're truly what the One Church calls, 'at one with creation.' Now go speak with your brother."

Legs of Jell-O carried me to the door. "Calamity, hold on, he'll be able to see through," said Lightfast.

While he darkened the Picture Window again, I asked Secret, "What will you be watching for?"

She waved a hand, "Oh, my mindware's a real tangle. I see

deeply. I'll see more of the boy in a minute than your mother saw in his whole lifetime."

CHAPTER TWENTY-THREE

HIS DOOR SWUNG HEAVY AND I stepped into his cell. From this side, the Picture Window appeared to be thick Plexiglas running wall-to-wall. From seventy floors up, the view looked out on a twinkling nighttime cityscape. The com-vision running the Picture Window made guests think their stay was in a very different place. Now I understood the hallway's disguise.

Jeff still faced away from the door. "Leave me alone, terrorist."

"You already are," I said quietly.

He rolled onto his back as if to see me, but his eyes remained closed. Then I remembered his pierced eyelids.

"So Cain's back to finish off Abel."

"Thought you might wanna know how Mom-'n-Dad are."

He knifed a vicious smile, "Safe from you. You got away though. Too bad." The cell clouded with the acid stench of Judas.

His words cut deep, but I'd locked my emotional dungeon's doors before opening his. "So you did know. I'd hoped they were just using you. The Nero-hero helped bag some real-live saints." If I gave him room to rub it in, he might spill something useful.

He tapped his chin. "Saint is such a pleasant word, why not use, oh, . . . terrorist? You people are unsafe. You belong in Re-habs."

Razz. Again, this was pure Jeff: no fallen angels. How'd he slide so far so fast? I thought of his spirit's madness. Making me feel worse must have made him feel better. "I think the PKs used too much soap in your brainwashing. So what's the story? Where's Mom-'n-Dad really?"

"I'm the prisoner, but I'm holdin' the cards, huh? What makes you think I'm gonna tell you anything when your friends treat me like this?"

"Now that's the real you. Lookin' out for number one. What makes you think I'm gonna believe anything you tell me?"

"Your friends did." More gloating. He steered his pride to run me down.

Time to flatten his tires. I stopped hiding my hurt. "You make my point for me. Your word's as good as the boy who cried wolf. And they're not my friends. His blood's thicker than yours or mine. They're family."

He cringed in mock hurt, "Is my brother the terrorist pretending we're not family?"

"You've already done that. I'm telling you His blood's a stronger bond than DNA. There's love here. These people are my family 'cause He's our Father."

"Wow, you're right at home in the cult compound."

That's enough, Calamity. Get out of there. The concern in Lightfast's rumble told me he knew my spirit's wounds.

Secret's done already?

She got what she came for, he said.

This had broken down into an exchange of insults anyway. I turned to leave.

Jeff's tone shot way up, "So, what, are the terrorists gonna torture me?" That one sentence was a call for help. His poor twisting spirit. Loneliness tainted the air. Pity battered its locked door in my soul's dungeon.

I paused, not bothering to face him, "Emptiness will do that. You'll be left to your own free will. Nothing delivers pain like personal freedom. You're in my prayers." I closed the door on him without even offering him a stick of gum. I was glad I didn't get the chance to see his soul in the Web. He'd become monstrous enough in person.

The viewing room's door opened and Lightfast stepped into the hall. "You okay, CK?"

I removed my com-shades and rubbed my eyes, that I knew bore a blue tint. "Just upset. I almost wish he and I weren't brothers."

"Certainly. Forgive him though." I frowned at Jeff's door. "That's His order to us for our own good. Feeding your brother's guilt to emptiness will eat your own soul and heart. Knowing Jeff's sad state does make forgiving him easier."

The Spirit added, *Matthew 6:12-15*—the stuff about the unforgiving not being forgiven. I prayed He'd give me time to work on this one.

I'd just began dialing the Boss when Secret faltered out of the little room and grabbed Lightfast's arm. She leaned on him, wheezing air. Glassy-eyed, pale and damp, she looked like her reason for living had called in sick.

I put the Boss on hold and hurried to take her other arm. "You all right, ma'am?"

Lightfast answered for her, "Her strength is gone. She needs rest. Reading minds is exhausting. I'll get her to the stackhouse." He handed me a chip. "Here's the goods. Go see what we've got."

e-girl loaded the CV's chip drive, and willed its data onto the screen. Angel glitter, the first I'd seen in our mission, swirled nearby. "Hey, howzit goin'?"

No reply.

A line map appeared and grew in detail. I tore my attention from the angel and keyed my com-shades to view the blueprint in three dimensions like a Web site. It grew into a small freestanding commercial building with a basement. Its basic design could have been home to a hundred different businesses. I sent it into a slow spin to take in the big picture before going inside. The basement loomed cavernous.

"Can you chase down a history on this address?" She shot me her does-the-Pope-wear-a-funny-hat look from the tops of her eyeballs. "Kay, fine. Don't go all Hackee on me. Check all traffic in and out since the church bust. Please. Pay attention to deliveries."

She tilted her chair, "Thirty seconds."

Queen's English came from behind me. "Calamity: thought you ought to know your brother's being released."

An' stay out, Nero-hero. Then I stiffened and turned to Grandpa, "Won't he be able to give us up?"

"Secret modified his short-term memory. He thinks he's been playing Snakes and Ladders with Winston Churchill and Margaret Thatcher, or something." He studied the CV from over my shoulder. "Is that where the church is being held?" The CV screen showed my com-shade's view.

"Dunno." Parts of the place were left out while others carried life-like detail.

"I thought Secret was to read his mind?" he complained.

"She did. This is where Jeff *thinks* they are. Check this out. The photographic parts all connect."

"If the lad's mind can see such detail, he's seen those places. He's walked through there. Well Pup, you've received a PhD in the FBT. What's your expert opinion?"

Hopes of our parents' rescue faded. "Skunked again. It's another trap. Look at the basement entrance. We'd have to enter through this long cement hallway. They seal off the ends and it's a coffin."

"I see what you mean. But, in itself, that fails to prove anything."

Swiveling the chair I dropped my chin to look at him over the top of my com-shades. "There's something else. Even if Jeff was working with them, why show him the church's location? So we could get it out of him. And go there again."

"Indeed . . ."

e-girl's chair squeaked. I watched angel glitter as she spoke. "All right, here's a thumbnail. The place was built in 2018 when work-place-crash-sites were just gettin' big. The king-sized basement was an employee apartment-bloc. The building's privately owned by local slumlord Trevor Stevens, who happens to be Alderman of Chicago's Ward Twenty-One. Last business to rent the place, a junk shop, cleared out last month. New renter leased two days ago. They paid one month's rent from a local dummy account. I chased the funds through a series of fronts, to the European Central Bank, and ended up at—safety your pistols—the International Bank in Brussels, Belgium."

Grandpa whistled.

I'd expected to hear she'd hacked an FBT tie-in, but walking a trail that ended at the One State capital sent my mindware spinning like a spider on a porch light.

She allowed our ears vent some steam before she continued. "As far as traffic, I checked archives from the last week and the place sat empty as a summer vacation classroom. Until yesterday. At which time grunts unloaded six white unmarked cargo vans, then left. At ten AM, four delivery boys dressed like accountants unloaded another van. Three-in-the-afternoon they were still there when a Chrysler New Yorker spit out two suits and our big brother. Twenty minutes later, everyone left, the New Yorker first, the van shortly after. But that's not all. Last night after sundown, peacekeepers unloaded enough weapons and ammo boxes to outfit a division."

I put a hand up, to stop her. "Enough. The church wasn't taken there. Food and medical supplies woulda been delivered, not military hardware."

Grandpa nodded, "Agreed. Ambush two, the skunking sequel. But the One State money trail concerns me."

"Why?" e-girl asked.

"It could mean Disciple involvement," said Grandpa.

"Judas'd be the only Disciple who'd join the One State," I joked.

Grandpa didn't laugh. "The Disciples are One State commandos. It's rumored they work magic."

I rubbed my face with both hands. "I'm too frazzled to even think about it. I need zzzs bad. One more thing before I'll see any downtime, though. How do I get in touch with the Surfers?"

He snorted, "The Surfer's Elder is . . . ahh . . . irritable. It would be far more pleasant for you if I passed along a message."

"I would, but what I need is a question and answer session. I really need to speak with him."

"Her. She's known as FairFax. The enchanting e-girl aside," he nodded at her, "Hacks tend to have a charm deficit, and FairFax is their queen. She's embarrassed that someone outside her court exposed the FBT database difficulty. You've already trodden on her toes—now you're asking her to waltz?"

"Yep."

"Consider yourself warned. e-girl, please get Calamity Kid on her dance card."

CHAPTER TWENTY-FOUR

e-GIRL AND I LEFT THE MISSION through the sewer grate that we'd first entered all those years ago. Or so it seemed. Our little stroll-in-the-rain made me sigh, then yawn. "Sis, I'm behind on sleep and a Sandman's reformation download doesn't include CV-geek mindware. Tell me why we're walking a mile to surf the same Web you can surf from the mission."

Just to tick you off. We CV Geeks are like that. Use thought speech, it's slick!

"You gotta get out more. I've barely got the energy to use my lips. I just wanna get this over with and unwrinkle my eyelids."

"To answer your question, a Sand-geek told me we gotta change up our routines or the FBT will come callin'."

I just didn't know enough Hack stuff. "So how's this help?"

"A chat between two reformed Hacks is slack. But Web-chat's privacy is like telling secrets with a bullhorn in the real world. Anyone with ears can listen in. Even if I set it up as private, other Hacks could chase, trace, and scan."

Note to self: add Hack-slang to mindware's fluent languages. "You mean trace it back to the mission?"

"Possibly. And spytap."

I guessed spytap meant eavesdrop in English. "So what homepage will you hack from?"

"Stuart's Super Stack." The motel chain had the reputation of being the cheapest crash site this side of a park bench. Everything about triple-S was bargain-basement, including their security.

"Aw, c'mon, girl! Gramma could hack a Stuart's homepage!"

She puffed up like infected bee-sting, "Not on my watch, Sand-Kid. Even Serene was impressed with my scope."

"She likes your mouthwash?" Yeah, I know it was too easy, but trying to figure out her slang had fried my brain.

e-girl rewarded me with a groan, "No, pinhead, a Hack's scope is how well she senses things in the Web. I can even see shadows, which is another reason why we're goin' to a Stuart's."

I squeezed my eyes shut and shook my head, "I can see shadows, too."

Her patience leaked out under pressure, in a my-brother's-an-idiot sigh. Words trickled off her tongue slower and sweeter than dribbling honey, "Kay, in English."

"I'd like that very much."

"A shadow is someone hacking from a high-tech network of virtual input hardware. They're very hard to detect. I'm getting into the habit of runnin' back checks. You know, checkin' behind me. 'Specially since you said we gotta be careful. Today I was homepage bound, when I caught a shadow tailin' me. I panicked and dumped to shake 'im." She slipped back into her native tongue.

"Which means you're no longer dating this shadow?"

Her eyes rolled a silent Duh. "I turned off the CV."

Even a not-Hack like me knew that wasn't good. "While still in the Web? I thought that was dangerous!"

"Can fry a girl's short term memory. I yakked hair-balls like Chewbacca's cat before crashin' for hours. Serene says I came out okay though. She gave me some tips for next time it happens. Anyway, she caught a shadow lurkin' our homepage twice more."

I suspected the worst, "Then someone's figured out the mission's Web access?"

She shrugged, "Dunno. We told Grandpa."

"Razz. Any idea who it was?"

"Not sure. It takes so much ritz state-of-the-art hardware to shadow, that the Hack who can is big-time. Even FBT Hacks aren't bankrolled for that." She rubbed her fingertips together, "That's free-market dollars. If the One State's got shadow work they subcontract it."

"The One State money . . . this shadowin' stuff smells like that Brussels' money you found. Please be very careful."

"I am. That's why we're here."

We walked up the wheelchair ramp. An old brass bell hung on the inside of the clear Plexiglas door and swinging it bounced the clapperless bell with a loud crack.

I'd just opened Hell's front door. A rushing reek of vomit, unwashed feet and cheap air freshener blasted my sense of smell. My sister gagged, for the second time today, like Chewbacca's cat.

The stench burned halfway down my throat before my mindware could adjust. Against our better judgment, we approached the desk. e-girl used her ID-chip to pay the $88.00 double rate for an econo-stack.

Our footware made sticky noises down the hall as we headed for our row. We passed a group of comfort-stacks near the public restrooms. Only three of them wedged between the ceiling and floor, giving guests room enough to sit upright. We, however, wanted to save the Body a few bucks, and arrived at economy coffin number 1089. It was a sideways phone booth.

"Oh, goody gumdrops."

"Yep."

In we squeezed. I cranked the shutter-door shut, elbow-bumping her with each crank. "Ouch! Stop! Quit it! Kid! Errr!"

I got to choose the meeting place, as long as its address began with a www, of course. e-girl loaded up *Peacekeeper*. At my request, she customized a playing field that copied Sunshine Chemicals' ambush alley in cyberspace. I logged into the game with virtual goggles and gloves.

Standing there brought it all back. Legacy's sacrifice slagged my mood, and I wished I'd just chosen a chat-room with soft sofas. I checked the Terrorist Webwire from my virtual com-shades to kill some time. A list of our captured Sandmen named everyone except Legacy. Even running a Web chase only turned up his wanted poster.

A motor sounded in the distance. E-girl had processed no random vehicles into the playing field, so I knew FairFax had arrived.

Boss, I come to you in the name of your dear Son Jesus, and through the Spirit. Please guide my heart and tongue as I meet with a tricky saint. I'm here as your slave through this test. Teach me or use me as you please. Your will be done, and to you be the glory, Amen.

The Spirit surprised me with a reply. *If I speak in the tongues of men and of angels, but have not love, I am a resounding gong or a clanging cymbal. If I have the gift of prophecy and can fathom all mysteries and all knowledge, and if I have a faith that can move mountains, but have not love, I am nothing. If I give all I possess to the poor and surrender my body to the flames, but have not love, I gain nothing. First Corinthians 13:1-3.*

e-girl's attention to detail impressed me when a yellow Subaru Baja pulled up to the wide alley. I breathed deep and focused on being in the Spirit's love.

Three angelic women got out while e-girl's fiery stare tried to set their backs on fire from her place behind the wheel. She pulled away, chirping the tires, and wearing such a sour face it had to be wrapped around a mouthful of virtual lemon smoothie.

The women burned white hot, like the first time I saw Serene and e-girl in the Web. Just as I decided that Christian souls dressed in His glory had to be the most magnificent thing this side of the real world, two looked pointedly around the virtual alley and exchanged snobby smirks. Beauty suddenly dimmed to empty dazzle.

One smirker spoke with the kind of paid-thrill voice employed by CV announcers while uttering the phrase, *"Order-now!"* She said, "Cute site. You burned up ace saint time to bring us here?"

This was gonna be harder than I thought. I swallowed hard to clear my own mouth of lemon pulp, then forced a smile at her rudeness. "You're FairFax?"

Still way-too-excited, she said, "And you're Calamity Kid." She swept her hand at her friends, "My assistant, Sleuth and the chase artist, Tracker."

Tracker, the one who hadn't smirked, smiled nicely. "I'm head Hack on the church search."

"I'm grateful for your efforts. Thank—"

FairFax crossed her arms and cut me "Please get live, cubby, 'n tell us why we're not better spending our time." Plastic had been poured into a mold to form her smile, and when she stopped speaking her face defaulted to the fake expression. If her eyes weren't gold, I'd have taken her for a Nero Symp.

I gave Tracker a wink, careful to avoid triggering an overload attack. "First, please give my thanks to the Surfers who put the FBT file into mindware format. The One State goes by the book, and thanks to them, I now have the book in my head.

"Which is why I needed to meet with you. Because of that file, I now have information about the kind of place where the church is being kept. I think I can narrow the search."

Doing the plastic smile thingy, FairFax narrowed her eyes and cocked her head.

I continued, "Our Cell had snatched someone we thought

might know where the church had been taken. Turned out to be a false lead, so we're back to square-one. You need to know that we're not under any time limits. Until a terrorist search is over, prisoners are kept on ice in case they're needed for public appearances. We've got two years from the date they close the case. Because the FBT must have spin control, the church is drugged and monitored, but they're getting top care.

"This means they're someplace with cutting edge med tech. First, we need to chase where the FBT might have facilities. Think anywhere. Hospitals, clinics, universities, private labs, even FBT HQ. Once we have a list of these places, we scan for new changes. All this went down less than thirty-six hours ago, so new patients, bed changes, shipments of monitoring equipment or certain kinds of drugs, anything at all might be a clue. Look for Jane and John Does, or maybe odd code names.

"Since they know you can hack any Webbed systems, all their data will be very hidden, maybe even coded. Get Field Hacks to chase and scan medical records in off-Web systems. They might be listed under their real names in those places. Please pass Serene or e-girl any fatebreakers. Questions?"

FairFax spoke right up, "Yeah, how do you like being famous?"

"What?"

"You're the talk of the Body. The too-small-to-be-a-Sandman cubbie who's been here for a whole two days, and is already running the place."

Her happy-voice burned my cheeks. The strump made me wish I could have gum in the Web just to not offer her any. Here I was trying to waltz and she discos? "Look, I've been trying to help by using what I know to--"

"That's what cubbies spin to themselves. The underground dodged extinction for giga-months without you. You don't have to force this personal church hunt of yours. If it's meant to be, it'll happen."

Is that how I'd been acting? I had to wonder. Then the Spirit spoke. I listened as it gave me chapters and verses. FairFax took my silence to mean she was right. She and Sleuth exchanged more smirks.

I turned and called over my shoulder, "Follow me. I want to show you something."

They paused before their virtual footsteps echoed mine. I slowed a bit so they'd catch up before I reached the trigger point. I crossed an invisible line and dozens of rooftop snipers opened fire. The ambush broke all over again.

Serene had said FBT agents couldn't win a fight in the Web, and I now understood why. In the second's fraction it took *Peacekeeper* snipers to get off a round, the Hacks gashed cyberspace. Erased programmes gashed Web-space. Black voids tore up the sides of the buildings, past rooftops, and into the sky. Impressive as it was, there were far too many bad-guys. As e-girl had arranged, the surviving bullets stopped centimeters from targets.

I faced FairFax. Her cyber chest gulped air and I knew my point had struck home. Wherever lay her creation body, it had just been juiced by enough adrenaline to lift a Land Rover. Her plastic smile finally melted, and her red-gold glare threatened to erase me.

I began only after setting the coolness of my tone at dairy freshness. "You're in a simulation of last night's ambush. This is how I Sherlocked the fake FBT database fatebreaker. You're grudging me 'cause one of your own shoulda scanned it. Woulda been scads nicer for everyone, 'specially for the fifteen Sandmen who fell here."

She opened her mouth to splash me with her red-gold brimstone, but I kept spilling chilled milk. "Sis, I'm doing my best to play my little part in the Body. If my tips are slag, don't use 'em. Or talk to my Elder about his understanding of the Parable of the Talents. When I crashed this wedding party, I took a seat in the back. Grandpa's the one who called me up; I did not ask for this.

"Yeah, this rescue is personal. I hope to spend this much energy on every job I saint. But if wanting to save my parents makes me a little rabid on this one then sue me, 'cause I'm just another sinner."

All the way through I'd kept my tone soft. I wasn't trying to tell her off, just make her think. "I can't know the path you've walked, but don't forget that, 'whoever humbles himself like this child is the greatest in the Kingdom of Heaven.' I'm here to serve by helping, not ordering people around. His will be done, not ours."

Before FairFax could reply, I disconnected and took off my goggles.

CHAPTER TWENTY-FIVE

MINDWARE ADJUSTED MY EYES TO the stack's soft light and I sensed e-girl's fuming. The same way you can feel the sound of a stereo's thumping bass, I felt my sister's frenzied scent. "I almost dumped that strump off the server!" she spat.

I tried to face her, but we'd crammed into the stack like Spam in a can. "Pleasant, wasn't she?"

"I *never* thought we'd find that kinda pretty-clique in the Body!"

I put my head down and couldn't keep my eyes open. "Grandpa warned me about her. You didn't know?"

"No, I didn't know that my Hack boss was a pretty-clique snob! You've grown scads, Bro. You came off kind, caring, and genuine. You played her absolute-zero."

"I wasn't trying to play her. Genuine was my exact intent. I'm so glad to hear it worked. Let's ride for mission."

Her face scrunched, "As long as I'm set up and shadow free, I've got a few things to take care of. You need your sleep though. Go ahead without me."

I squeezed dried-out eyelids and decided I didn't need to be told twice. "Too slagged to argue. Hymn to Him, e-girl."

"Word, Calamity Kid," she already sounded distant as her senses drifted Webward.

I cranked the shutter, careful not to elbow her with every turn, and inchwormed out of the stack. My dragging boots made sticky noises toward the lobby.

I faced a long walk home, but at least I could get my nose working again. I'd gotten so used-to scent, I was blindfolded without it. Leaving the bell to smack Stuart's front door, I relished Chicago's fresh industrial smog. Stackhouse stink stuck to my clothes like wet smoke.

* * *

My boot-steps rang lonely off the urban canyon. Rain was on a coffee break. Overcast clouds lurked too thick for moonlight, and too high for city-light's reflection. I made the mistake of cutting through a dumpster-lined alley. The intensity of rotting garbage warned that local bacteria colonies, currently obsessed with cell-division, had an Imperialistic stratagem for ruling the metroplex. Amazed at topping Stuart's stench so soon, I muffled my sniffer.

Then the whine of a small electric motor told me I wasn't so lonely after all. It sang far above normal human hearing, and some distance behind me. Its pitch sounded familiar. I kept on as though I hadn't heard it.

My senses strained for clues. Surrounded by stink that could hide even Stuart's floor, it didn't matter if I switched my nose on or off. Sight and sound hauled empty nets. I replayed the noise and matched it against my audio database. "Analyzing . . ." flashed across my com-shades. Just as my electromagnetic perception lit-up like a night-game at Soldier Field, I read, "Match found: Goliath gun mount."

Jumping straight up, I raised both hands and fired my grapples. They anchored three stories up and I set the high-speed winch to reeling cable. Gravity lost its grip as I did my best impression of a champagne cork. The nylon dumpster below jumped and kicked. Bits of brick and mortar spattled against the plastic as high velocity rounds punched random holes in the wall.

Two stories high, I rewound the grapples and shot one at the fire escape directly ahead. I swung forward as gravity hauled me back down. Heavy machine gun bursts revealed multiple bad-guys, but avoiding projectile acupuncture had me too busy for an accurate roll call.

They ceased fire, which meant they were tracking me. Time to dodge again. I doubled the cable speed and wind rushed my face. Bullets popped rows of holes in the bricks behind me. Razz, their targeting systems were fast!

Now that I'd been airborne for a whole three seconds, my mindware worked up a blueprint. The good news was that I knew where they were. The bad news was that there were three Goliaths. The really bad news: two crouched ahead of me, and one closed from behind. That put me in crossfire. The worst news of all, EMP grenades and flash strobes wouldn't do it this time.

These had been modified.

Note to self: have no-news-is-good-news tattooed on forehead. I'd forgotten all about that.

The first-story alley wall rushed at me. With only two meters of cable left to reel in, I released. My velocity gave me three running strides before I had to push off the wall with both legs. Once again I'd become a story problem for their targeting systems.

Grabbing my knees in a tuck, I spun two somersaults before hitting the ground. Landing feet first, my knees worked as shock absorbers. I rolled once and changed direction by launching straight up in a corkscrew spin. Another machine gun burst raked the alley where I'd have been rolling. In story-problem land, I was a trick question.

Ticked off tired of trigger-happy Neros using me for target practice, I cut the two high-explosive rounds I kept in each clip to the head of the line. My own targeting system marked Neros as I spiraled. Baby Eagles flicked out.

The Goliath on my tail took one high in the chest, and the explosion slammed him down like a Yahtzee cup. He still had game, but his dice would rattle before he'd be ready for another turn.

My nines had holstered before my other two rounds blossomed. Even though the fireballs hid the other Goliaths, my mindware had forecast their movement and fired a grapple into the ground behind the left Nero. I reeled cable, timing my flight so the blast flared out just as I arrived.

I crashed into the chromed hulk. We sprawled ankles over elbows as my grapple rewound. His partner's gun mount tracked me, but as I'd hoped, he held his fire. Their armor couldn't stop the armor-piercing bullets they used. Either these two were buddies, or I'd bowled over the guy whose turn it was to buy donuts.

Again I discharged a grapple, stopping it just after it passed the standing Goliath's knees. Yanking my arm caused the thin cable to whip around his shins and stick the grapple to his armored leg. The motion effectively tied his shoelaces together. He tried a step toward me and toppled forward.

I'd turned just in time to see the steel fist coming as it clipped my jaw. Little dots swam in a tinny taste of blood. A metal hand clamped my wrist in a vise, dragging me closer. I'd counted on this part.

Mindware lowered pain's feedback level so I had to be careful. I could break bones and barely feel it. He drew me close to reach for my throat. That's when I tore a small metal plate from the center of his chest, exposing his own grapple unit. Cold steel fingers brushed my Adams apple, but the thought's quicker than the hand and my Electrocutioner discharged.

The shock rode his grapple cable into the suit. The charge passed through unshielded circuitry on the way to zapping donut guy. I heard a small crackle. The suit's audio pickups never did. He locked up stiff as a Capone on Judgment Day.

Off to my left came the metal-on-metal click of a spring-loaded blade and I heaved several hundred kilos of rigor-Nero toward tripped-on-my-laces man. The ankle-wrapped Goliath blocked flying donut guy with one arm, and hacked at my cable with a forearm snap-blade that jutted from the other. I somersaulted behind him and looped cable around each of his wrists. Running a coil from his neck to his feet, I pulled tight. His body arched backward, hog-tied.

Yehaw!

He squirmed to get his gun mount on me. I jerked him around by the cable till we were near the alley wall. Scooping a handful of pebbles and grit, I flipped him over and trickled it down his gun barrel. Only then did I order my left grapple unit to crimp and cut the cable. Two down, one to go.

Forty meters away, the Goliath with a blackened chest found his feet. I walked slowly toward him. The few seconds he'd taken to remember what game he'd been playing were all I'd needed to take out his two friends. That fact rattled his dice even further as he planned his next move. Thinking wasn't his strong suit, so he settled for spearing me with his best I'm-an-intimidating-and-dangerous-high-tech-weapon-so-be-afraid look. Twenty meters from him, I stopped. A soft night breeze clattered a drive-through cup past us. All that interrupted our staring was a loud bang from somewhere behind me as common alley grit blew out his buddy's gun mount.

His audio transmitter made him sound as inhuman as he looked. "Stand down, Jesus freak!"

I smiled. "You're alone now. You know you can't take me. Hey, do me a favor and say 'Danger Will Robnson!'"

"Last chance, Fundi, or I put you down."

"Mmm, my mother's ugly and she dresses me funny?"

With all the humor of a death-row convict, he stomped toward me.

"You're gonna embarrass yourself."

I moved backward to buy him a few seconds. "I just wanna be on my way. I can do that without slaggin' your shiny silver suit." I held out my arms in a gesture of peace but he stomped mechanically closer.

"Flippin' rat-terrorist!" he droned. At the word terrorist, his hand shot out to aim a snap-blade at my chest.

Overdrive.

In a swirl of coat, my blades sang from sheaths. I deflected his spring-loaded sword with an electric pop. We bled red sparks down the alley. When I spun to slash at his open side, he sat and rolled a backward somersault.

I pressed on with a scissors attack before he even had his balance. "Live by the sword, die by the sword," I explained, but he blocked in time. I lost him in a spark shower that even filled the electromagnetic with a static burst, but my mindware kept up the attack.

My body moved well, knowing what it was doing without my will. He kept giving ground, so I kept taking it. His attacks were a bit slower than mine, but strong. His blocks came steady and he didn't seem to be tiring. The thought that he could outlast me crossed my mind. *Walk in the Spirit.* My focus, serving Him by being where I needed to be, filled my mind and choked away all doubt.

A rabid two kilo bee stung my back.

I arched backward.

The crack of gunfire.

Another sting, another crack. The Goliath swordsman stepped back, watching me. My body shut down the pain. My nervous system went cold-empty numb. I told my legs to move, but they didn't listen. I pitched forward, twisting as I fell, to see behind me. There stood a shirtless man in knee-length black spandex shorts. Next to his cheek, in a two handed grip, a smoking pistol pointed toward the black sky.

That was the shooting style FBT agents were trained to . . .

CHAPTER TWENTY-SIX

I SLIPPED OFF THE CV VIRTUAL-training rig and whole-body stretched in one of the mission's CV recliners. Being bested by Neros, even in a training procedure, made me frown. *Note to self: Neros in Goliath suits don't get a full shock through their grapple units.*

By setting the simulation to outfit the Goliaths with every available aftermarket upgrade, I learned that an FBT trained operator could escape a crashed suit. Donut-guy had quietly squirmed out and napped me.

After returning from Stuart's Super Stack, I'd crashed long enough to fully recharge my batteries, filled my belly, and ran the training programme.

I didn't want to slag myself so soon after resting, so I closed the simulation. The virtual reality exercise still burned in my muscles, and reminded me of track practice. I reached down to rub at my legs and noticed my shoelaces looped around the chair-frame and tied together. Overnight, Tinker had gone from Oscar-the-Grouch to Fozzie Bear.

A motionless Serene worked the Web from the recliner next to me. I wanted to thought-speech her, but she wore concentration's frown. Hacks lying flat in recliners appear deceivingly relaxed, but their faces are billboards. Her laces had also been tied together.

I left them that way, and made for the sofa pit to check the Terrorist Newswire, exchanging nods with two saints chatting in the mission's armchairs.

Stretching out in the empty pit, I tweaked the volume and chose the only story not told by Delisha Lix. A shrink prattled on about the ten ways to tell if your neighbor's a Fundi. Sidebar links and a scrolling-ticker carried nothing but Sunshine Chemicals related stories. *Terrorists out of Sominal—they'll use live ammo! National Threat Advisory Goes Orange!* and *FBT warns of terrorist retaliation for sandman bust!*

The Newswire would beat this until ratings dropped. Then something else would explode.

Disgusted with e-person lies, the bookshelves caught my eye.

Murdered by CVs, collating printers, e-books, POD vending machines and reading glasses, real books had been endangered since before I was born. I wandered over and burned twenty minutes picking out a novel. One stick of Winterfresh later, I ended up with a paperback by some guy named Peretti, and settled into an armchair. I was reading the first page for the third time before I realized I was reading the first page for the third time.

Note to self: Tell Lightfast mindware needs to make waiting easy. That would be like lifting a wait from my shoulders. I've never been good at waiting. There was just too much flying around in my well-rested mind. I'd hoped to have heard from the Surfers by now. Nothing.

Admitting that even Dr. Kevorkian had more patients, I put the book back. *Serene . . .*

She sounded annoyed. *Calamity, I told you, you'd be the first to know when I found something.*

I just wanted to let someone know I'm headin' over to Terminal. Since Legacy is MIA, contact with Tough-x falls to me.

That softened her. *Oh. Time draggin', Kid-O?*

Yeah. Dragon so bad it breathes fire. And nobody's checked in over there in awhile, so it'll gimmie somethin' to do.

Her tone went flat as she went back to work. *Kay. I'll be in touch if we need you.*

I braved light rain on a longer route, and approached Terminal from the south side. Melancholy clouds had me thinking of Legacy all the way here. How can you miss someone you barely knew? Angel glitter sparkled the gray building with magic, and I nearly smiled. Two more security cameras had been added. Their short overlapping sweeps made it impossible to approach without being seen. Knowing my socks were safe, I splashed through the running puddle water that trickled through the gravel parking lot, and opened the front door without knocking.

The scene that greeted me did make me smile. Children romped as I flapped raindrops from my coat. Young women waded hip deep among them.

Construction stormed the far end of what used to be a dance

floor. Men in tool belts swarmed a plastic and steel skeleton that reached to the rafters and filled the place with the smell of 'new.' Work frenzied as hard as the music that thumped from flip-coms, all tuned into the same audio-wire. The sound of teamwork's Golden Rule. A few angels swirled in here as well.

The best change though, was laughter. These smiling Tough Times faces couldn't belong to the same men who wanted to beat me to a smoothie-pulp only days ago. Humans of all ages had been introduced to joy, and their laughter rang thanks to Liberator.

The wonderful smell of home cooking wafted. Pork, baked beans, wild rice, and green salad. Workers sat around the bar area where Legacy'd gotten his coffee. Cooks and servers behind the bar talked and joked with those who stuffed away great gobs of lunch.

A thick middle-aged woman with round green eyes and dark skin came at me through the hubbub. "Hymn to Him," she said in a surprisingly sweet voice. The white apron tied around a worn cotton dress gave her an old-fashioned and motherly look.

"Glory" I replied.

Her smile smelled real, "Nice to finally meet you, Calamity Kid!"

"Oh. Um, thanks. Did someone tell you I was coming?"

"Well, since Legacy's gone missing, we thought you might be stopping by."

"Have we met?"

"I don't believe we have. My name is Matron."

I stood there giving her a puzzled look.

She broke out in a chuckle. "You don't know how I know your name! You've been on every list from the Prayer Chain for the last two days! It's usually impossible to keep track of someone we're praying for. But with you, all we have to do to get an update on the Calamity Kid is turn on the Terrorist Webwire!"

"Prayer Chain? You talk to Him, about me?"

"A thousand saints have been praying for you, little brother."

A thousand! FairFax was right. I really was famous. "I didn't even know there was a Prayer Chain. I need all the help I can get, so please pray-on! I'm so new I hardly know anything about how the Body's set up."

"Need to know basis. Have a seat and maybe I can clear some

things up. Come, sit." She swept an arm at a pile of cushions in a calm corner.

She explained as we walked. "Many don't talk for security reasons. The less we know, the less that Neros can get out of us if we're captured. I'll tell you some basics though. The Body's made up of hundreds of Cells. Some specialize, but most are Muscle Cells like yours, made up of different kinds of saints. This way if one Cell is caught, a dozen others can step up. Some saints belong to several different Cells. I belong to this Shelter Cell and to a Prayer Chain Cell." Then she chuckled. "There's another woman in the Prayer Chain who's even the Elder of the Body Surfers! I don't know how she finds the time."

My eyes bulged "FairFax?"

CHAPTER TWENTY-SEVEN

YOU KNOW FAIRFAX?"

I sat cross-legged on a large yellow cushion. "Met her today. She doesn't like me very well though. I didn't think I'd find anyone quite like her in the Body. Why is she . . . the way she is?"

Matron's eyes smiled sardonic. "Her faith is weak. She and I have spoken of it before. She works on it, but it's hard for her. She hopes her work with the Prayer Chain dulls her sharp edge."

"I don't understand. How can one be reformed, and not know He's there?"

"A weak faith isn't just doubt. Mindware meshes poorly with a strong will."

I considered that. "So if someone can't ignore their own will, they ignore His?"

"Right. To the rest of the Body, that person seems selfish or rude. Their spiritual handicap is plain to us. Some people's weaknesses are easily seen. It's a blessing really, because others in the Body can hold them accountable. Nobody can call you on unseen failings, so there's only personal accountability. Few have the discipline to address their own greatest weakness, so invisible sin usually festers."

"I used to see lots of gray areas in life. That way it was easier to do what I wanted. I made excuses for weaknesses. But reformation's centrifuge separated my gray into black and white. Only now can I see how dead my faith was. I thought it would be that way for everyone. To be reformed but still serving emptiness seems impossible."

"Goodness, no. Our mindware helps us to better live His law, but we're still fallen. FairFax struggles to make Him her Master with her every breath."

I leaned forward on my cushion, "But isn't submission what it's all about?"

"But what if submitting was your own greatest weakness? Even reformation can't really help strong willed people. They really are handicapped."

"Razz, FairFax can't walk in the Spirit, can she?" The memory of that hard lesson took my eyes to Dragoon's classroom: Terminal's loft.

Matron saw my glance and laughed. Hard. "Serene told me about your first Spirit walk in the loft. Speaking of, let me show you around."

"Do you think FairFax will ever get over it?"

"Perhaps. But I only brought her up as an example. I think if we go any further this becomes gossip. You know what James Chapter Three says about the tongue . . ."

I flushed. "Verse eight's the strongest. 'but no man can tame the tongue. It is a restless evil, full of deadly poison.'"

I'd been all ready to slag FairFax. "One of my own hidden weaknesses I guess."

Matron dropped the topic and turned on her cushion. "We only need a few saints to run this place. There, see the tall older man in the white T-shirt?" She pointed where two men stood. One fit her description. The other was Tommy. "That's Rock. He's the Elder here. He's part Pastor, part Sandman and part Drill Instructor. He works with shelters' leaders." She paused, searching the crowd. "Somewhere around here are our Healers."

I'd not heard that term before, "Healers?"

"Many teachers, nurses, and med students who join the underground become Healers. Their mindware's set up for healing and teaching."

She hadn't mentioned the most obvious healer. "What about doctors?"

"Most doctors have so much invested in their practices, they find it hard to leave the One State Medical Plan.

"Oh, we also have a Field Hack in the back room who runs security. Those who come to us do the rest. They work as teachers' aides, chefs, maintenance workers, and recruiters."

That was the part I didn't get. "But why? I mean what drives them to work?"

"Two reasons. One, for the first time they have hope. A point to begin rebuilding their lives. This is their neighborhood, family, and friends. Once they see what we're about, even the worst gangers come around. In fact, the worst gangers become the best saints. Their passionate violence is most easily turned into compassionate action. They care. It's because they care that places like Terminal work. Just don't razz them."

"Noted."

"Two, empty stomachs. 'If a man will not work, he shall not eat.' Second Thessalonians 3:10.

"Because of these, a shelter can run on a handful of saints. We teach them Liberator's orders. These people work for Him with everything they have, and in return He'll get them everything they need. The rules are strange to them at first. We start with the laws that families must have. You know, the Ten Commandments, no substance abuse, sex only in the marriage bed, and so on.

"The construction, there," she nodded toward the other end of the building, "is one of the perks of marriage. It's a room-sized stackhouse. All families get their own. The man is taught that in his every action, he's to treat his wife as a queen. The woman's life becomes service to her husband. Ephesians 5:22-33 is the model for marriage. The only person more important than the husband and wife is Liberator. We teach them Liberator's way is right, and their old ways are wrong. Because of Liberator value, they have value. This they can understand."

"You're telling me street gangs accept this overnight?"

"Don't underestimate the effect of hope on the hopeless. Only a few left Tough Times. Gangers are used to teamwork, with rules coming down from the gang boss. Then they start to see how His laws help them."

She held up a finger and cocked her head, "James 2:15—17 is another must for outreach."

As I recited it, she closed her eyes again, this time bowing her head as though she listened to a Mozart concerto.

"Suppose a brother or sister is without clothes and daily food. If one of you says to him, 'Go, I wish you well; keep warm and well fed,' but does nothing about his physical needs, what good is it? In the same way, faith by itself, if it is not accompanied by action, is dead.'

"That's what you see here. When they see the Movers bringing everything in, these people are kids at Christmas. When they see Liberator's three squares a day, the only thing bigger than their eyes are their smiles. When Healers take away their chemical addictions, they see. Rotten teeth are cured and they see. Medical care, dry heated stackhouses, clothing, nobody's shown them love like this. They've been used to Junkman. Rescuing people is one-soul-at-a-time work which is usually slow, but Lost Warders understand the difference between a need and a want. He uses us to serve hundreds of them every week, and they come to us so fast, we never have enough space."

I found myself nodding as she spoke. "He's really given us something here. What you're doing's gotta feel great. You must love waking up in the morning. One question though." I dropped my voice "You keep saying Liberator. When do they learn whose love they're really seeing?"

"When Rock feels the time is right, he tells them who Liberator is. Usually a couple weeks."

A young man jeans and a black Railgun concert-tee flopped down on cushions, shaking his head. "She talkin' your ear off? Matron, one day you're gonna use up all those words he gave ya and have'ta go mute 'til your homecoming."

Matron slapped his shoulder, crossed her arms and faked a bothered look. He turned a smile on me. "What she's tryin' to say is in this day and age, you treat a person like a person, they're gonna notice." He extended a fist. "I'm Logic."

"Calamity Kid." We knocked knuckles. "You one of the Healers here?"

He lay flat on his back and closed his eyes. His pierced lids had been fitted with rings like Jeff's. "Ya-hah. Logic's in da Terminal 'cause it's where Boss put me."

I nodded. "All right lessee if you two can answer this. The Body's got more supplies than Neros have nasty. Where's everything come from? Who's payin' for all this?"

A thirties-something man and a woman sat as I asked. Either the Movers had delivered a case of Railgun concert-tees, or these three all attended a performance in the L.A.-S.D Metroplex.

Matron answered, "Undercover Christians will have to answer for trading a part of themselves for One State comforts, but He uses them to give the Body of Christ its tools. Saints called Links live among them. They pass along dollars, goods and manpower that are donated by One State Christians. There are even a small number of unbelieving sympathizers called symps, who support our cause as well. Millions of Fundamentalists and Symps out there pay for our work."

"Wow. I'd grown up with home church parents who collected a lot of offerings. I had no idea they were supporting the Body. All the same, I'd rather have been here in the underground."

Thirty-something woman said, "It's pretty easy for a young couple to believe raising kids in a houseful of comfort is better than a Lost Ward alley."

"Oh, don't get me wrong, I'm not blaming them. But why would He put them into a spot where we'd have to make that kind of choice?"

Thirty-something man cleared his throat. "I've always found that problems of honor are usually created by our own sin. In a perfect world, your parents should've left the One State before making a family. In our fallen world, people have free will to make bad choices."

The woman hugged her knees with both arms, "Well that's harsh! My mother used to say the only difference between Fundamentals and unbelievers, is that we *know* we're sinners. When you put yourself between a rock and a hard place, you grit your teeth and live with the results."

The conversation had stayed low, but now Matron spoke a little louder, wrapping things up. "He's made us who we are, given us what we need, and put us where and when He wants us. Along the way we find the good and bad in the world and in ourselves. It's up to us to understand that He's teaching. Only we can decide to walk in the Spirit."

"Keep Him first, treat everyone we meet as we'd like them to treat us, and His will be done," advised the woman.

Logic added, "We serve, in love. We get the Word out. We meet people where they're at." He pointed.

Thirty-something man held up an index finger, "One soul at a time."

"Well, if you know a tree by its fruits, you guys are all fruit trees." Chuckles all around. "No, really, this is a great work. Places like this are what it's all about."

Matron dropped the bomb, "You've spoken truth, Calamity Kid. I just hope we can keep Terminal going."

CHAPTER TWENTY-EIGHT

THE THOUGHT OF TERMINAL shutting down raised a thought balloon over my head. It contained a heavy handed scribble, "What?"

Matron gave a long worry-scented sigh. "A Muscle Cell's rescue efforts hurts Capones. By changing their gangers, we replace the neighborhood's rule of crime with the rule of His law. That costs them money.

"At first the crime lords didn't know how to deal with us. They'd try to take their businesses back, but couldn't beat our Sandmen. So they tried calling peacekeepers. That didn't work any better. Now it's the FBT. The Capones use the One State to get rid of us. Then they move into another building and resume control of the neighborhood. We take the new building, and they call the FBT again. I'm afraid that's about to happen here."

As she spoke, I spotted Junkman. Like king-of-the-hill, he sat on a pile of cushions among the playing children. I pointed him out "I bet Junkman would tell us. It surprises me but he looks to be dealing with Terminal's changes better than I'd expected."

The thirty-something woman made a problem face. "Yeah, now. He's only been this way for a couple of hours. He snubbed everyone at first, and just played with his flip-com, all bigger-'n-better than us. Because he wouldn't work with Rock, we wouldn't let him eat with us. He fixed his own food and crashed. When he woke he was no different, but after a few hours he got bored. He sat in the loft, at the railing, for hours, watching us work with the grade-schoolers. That little girl sitting next to him—" She nodded. "—went upstairs and talked to him. She took his hand, brought him down, and introduced him to her friends. All he's done so far is play with the children."

"Hmmm." I stood, studying Junkman. "Thanks for the talk, guys."

"Whatcha gonna to do?" asked Logic.

Matron whispered thought speech, but I picked it up. *His job. He may be small, but he is a Sandman.*

I kept my eyes on Junkman and made like I hadn't heard. "His will be done, everyone." These people all made my gum-list. Even Matron, in spite of her *small* comment. I tossed Logic my mostly full pack of Winterfresh Extra.

They bid me providence.

Junkman paid such close attention to the kids that he hadn't noticed my approach. I circled around to come up behind him. I wanted to see his spirit up-close.

He had Jeff's twisty-rod shape, but his red was bright like a stop sign. Also like Jeff, the poor guy twisted inside out so he could only see inside himself. A pink section stretched fearfully toward the little girl's skinny yellow spirit. It moved like a dog sniffing a new dog's scent.

I slipped in close enough to touch him. "Hello, Junkman."

His animal body jerked like I'd dumped ice water down his shirt. His spirit rod yanked away from the girl, darkening to infection purple before going black-'n-blue. He squirmed even faster.

My breath drew heavy, more from his honest emotion than the effort. I had to see one more reaction. "She's dear to you. Nice to see you can still care 'bout someone beside yourself."

He shuddered, twisting inward even tighter. A blood-red blotch appeared on his center section. The spot stretched to form a line. In a second's fraction the line ran end-to-end down his whole spirit-body. It thickened and red liquid oozed from its center until it dripped.

"You people use love as a weapon. That's one of the reasons everyone hates you." Junkman's growl stank like hot rubber--hatred's scent. The blood-red liquid dribbled in a thin stream.

I stepped back in shock. I'd hurt him. Badly. My FBT mindware file included a personality-typing procedure that Neros use to hack heads open. I called for a breakdown of everything I'd just seen, and a report immediately appeared on my com-shades:

It is 97 percent probable that the little girl brings back a memory from the subject's past. The memory had melted the subject's hard shell. He had reached out to her because he trusts her. Viewer's entrance caused subject's shell to reappear. Observed wound too large to be caused by stimulus; stimulus reopened an old wound.

I marveled at this mindware tool and filed it for reference, but Junkman bled, and I was the child of the Heart Surgeon.

I came around in front of him and dropped to one knee, meeting his dry-ice stare. "You're right. We have this list of rules we try to live by, but like everyone else, we're human. That means we don't always live up to them. What I said was cruel. I hurt you, and for that, I'm sorry."

Icy eyes widened a bit. He searched me silently. I began to wonder if he could see my spirit when he finally squinted, "I don't know why, but I believe that you're truly sorry."

I smelled that he might open to me as he had to the little girl, so I pushed. "I think I've judged you unfairly. I wanted to ask you about your Capones, but this is more important. Who does she remind you of?"

Ice splintered away as he squinted at me. "Who are you?"

I waited.

He rose "What the Hell. Let's talk."

I followed Junkman to the door that led to the private rooms. It opened into a hallway, a set of steel shelves just inside. He snatched some items as he passed. The hall turned and he opened the second door on the right. We entered a restroom, two meters square, single toilet and sink. He closed and locked the door, then went to work duct-taping towels over the door crack. When he'd finished, he stood on the toilet and taped another towel over the vent fan. Stepping back to the floor, he drew a small red cube from his pocket, tapped some buttons, and placed it in the middle of the floor.

Junkman straightened-up, crossed his arms, leaned against the sink, and immediately spoke, "Six years ago I was a purchasing agent for an import firm. The One State placed our family of three in a four-bedroom home at Oakbrook Estates, and leased us two Lexus Starlings. My wife spent her time raising our four-year-old daughter, Anastasia, and shopping with her sister. As it turned out, wifey had too much time on bored hands.

"After work one evening, I pulled up to the neighborhood security gate, as I'd done a thousand times before. But this time I was dragged from my Lexus at gunpoint. Peacekeepers took me to O'Hare, and I was flown to D.C. to await my trial as a Fundi terrorist.

"Seems the little lady had joined a home church outside the Estates. I wouldn't have cared, 'cept the pastor day-jobbed with the FBT. The evidence against us was a box of pirate Web chips, FBT surveillance chips, some old Fundi hard-copy, and a hard-copy New Testament with my wife's handwriting all through the margins.

"They tell me she died in a Rehab. I hope her bored-home-maker-adventure was worth it because Anastasia's growing up somewhere without us. Without me. All the Federal Bureau of Children will tell me is that she's in a good home. She was placed with a foster family who adopted her while I was in Rehab without my citizenship. I've made a living out of finding things for people, and even I can't track down my own daughter."

I said "That's like—"

"So." He spat the word at me like a bullet. "The only people I hate worse than the One State are you Fundis. I lost everything in your little holy war. Since then, I've started my own business. In the time it's taken me to build up Terminal, I've met three Fundis looking to join the Body. Each time I took them in and called the FBT hotline.

"Now you walk in here and take everything I've built. I pay dues to the local Capones, so I let them know why they won't be getting my payments anymore. They took it to the FBT. The FBT wants to know more about your shelters, so they bugged the place."

That fit with standard FBT operating procedures, but the Hack running security couldn't have missed bugs. "No way. How'd they get in without . . ."

He explained in one word "Houseflies."

I groaned. Tiny remote surveillance drones. "Razz. That explains the towels and duct tape. But why tell me all this? You gave up Terminal to the FBT just to get rid of us, and now you warn me? Why?"

He looked to the wall that separated the tiny bathroom from the room full of children. "When I ran this place, people came to Terminal to escape life. They thrilled at the risk of visiting a black market club—a place to escape. To be whoever they wanted for a few hours. In two days I've watched you Fundis turn this into a place where people rebuild their lives. Lives that they won't want to escape from. Like the life I used to have." He swallowed hard. "I trapped people into working for me by finding out what they wanted. People work here because you give them what they really need.

"That little girl you saw me with, Auburn. I've never seen her before today. Her mother sold her to get money to buy my crax. She escaped from the man who bought her, and has been hiding, no, living, in a dumpster . . . until yesterday. She said the dumpster wasn't so bad except for the flies. She's glad there are so few flies here. She looks so much like Ana." Again he swallowed, his eyes glassy.

"Now that I see what you do, I don't want it to end. This is the best I've felt since my family was taken from me."

Where was he going with this? "So what, you want to join us?"

He laughed. "I'm no Fundi. But I guess I've become a Symp. I'll work with you."

Right. And I'm Abraham Lincoln. "What about your Capones?"

He shook his head, "Forget 'em. Listen. I'm your exterminator. I can sweep this place clean of bugs. I've got a gizmo that fries their sensors. When they send new ones, this device can also feed 'em whatever I want 'em to see. I've got image-chips of this place, empty. They'll think that you cleared out. I never turned that thing off, it's how I stayed in business all these years. Your people unplugged it, but I've still got it. It's a few blocks away at the U-Lock-Storage-Barn."

I motioned at the door, "Let's go then."

He picked up the red cube.

"Hey, what is that?"

He held it up between his thumb and index finger. "Pocket static generator. Hides sound waves. Just makin' sure the bugs won't know what's about to hit 'em."

Drizzle misted my com-shades. I turned my collar up against cold rain, hoping we wouldn't have far to walk. I'd smelled half-truths in the bathroom. He wasn't outright lying, but this wasn't the whole story. I decided to give him some room and see what happened.

We started down the sidewalk about the same time a car turned toward us, one block up. This area had so little traffic that I gave it a casual glance before looking back down at the sidewalk. I studied a visual snapshot on my com-shades. A new Lincoln Town Car in this neighborhood? Both windows on this side were down . . . in the rain. It carried three people, both passengers riding next to open windows. It needed one of those pizza delivery rooftop signs, Guido's Drive-By Shootings.

The Spirit told me I'd pegged it: *Be on your guard against men, they will hand you over to the local councils. Matthew 10:17.*

From my vision's edge, Junkman peeked at the car, then stole a glance at me.

CHAPTER TWENTY-NINE

THE SPIRIT ADDED, BUT I TELL YOU, do not *resist an evil person*
. . . *Matthew 5:39.* He's the Boss. It surprised me at first, but the
more I thought about it, the more sense it made. If I fought or fled
I wouldn't know who they were, or what they were planning. As
the motor grew louder, Junkman edged away from me. Scanning
the electric and magnetic fields created something like a photo
negative in my mind's eye.

The gun barrels that poked from windows made me focus
closer. When their trigger fingers tensed my mindware made me
bulletproof. Jackhammer popping of full automatic fire filled the
air. A Sandman's mindware is able to analyze gunfire, so I knew
they fired tranq rounds from HK nine-millimeter machine pistols.
They wanted me alive? *Why on Earth?*

My com-shades streaked the air red with bullet paths.

The idea behind firing fully automatic weapons from a moving vehicle is to fill the air with so much lead that even a monkey
could hit something. Aiming is pointless. The monkeys pegged
me with three rounds. Even though my reformation stopped the
tranq, I didn't resist the evil person, and went down like I'd been
hit.

The Lincoln curbed.

Mindware's wisdom had taught me that a shooting stirs up
strong emotions in witnesses. Sadness, excitement, fear, and anxi-
ety are the top four, so most of what I smelled was normal. But
the stink of a Goodyear factory that had fallen into a volcano?
Extreme hatred came from Junkman, who moved closer. Even
though I faced away from him, my other senses painted the picture. When he kicked me I knew it was coming.

He hissed through gravel teeth, "That's for Anastasia!"

That part of his sad story appeared to be true. *Might be hope for
him yet.*

The back seat gunman tortured Junkman and I as they loaded

me into the car. "Razz, it's a runt! You needed help with this?"

Laughter.

"Kinda small for a Sandman, ain't he?" the same voice added.

More laughter.

When they sat me up in the back seat instead of the trunk, mischief slipped from my soul's dungeon. Being a runt and all, it'd be easier for my stubby arms to reach laughing boy from here. I nipped my tongue's tip, to mug a wicked grin.

Capones sat next to me, back doors slammed, and we rolled. Nobody said a word, but the front seat shooter screamed with brain-wave activity. I cracked an eyelid and peeked between lashes. He wore a silk business suit, not a gen-one wetsuit. Probably Armani reformulated Kevlar. Capones sportin' gen-2 BW tech? That didn't click. Why had Dragoon been stylin' gen-1 if they could have sent this guy?

I counted ten city blocks before the BW signal hushed. Armani-man broke the silence, giving orders in a cold quiet voice that was used to power. Used to giving orders. "Cruise control's processed, so let the car drive. Capture-one bagged the Elder, a Tech and two Hacks. They're in transport. We'll meet enroute. Dispatch us to Midway, and you'll be free to go."

I considered running a mindware check on my hearing. Grandpa, Serene, e-girl, and Tinker were all in the mission when I left. Our new Muscle Cell, slagged already?

Armani-man had to be FBT. Capture-one, transport, and dispatch were all terms straight from the FBT handbook. The crime lords and FBT, working together? Then I remembered Grandpa talking about Disciples. A super-spy on our case?

Junkman's voice came from my left, "When do I get Terminal back?" Silence. "Fine then, just gimmie the reward money."

"You get nothing," the suit mumbled.

Junkman's voice rose. "The deal was Calamity Kid for Terminal!"

I'd heard enough and their drama distracted. I got live.

My right hand shot out at Armani-man's neck to discharge its Electrocutioner. He jerked and went limp.

My back seat buddy tugged at holstered pistols with the ol' basic reflex-one-point-oh. I crossed my arms on my chest, flicked twin nines into my palms, and demonstrated the advantage of upgrading to reflex-three-point-one.

Junkman and buddy responded to my tranq rounds by quietly slumping in their seats. Well, perhaps they'd be impressed when they awoke.

The wheel-man made the mistake of using both hands to tug at his weapon. This told me the Lincoln still ran on cruise control. I napped him too.

"Asleep at the wheel. What a Calamity!" I said to Armani-man. Crossing my arms on the back of his seat, I rested my chin on a forearm. "Betcha think twice next time you give a Sandman a lift."

Poor Nero now jerked around, trying to shake-off the effect of my Electrocutioner's shock. I pulled open his suit-coat to make sure. A gen-2 pack rode on his belt.

"Hate seein' ya in such a state," I lied. "Let me put you out of my misery." I winked, and he bounced satisfyingly off the wind-shield.

I enjoyed that part too much, asked forgiveness and help with my intolerance for Nero's lost souls. Then thanked Him for the chance to save our cell.

I unclipped my chip-tool from my belt and scanned the back of Armani-man's left hand. He I.D.ed as Michael Perkins, Arthur Anderson accounting. *Yeah, right.*

Cruise control showed us headed for Midway airport. We'd rendezvous with a convoy of three peacekeeper Humvees on the way. I could only come up with one reason we'd be going to an airport. They intended on taking us to Washington D.C. to face treason charges in Federal Court.

I tried to thought speech Serene. No answer. I tried Grandpa, Tinker, and e-girl. After what I'd overheard, my hopes were com-chip slim. I got what I expected. But as I made those calls, a brain-storm gathered. Deep purple with five mile tall thunder-heads. Lots of lightning.

This felt like what I had to do. Wasn't like I had time to take a saint-poll. Most of the saints I knew were a bit preoccupied any-way.

I tried to alter our directions, but the touchscreen's security read only authorized fingerprints.

So I used the wheel-man's limp arm to poke at the screen.

I needed some tools. They'd used AK machine pistols on me,

and those might be useful, but my brainstorm required more. When they loaded me into the car, the smell of gun oil and powder fumed from the trunk. I tore out the rear seat's backrest.

Bingo. The trunk held an arsenal. Their Remington 875 semi-automatic 12 gauge semi-auto shotgun, and Freedom Arms GL-7 grenade launcher would do very nicely, thank you.

For ammo, the Remington was already loaded with five tranq-splinter shells, and there were *cases* of grenades.

I also pocketed a medical injection gun, and a box of anti-tranq. emergency road flares gave me a dangerous idea; I stuffed a few into my other pocket.

I thanked Him again as I readied non-lethal weapons. He'd put me in the place I needed to be, with tools and talents. I thought about Galatians 5:13, and twisted a bad pun at the Lincoln's roof. "Neros up, love-fifteen, my serve."

Cruise control kept the Lincoln in the slow lane, running just below the speed limit. The dashboard clock showed our rendezvous with peacekeeper Humvees in two minutes.

The directional came on and we turned onto the Tri-State Tollway's entrance ramp. The Town-Car veered far left. The emergency shoulder gate opened at our approach and we whizzed through.

Wind in my face gagging me. I'd taken out the Town Car's windshield with my new Remington. Low clouds, but no rain. Perfect weather for a hi-jacking. All part of the brainstorm.

We merged into six lanes of 120 Km/h NASCAR wannabees.

Three olive-green Humvees made me reach for my pack of Winterfresh Extra. Then I remembered giving it away. They cruised the far left lane, and a bit behind. Perfect timing. Traffic gave them plenty of space. I took as deep a breath as wind allowed, and bolted dungeon doors.

Giving the Boss a final call, I squatted on the wide front bench-seat. The Remington, and the Freedom Arms GL-7 pointed downward under my coat on crossing shoulder slings.

The Town Car changed lanes and slowed, preparing to merge between the second and third Humvee. As the lead vehicle passed me, I got a close look at the four peacekeepers in the rear-facing seat. I raised the GL-7. Much to my delight, they put on their best hey-he's-not-supposed-to-do-that faces.

I beamed pearly-whites in a, yeah-no-kidding, grin. WHUMP! WHUMP!

Two Crashmonster tranq grenades punched through the soft clear plastic zip-in panel that sealed off the back of the Humvee. Each was rated for 500 cubic-meters, so I just filled a buttoned-down Humvee with enough non-lethal tranq to nap a 767 passenger jet—baggage handlers and flashlight wavers included.

The gas was invisible. My lullaby wasn't. Neros sagged asleep.

I re-checked the *on* position of the GL-7's safety, took another deep breath and keyed my com-shade's stopwatch.

This is where things got real tricky.

I sprang onto the Lincoln's hood and leapt off the driver's side.

Mindware hit overdrive, adjusting to make up for the 120 Km/h blast of air. I scanned inside the vehicle while airborne. The six-person FBT team all wore first generation wet-suits. Grandpa drooped lifelessly between two front seat Neros.

I landed perfectly on the Humvee's steel hood, facing forward like a life-sized hood ornament. The smart soles of my boots bonded with the metal and I released the grenade launcher's shoulder sling. Time to play the ol' ring-the-bell-and-win-a-prize county fair game. Holding its barrel with both hands, the GL-7 arced over my head to slam into the front bumper.

The bell rang. Airbags in the front and middle seats mushroomed, forcing four pistol-drawing Neros against backrests.

Pillow-fight!

Flipping the GL back around the way it was meant to be held, I stepped around, re-bonded my boots, targeted the rear Humvee and clicked the safety to takin'-care-of-business.

WHUMP! WHUMP! WHUMP!

Three Insta-Dry black paint grenades splashed a thick layer across their windshield. I could tell their cruise was on because they didn't even swerve, but it would give 'em something to think about. I dropped a Day-Brite orange road flare over the passenger side before going back to work on my highway surfboard.

With a thought I drew a pistol. Careful not to shoot anyone, I put an armor piercing round in each corner of the windshield. Obeying the laws of physics, the glass pebbled, and blew into the front seat. I holstered the pistol and dropped another road flare.

This is spiff! I said to me, really starting to enjoy myself.

Yells, shouts, and billowing airbags convinced me that it was time to simplify things. "Nightcap, anyone?"

I hoisted the Remington, and blasted four squirming areas of airbag in the front and middle seats. Tranq needles tore nylon and rubber.

The driver had canceled the cruise, and slowed onto the fast lane's narrow shoulder.

Safety first.

I dropped a third flare, reached through the windshield, and cranked the wheel away from traffic.

Freeing my boots, I rolled off the passenger side.

Their Humvee sparked along the guardrail as I tucked into a ball and rolled down the fast lane.

CHAPTER THIRTY

THIS IS WHAT THE ROAD FLARES were for. Mindware clocked me at 49 Km/h. Yeah, that was stupid. I thought the bulletproof-thingy was spiff. My mistake.

Pretending to be a bowling ball on pavement is a really bad idea. Really bad. At 49 Km/h, even reformed senses can't track which elbow, cheekbone, or knee will next kiss concrete. Bumps and bruises heal fast if you've been reformed, but trauma, contusions, and lacerations *hurt*.

I lived. Coming up in a crouch, I set a weapon against each hip. Thirteen paint grenades splashed Humvee windows as they sparked down the guardrail. The GL-7s ammometer read 02 when a frogman jumped from the middle Humvee's rear door.

According to 'the book' he wanted to surprise me.

My 12-gauge thundered. His needle-nap made the vehicle's last frogman rethink the whole jumping-out thing.

My last two grenades were Crashmonsters. I took aim at Humvee-three's plastic panel. WHUMP! WHUMP!

Never thought I'd say this, but I was beginning to like

peacekeepers. They were easy.

Only one frogman to go, but I had to leave enough time for escape before back-up arrived on the scene.

My empty firearms hung from their shoulder slings, and I leapt to the third Humvee's rear passenger-side door. My knees absorbed the shock of landing. I yanked it open and winked a scorch at the back seat frogman.

The air between us shimmered. His groping hand found a door handle and he tumbled backward out the driver-side door and over the guardrail. This slagged my scorch.

I leapt a somersault over the Humvee, drew my blades and landed facing the vehicle. He'd hit the ground rolling, but froze at the sight of my naked steel. A millimeter separated his cheek from my sword-flat. His soul colored that shade of yellow commonly found in wet diapers. He reeked of fear and trembled so the handcuffs on his belt made a tiny jingling.

For effect, I took off my com-shades and drilled him a rabid 24-carat stare. "Game over. Got an idea. How 'bout instead of me playin' scorch-the-Nero's-behind, you take your boss a message?"

He nodded stiffly.

"Tell him, Calamity Kid said y'all ain't ace enough to trump the King of Kings. I won't bow to a false god, but you're all in my prayers. Got that?"

Again, he nodded. Crab-scrambling sideways, he clamored to his feet and ran off.

As he ran, I noticed out that the word "German" blinked on my com-shades because that was the language I'd just spoken. This mindware stuff was ab-zero cool.

I swept the vehicles for guns and supplies, and loaded up the Town Car. Of all vehicles, this was the one least likely to be bugged. I traded Junkman and the other Neros for e-girl, Grandpa, Tinker, and Serene. Grandpa slumped in shotgun position.

As we merged into the gapers' delay that had piled up, I drew the injection gun and shot Grandpa with anti-tranq. I wondered how long it would take to work, for about a half a second. He groaned.

"Grandpa, you alright?"

"Ugh . . .Wait . . ." His fingertips massaged his temples.

A few seconds was all the wait I could give him. "The book says a Humvee's CV calls HQ when its airbags pop. That happened four minutes ago. We're southbound on the Tri-State. Cruise control says Ward Fourteen. Providence may get us through one checkpoint before this car's a Nero magnet so I need you to get us lost in a Lost Ward."

"Take the 99th street exit east."

"First thing, Terminal needs some immediate security improvements. Tell Matron those children are due a field trip . . ."

"Sorry I can't do bedder fer you guys." The man I knew only as Jimmy had broken down some cardboard boxes and laid them flat to cover the stained and sticky floor. "Over on da shelf is some tablecloths. Da tick plastic kind you can wipe off. Use 'em fer blankets if you get cold. Godda get back before dey miss me."

I slapped him on the shoulder, "Could be worse, thanks for the bolt-hole. You da man." Jimmy closed the door behind him. Until we figured out what had happened, this greasy spoon's storeroom was our new crash site/ mission. Scads of boxes, cans, and jars sat stacked on steel shelves. Not yet trusting the floor, I used one of the bigger boxes for a chair. When Jimmy hit the lights, roaches rippled the floor like wind on a wheat-field. I hid my disgust by looking for a bright side. Even if the Neros Sherlocked our site, they'd rather let us go than risk death by cockroaches.

Serene and e-girl made us guys look like mopes by kneeling right down at the room's cable outlet. They had too much to chase for roaches to stop them. For one, we needed to know if the whole Body was live with attacks, or just our Muscle Cell. Serene had to network with FairFax as well. They plugged in thingies on their belts and hacked the Web. We were out of range for thought speech. Grandpa tried a couple of Elders he thought might be nearby, but came up empty.

Tinker kicked at a crack in the floor where some roaches had taken cover. "Rotten oozin' scobs— Kid, did you mind-fax me?"

"Not me."

Grandpa followed my lead, and pulled up a box. "Did you contact any of us?"

"No, why?"

They looked at each other. Grandpa answered, "We all received Calamity Kid mindware text messages that summoned us to Terminal. We were lured into the open."

"Right before we got sniped!" Tink scowled.

"Calamity said they've been routing us. Either they crunched our travel times or . . . e-girl had informed me of a Web-shadow. That's the more likely scenario."

"Maybe that's how they got you two, but I was ratted out." They listened as I told the story of Junkman and my capture. My description of Armani-man yellowed their eyes in interest.

"Armani-man, as you call him, could very well have been a disciple . . ." Grandpa stopped to gawk at e-girl who began bouncing like a tribal native at a war dance bonfire.

"They got 'em!" She clamped a CV chip between her thumb and index finger.

"Got what?" we all asked at once.

"Mom-'n-Dad! Surfers found 'em!"

CHAPTER THIRTY-ONE

I'D HEARD THAT BEFORE, BUT my heart still flipped in my chest. "Where?"

"They got 'em! They got 'em!" I knew she'd gotten some pretty solid data to be this worked up.

"Sis! Take a deep breath and explain in English. Please!"

"The Surfers chased and scanned the leads you gave 'em. A few places only had research and billing databases online so some Field Hacks got live. One of them Sherlocked a private clinic with a whole floor disabled from core security. Video archives were right up your alley.

"All systems were fine until two days ago when some suits pulled up in a New Yorker and met with the head of security. Soon as they left, the third floor cameras crashed. Then truckloads of men and equipment showed up and headed for the third floor. A few hours later, just after our church bust, their entire security system went offline for over a half-hour. Since then, nothing. Third floors even been locked out to the elevators. The place is a stone sealed tomb!" She resumed her pee-pee dance.

I punched thin air. I turned to Grandpa, "I gotta plan the rescue!"

Grandpa smiled. "Your mindware won't permit rest until you've done so." He stretched out on the cardboard, flapped open a tablecloth-blanket, and winced his eyes shut. "Mine, however, bears no such strategic burden. I cannot speak for everyone, but I'll be collecting forty winks in hopes of eliminating the tranq headache that swallowed Liverpool. Who intends first cockroach watch?"

I plugged the chip into my com-shade's jack, and leaned back against a shelf. Mammon Clinic's laundry service turned out to be subcontracted to a Symp, so the field hack had ghosted security in a load of clean sheets. After Sherlocking their system for five hours, another laundry truck ghosted her back out.

It took only minutes to see that the file's field hack was an e-artist. I had every detail I needed, and worked off the electron Mona Lisa slicker than cooking oil on Teflon. Thirty minutes later, I pocketed my com-shades and rubbed my eyes.

I roused the drowsers and ducked the complaints thrown my way, including Tinker's speculation about my parents' marital status at the time of my birth.

They gathered around the crude line map I'd scratched onto a piece of cardboard. I tapped several rectangles at the map's center with the screwdriver I'd used as a pencil.

"All right, this is our target. Mammon Clinic sits smack in the middle of 12,000 wooded acres. In the world of modern medicine, this place is famous for having wizards as doctors. Naturally, their kinda' care goes only to those who can afford the very best."

Tinker scowled and rubbed his beard. "Mammon Clinic. The Department of Wealth and Hellfare. They rebuilt Mayor Daley the Third's heart a couple years back."

My screwdriver aimed at him. "And that's my point. Some patients are rich *and* famous. So let's say the mayor's enemies want to slip him a permanent Mickey. Or the Webwires won't leave him alone. A man like that needs privacy. Heck, even the rich ol' uncle Freds out there who've left stuff to a barrel of rotten apples need bodyguarding. Mammon's med care's ace, but right behind it is their rep for patient privacy and security."

"That begins at their property line with this." I pointed to heavy gouges running around the map. 'That's a seven-meter razor-wire fence juiced with 50,000 volts. Tink, on your way into Mammon, heat up that thermite torch of yours. Cut us a three-meter hole. The fence has tensioners and an alarm circuit so clamp circuit leads across your cuts, or you'll become security's excuse to field test live ammo."

Tinker gave me his best I-hate-electricity look. "I'll wear rubber-soled shoes."

"Over the fence, the forest has a few thousand of these little guys." I tapped the dozens of holes I'd punched in the cardboard. "Gray weather-proof domes 'bout eighteen centimeters across."

"Mines?" guessed e-girl.

Tinker hung his head, "Worse. Man, I hate those things. They hold all sortsa stuff: motion sensors, electric eyes, thermo graphics—"

"All of the above. Nice thing about Hacks is they see security systems from the inside. That's also how we know about their guard dogs," I said.

"Pit Bulls?" guessed Serene.

"Too low budget for this set-up. Try genetically engineered Greyhounds; datafile says they've got a gator's jaw strength, sensory wiring of a wild turkey, and jaguar claws . . ."

Her hands fell limp on her lap, "Great; Hell hounds."

". . . that can hit 60 Km/h over rough terrain," I finished. "Moral of the story is we'll be going in through the front door rather than over the wire and through the woods."

"Great moldy scobs! Why'm I riskin' my anatomy with the fence?"

"That's our escape. The gate's the weakest point for entry."

"That will be no small task." Grandpa raised an eyebrow. "If they've visitors of the Bureau inside, the guest list will be quite discriminating."

"And that's why I need you to contact your Symps at Vader's Inc. and Arrow Laundry Service."

His eyes got round beneath frowning brows, "How in the blazes do you know—"

"The Field Hacks' report included Symp contractors doing business with Mammon. We'll need both their elevator repair and laundry services. Oh, and please set me up with a Healer for the entry team as well."

"Done."

I nodded. "Now, Mammon's systems are self-monitoring. When something breaks, sensors automatically trigger Web service calls. A couple hours before kickoff, e-girl will hack the maintenance elevators' sensors, triggering a call to our friends at Vader's Inc. We'll need one of Vader's trucks, a driver, uniforms, and ID files for Vader employees already logged in Mammon's security system. That'll get Serene, Tinker and their driver into the basement to access the maintenance elevator. Utility access and CV hardware are just down the hall."

I sat back against the shelf. "Here's where things get tricky, 'cause building security's hot-'n-heavy. Their system reads ID chip signals to pinpoint not only who you are, but also which restroom stall you're using. If you don't have an ID chip, lights start flashing in the security office. If your ID's not in the system, lights start flashing in the security office. If you go anywhere your ID isn't cleared for, lights start flashing in the security office. Get the picture?"

Tinker and Serene both nodded in boredom.

"The vader's master controls are in the CV room. The CV room's lock will be expecting you, so your IDs will open the door. This is where Serene gets live. Live is made up of five parts. One, get us cleared so we'll be authorized to enter the building when we get there. Make sure their system reads our ID chips as top clearance."

"You guys'll be workin' the third floor. Wanna be FBT?"

"Spiff, that'll do nicely. Two, freeze a view of the Arrow Laundry truck on the basement entrance cams.

"You'll get out of the Vader truck at 10:10 p.m. e-girl, a Healer, nine Movers, and I will follow in the Arrow Laundry truck at 10:18 p.m. That gives you eight minutes to unload your tools, get into the CV room, and complete one and two. Any problems?"

Serene served her best look of chilled calm. "By 10:18:01, they won't know if you ride in on elephants."

"Good. Our truck can't leave until we've unloaded. It's gonna look suspicious if the laundry crew takes too much time, so by 10:20 p.m. both trucks should be pulling away. Three: central security's office has cam views of the whole place. Their third floor screens have been blank since the FBT moved in. Rig the system to make sure their monitors stay blacked out, because number four is bringing the third floor's system back online. While we're un-loading the truck, use the system to get the floor's security layout. Count Neros, and check their armaments so we'll know exactly what we're up against. I'll get a report from you before headin' up to secure the floor.

"Five, slag the outer defenses, but be careful. I said this sys-tem's hot-'n-heavy. Disabling any sub-system makes more of those lights flash so only adjust things, don't turn anything off. Raise temperatures in heat pick-ups. Speed up the meters/per sec-ond in motion sensors. Blind sec cams with recorded loops."

"Got it," said Serene.

"Now we're not just bringing Tinker along to flirt with electric fences. All Mammon's elevators have been cut-off from the third floor. This includes the maintenance vader you came to repair. Tink, we need to get to the third floor."

He looked at the ceiling and scratched his hairy neck. "I can lock out the lift on the basement level, open the ceiling hatch and rig a cable ladder to three."

I nodded, "Slick, but be quiet about it. I'd bet a whole pack of Winterfresh Extra they've got BW tech ears on. After I secure the third floor, get e-girl up that vader-shaft. That puts you both in a maintenance room. e-girl, you'll find the floor's isolated CV hard-ware in this room. Scan that system for FBT security upgrades. Make sure we've got no surprises. Then tweak the settings in pri-vate rooms so no one will know when we start snatchin' patients. IV tubes, heart monitors, and temperature sensors are all bugged with screamers in the nurses' station. Also, pressure pads trig-ger alarms when a patient leaves the bed. After that, make it so Mammon's system reads the church's IDs as FBT-clearance too. We don't want lights to start flashin' on their way out.

"Tinker, while e-girl's hackin', remove the main exhaust duct's access panel. Climb that duct and remove the rooftop panel as well. That's our route to your fence hole. When you're done with that, make sure the elevator car's locked to the basement level, and burn off its roof with your torch."

"Oooh, a cus-tom convertible!"

Serene shot him an oh-grow-up look that set him sniggering.

"When the rest of the team finishes their jobs, we lower the church down the elevator shaft and drop them in the waste dis-posal unit."

Everyone looked at me like I was joking. Tinker verbalized their thoughts. "You're rescuing these people, so we can throw them away?"

"Something like that. Then we're outta there. The FBT walks a floor check at the top and bottom of every hour, so by 11:00 p.m. we're dust.

"Questions?"

"Why don't we skip the part where I try to fry my bacon on their fence, and we all just take off in the trucks?"

I shook my head, "Never leave the same way you came in. If they're on to you, your escape route's cut off. So we'll be goin' up and out the air-shaft, down the fire escape, and through the woods. A van will be waiting for us outside your fence hole."

Serene raised a finger, "Uhhh, and the Hell Hounds?"

I grinned to let her know I hadn't forgotten that little detail. "We're pole position on the food chain for a reason. The Rovers' senses will stop at raw meat. Included in everyone's gear will be a freezer Ziploc containing five kilos of butcher's scrap."

Grandpa had been rubbing his chin as I detailed the rescue. He finally voiced his thoughts, "Calamity Kid, I regret to say I cannot back your plan."

CHAPTER THIRTY-TWO

I SEARCHED, BUT HIS FACE SHOWED no hint of a joke. His kindhearted smile told me that frustration and distress had pulled a soul's-dungeon jailbreak and now danced across my face. "Why not?"

"You lack adequate muscle in the event that things break down. Counting drivers, you've got sixteen saints entering an FBT safe house. There's but a single Sandman among them, and an inexperienced one at that."

I paused before I explained my logic—didn't want to seem too quick to defend the plan. "I'm not going to argue the plan because it's mine, but I will argue three logical points.

"One, the Sunshine Chemicals rescue consisted of ninety percent Sandmen, and that meant nothing.

"Two, according to the book, the church will be lightly guarded.

"Three, our goal is stealth, not siege. There's only enough work for one Sandman; we don't need more bodies to sneak past watching eyes."

Grandpa countered, "That said, the team requires additional muscle in the event of a crisis. To that end, I shall accompany you." He spoke as though he were addressing a child. This usually ranked as a mild irritation. I'm a small man, just out of my teens, so I do understand people judging a book by its cover. But this time it cut me.

Silence settled over the group, and all heads turned to me. I eased a polite smile. "Then you've put me in a pickle." I leaned forward, kneeing my elbows. "Grandpa, I respect you not only as the Elder of this Cell but also as my elder, one older and wiser than I. You once told me you'd be wasting my talent if you didn't use me to plan runs. I speak as an advisor when I say you never had any business going into the field. Were you to join this rescue, I'd still be the only Sandman. He made you to run a Muscle Cell, not to muscle a Cell's runs. If this rescue goes as best as it possibly can, our gains wouldn't be worth risking your skills and talents in the field. If we get skunked, the Body needs you to lead Ward Three's mission. It's certainly within your power to insist on going, but first you'll have to remove me from planning runs. Doing my best means I can't allow you to risk yourself."

Like a tennis match, all heads followed the ball back to Grandpa's side of the net. I heard cockroach footsteps in the hush. If he were a CV, his fan had kicked on and his face had slipped into screen-saver. The wait put my breathing on hold.

Screen-saver still ran when he finally began speaking, "Further argument would come from loathing. I loathe to sit waiting for news of a run. My nightmare is staying behind when I could have made the difference on a failed operation. You've convinced me, pup. I'll contact the Symps as well as the proper Mover's Cell."

He winked at me, "I thank Him for lending you courage enough to fight for right. I stay in the mission."

Silently, I thanked the Boss.

Tinker blew a leaky balloon noise from puffed hairy cheeks,

"Industrial strength scads-o-drama."

I reached for a stick of gum. *Nuts.* "Anybody bring some Win-terfresh Extra?"

Serene stood, "Well, let's do somethin', even if it's wrong." She flipped me an unopened pack. I almost cried at the beauty of such self-sacrifice.

I thought the next eighteen hours would drag.

I was wrong. Our many preparations rocketed time's passage. All those hours of *Peacekeeper* took over and I worked from in-stinct. After not knowing if we'd ever find their hidey-hole, prepa-ration meant our parents' attempted rescue was finally close.

Grandpa upgraded our crash site to the local Mover's Cell. While things can always be worse, downgrading from our cur-rent crash-site would have been difficult. We traded our roach motel for a Mover mission stackhouse.

I presented the movers with the rescue plan. Their touch-screen boards worked way better than screwdriver scratches on cardboard. Nine volunteers later, I found myself hammering out details, checking equipment, and distributing supplies. I set up practice areas and task drills.

While I timed the team's best efforts at lowering tires down a ventilation shaft, Schlep, the team leader, set a plain brown card-board box at my feet.

"I thought you were at the bottom of the shaft. What's that?"

He shook his head, jiggling shoulder-length blonde curls, and shrugged shoulders that belonged on a Clydesdale. "Just runnin' a delivery. Tinker says Merry Christmas."

I looked at the box, considered its sender, then back to Schlep. "Whaddaya think, foam snakes gonna pop out?"

Schlep snapped off an eyelid-heavy get-real stare. "Foam? I hardly know Tinker, which is enough to know that guy would spring load real snakes." He backed away showing me the palms of his hands in mock fear, "Don't open it till I'm back down the shaft."

"Coward!" He left me chuckling to myself. Nothing happened when I nudged the box with the toe of my boot. Hey, you only live once, right? I parted cardboard flaps with bare hands. Tinker had taped a handwritten note to a Ziploc bag.

Calamity Kid,

You remember your idea for team communication during BW blackouts? Scrounged up some micro-coms. Had Grandpa track you down some sniper protection too. Hope it fits.

Tickle my tailbone, Delisha just called you runt on an international Web-cast again. The Nero from the Humvee musta told quite a story 'cause your head's worth ten million now.

Man, could I use ten million.

Tinker

Razz. I'd turn myself in for ten mill! Inside the Ziploc were enough micro-coms for the whole team. The Band-Aid-style flesh tone strips came in pairs. One would stick to an ear and the other over the throat, at the voice box. If we'd had these toys at the ambush, it would have had a very different ending.

Setting them aside, I held up a brown oilskin duster. The ankle-length coat bore an L.L.Bean Kevlar label. It looked just like Legacy's, right down to the zippered collar-hood.

I shed my army overcoat and slipped into the satin-lined armored-duster. It was a touch big, but most of my clothes were.
Note to self: name first-born child, Tinker.

My mindware had me crunching details for almost too long, but crashed me in time to be fully rested by zero hour.

At 9:00 p.m., we arrived in the utility tunnels beneath Arrow Laundry. The Movers loaded our gear into one of the company's white step vans—one of those stubby door-less delivery trucks. Riding shotgun in spring-fresh-linen-on-wheels brought back CV fabric softener commercials with teddy bears and clouds. We came prepped for danger. We left all fresh, breezy, and bouncy.

We rolled with nine Movers and one Healer hidden in the back. Only e-girl, the driver, and myself could be seen from the street. Belted into a folddown seat, e-girl worked invisibly from a pair of com-shades. Seeing her like that, wearing e-glasses, in a back seat, returned me to the night it all started, and what she'd impossibly hoped for beneath that bridge.

Here we were.

CHAPTER THIRTY-THREE

ARROW LAUNDRY'S DELIVERY DRIVER kept sneaking looks at me. The sturdy graying man wore navy blue nylon coveralls with a matching army-style cap. His name had been stitched above his security pass, *Travis*. We wore similar uniforms, but our tags; mine read *Temp Worker*.

I didn't know about the symp who owned Arrow, but Travis had to be a believer. There's a big difference between backing someone else's play, and putting your own neck on the block.

I caught him looking again and gave him a nod. "Thanks."

His attention went back to the road. "For what?"

"The lift."

He waved it off, "No biggie."

I stared out the windshield, "Then you don't know what's on the line. This means a lot. I'm not allowed to give an exact number, but you're saving dozens from rehab."

His lips twisted with frown as he shook his head. "I don't wanna know. Slagged world we live in." He gave his attention to turning a busy corner. "Never met uh saint before. You really wit da Body?"

"Yessir."

"Never spected I'd meet one uh you guys. What kinda' work you do?"

"Sandman."

"Tough guy, eh? I'da taught a Sandman'd be bigger, doh."

"You know, I've never heard that before," I offered him a stick of Winterfresh Extra.

That smoothed most of the wrinkles from his forehead. "Tanks, I love dis stuff."

"Me, too."

He worked on the gum, and seemed to be putting something together in his head, so I gave him some silence.

He finally said, "You're a mover and shaker. Tell me somethin'. It looks to me like da One State's too strong. You tink we gotta chance at livin' free?"

"We're a little outnumbered—say a thousand to one. They're better funded too. When the Neros need more money they just print some. And they've got some great toys.

"We've got a couple strengths though. For one thing, the Body's teamwork is so smooth that we really do function like a body. That makes us quick and slick. What they have in quantity, we make up for in quality. Man-for-man we're far better. Our reformation makes us super-human. 'I tell you the truth, if you have faith as small as a mustard seed, you can say to this mountain, move from here to there and it will move. Nothing will be impossible for you.' Matthew 17:20, 21. You heard that before?"

He nodded, "Uh long time ago."

"We can really do stuff like that."

He began a staring contest with the road and his silence smelled thoughtful, so I enjoyed the rare starry night. The clouds had moved off. This was my first time seeing the universe through reformed eyes. Planets, stars, nebulae, all so brilliant. Then I saw a dim blinking light moving in a slow straight line. A satellite. Tonight the Neros had eyes. The weather forecast had called for this. I'd planned to get our escape underground fast, but—

"So if God wants us-ta' beat em, we'll beat em?" asked Travis.

I shrugged, "Nothing can stop the will of an infinite being. His will be done. We can ask for nothing more powerful. But don't think of it as beating them. These people are going to Hell. This is no game."

He nodded and resumed road-staring.

I'd once been like him. Without mindware's cheat-sheet answers, I'd still have been like him. The wide world's vast unknowns once buried my mind. Time had stretched out so long behind me that 500 years used to be the same as forever. Now I understood that to be just seven or eight lifetimes. A finite moment.

Yet new answers led to new questions. Death for example. The thought of dying used to scare me more than anything, but now it had become a meaningless footnote on some future calendar. Death is when the caterpillar becomes a butterfly. Death had become a paradise beach condo.

But why? Why everything? Why the universe? Why us? What events lie beyond mortal death?

So now I lived truly fearless. Even respect for Him isn't really fear because I know Him to be good . . . pure, first-class, forever-love. Even if I one-day wither under His glare, I know Him to be just. If He gives me hard times, I can trust that they're like sweet potatoes. I may not like the taste, but they give me strength.

My brain announced what my eyes had been seeing, and reality flared. Mammon's huge fence slid past my window. Tinker's escape hole zipped by, invisible except for my mindware. In about an hour, God willing, a Department of Metro Works van would ghost us away from that spot. Of course, a rental fee would be made to the department's account.

A dim glow in the trees ahead marked Mammon's guard shack, and we slowed. Travis spoke up, "They're gonna look us over, so just sit tight."

I'd already known that. e-girl had checked archives from the nearby streetlight cams. With contractors and vendors coming and going, Mammon's wide-awake security had grown sleepy.

The term guard shack fit Mammon's security building poorly. The fieldstone and PlastiWood A-frame loomed bigger than my parents' town-house. Somewhere a Swiss Alp was missing a ski lodge. A steep sod-covered ridge took the place of the fence behind the building. The driveway entered Mammon's property through a narrow gap in the ridge. The security squad flanking the road sported Lumberjack-Ken's wardrobe and G-I Joe's arsenal. The bed-'n-breakfast decor clashed hard with shoulder slung Fabrique National .308 assault rifles, which pointed oh-so-casually at us from across a chain of tire spikes. Heidi meets the Gestapo.

A how-dare-you-make-me-get-out-of-my-chair faced guard appeared in the ski-lodge's doorway.

He stepped onto my running-board, poked his head in, peeked at the carts of towels and sheets and swung back to the ground.

Strolling back to the shack, he waved at the squad. A Ken/G-I Joe yanked the chain of tire spikes out of our way.

Very sloppy.

The silky black ribbon of driveway wound through forest. Flaming gas torches spaced along the road, and flickered the woods into deep shadow. We crested a small rise and breath caught in my throat. Mammon stretched out before us. Ivy-grown fieldstone manor houses must have been designed by seven dwarves. Shrubs sculpted into knights, guarded rainbow lit fountains. Stone gargoyles scowled from the main building's eaves. The place was a marble castle. If I'd not seen blueprints showing the clinic's walls to be constructed entirely of large Picture Window panes, I'd have sworn them to have been polished stone blocks.

Curious choice of architecture. The kind of medicine practiced behind castle walls was reason enough to thank Him for having a birthday in the twenty-first century.

Three sleek genetically-altered Greyhounds glided out of the shadows to pace the truck before veering off into Mammon's grounds. I also thanked Him for the invisible fence that kept the man-made monsters off of paved areas.

The road forked, and Travis followed the branch that wound around the castle's rear. Out my side, eight pairs of fir trees trimmed to standing ovals flanked a long reflection pool. An ivy-grown brick wall cut off my view as the drive sloped down to Mammon's basement entrance.

Travis stopped at the glass and concrete service doors. The Vader truck sat shrouded in shadows a dozen meters ahead of us.

I touched the band-aid at my throat, "Serene?"

Serene answered so calm, she may as well have been working from a CV back at the mission, "Their cams are doin' da loop-de-loop. Yak when Arrow-One's ready to roll."

"Wilco, Sis." I turned my head and raised my voice, "Let's get live."

Linen flew and saints popped out.

Travis panicked, "You're usin' two-way com sets?"

"Micro versions, yeah. Communicating with BW tech would be like shooting off a flare. Kay now, she's coverin' us with a recording from a past visit—"

Wide-eyed, he cut me off, "They'll pick up your broadcast!"

I showed him my palms. "Our head unit's on a random scrambler. All they could possibly hear is one garbled syllable before our system automatically switches to another frequency. Our broadcasts are masked to look like background interference."

He relaxed and nodded.

"Now, when we're unloaded, I'll look out that window by the potted palm tree and count down to zero on my fingers. That's when you pull away. On zero, kay?"

"Gotcha." He held out a hand. "God-speed, Sandman."

He had a firm grip.

"You know you're part of the Body too, right Bro?"

His eyes took on a deeper look, like we were connected. And we were. "You're just as big a part of this as any of us. Thanks again."

"No sweat."

"His will." I hopped out.

"Forever-'n-ever," he called after me.

CHAPTER THIRTY-FOUR

MAMMON'S AUTOMATIC GLASS DOORS slid open on my approach. I double-checked my ID chip on my com-shades. If we failed to fool their CV system, we'd be done faster than a microwave egg.

Inside the doors, plush rose carpet swallowed any sound my footsteps could have made. Everything but the floor had been coated with creamy yellow latex, and smelled of antiseptic pine trees.

Just down the hall, I found the CV room's door cracked. Serene knelt on the floor before blocky chunks of CV hardware. Sweat beaded her brow. "Cooked up that recon yet?"

Her arm arced like a ballet dancer's, and a chip sailed through the air. Had I slagged the catch, the com-chip would have bounced off my breastbone. Her mind never left the Web.

I left her door cracked behind me and plugged the chip into my com-shades.

Taking the third floor would be easier than I'd expected. The only thing that surprised me was how by-the-book these guys were. Absolute vanilla.

Schlep's voice sounded in my micro-com "The Arrow's nocked." That meant both trucks sat empty, waiting to leave.

I touched my throat, "On my order," I answered.

I headed to the window that I'd pointed out to Travis, as Serene piped up "Count us down, Kid-O."

I spoke on the micro-com while flashing my finger count for Travis to see. "Three, two, one, mark." On mark, I held a balled fist in the air and Arrow-One pulled away.

I waved.

Travis waved back.

Serene said, "The Arrow's away. Outside eyes are open."

The back door cameras were back on.

Sandman time.

Gear choked the hallway, leaning against the right wall in crooked Dr. Seuss stacks. I hunted down the shoulder duffel that I'd packed for this next part, and headed for the elevator.

I threaded my way past the team to the open elevator doors, bumping fists with Movers along the way. e-girl and Tinker stood waiting. Everything now depended on my trippin' the Sandman thing. This was the part that Grandpa fretted.

No pressure.

Tinker gave me a nod. Shouldering my bag-'o-tricks, the bearded tech gave me a boost, and I wiggled through the vader car's ceiling hatch. Before climbing Tinker's nylon rope-ladder, I dropped my gum on the car's rooftop. Hearing had to be ace.

Up I went. Tinker had wedged open the third floor's doors with a foam-wrapped screwdriver. I stepped into the maintenance room. He'd already removed the duct's access grill, and it lay flat in a corner.

I had to make like a mouse for this next part.

Rummaging through the sack, I came away with a string-wrapped foam ball. My hand wriggled through a loop tied at the end of the string while I peeked up the air-shaft. The hole smelled like rotting meat—sick people's fear. I sat on the grill hole's crimped edge and leaned in.

My eyes adjusted to the gloom so completely that I could make out the galvanized frost pattern speckling the dull metal. If I leaned in the wrong place, or bumped the shaft's side, the kink of sheet metal would slag everything.

I squinted. A telltale row of zip screws poked into the duct where it fastened to a wall stud. Leaning my palms at that spot, where the stud would support my weight, I stood on the grill edge. That allowed me to peer into one of the small ducts that ran through the third floor ceiling. Six meters in, light filtered through a ceiling grill marking my target. I wished I could scan the third floor sec cams with my com-shades to make sure the Goliath still stood beneath the grill, but the BW blackout made that impossible. A hole in the foam ball gave my finger access to the EMP grenade at its center.

Triggering the five-second timer, I rolled my foam-wrapped Nero-stopper into the ceiling duct. When it reached the grill, I gave the string a soft yank, parking the grenade on the opening. I slipped the string off my wrist, eased back onto the floor, and blew out the breath I'd been holding.

I crossed to the door and eased it open.

Overdrive.

My mindware flicked out both guns and dropped me into firing position. The hall's far side consisted of a meter-high clear plexi-rail, that overlooked the first-floor waiting area. I knew about the Greyhounds, but the creature floating beyond the railing wasn't on the Field Hack's recon chip.

Some thirty meters long, it could only be described as a . . . a dragon. Its head swung slowly toward me.

My fingers curled triggers—then I saw the cables.

Blowing out lungfuls of falling-backward-in-your-chair-twigit, I slumped back into the room to sit for a moment. Adrenaline valves eased shut, and my heart's hammer slowed its banging. I considered the size of the holes my four explosive rounds would have opened in the motorized sculpture. Large, I decided.

I crept down the corridor, thick carpet swallowing every sound. The building's grounds glowed in gas-torchlight through its three story Picture Window front wall.

A hallway opened to my left. Peeking around the corner, a Goliath stood beneath the ceiling grill. Well almost stood. Its toes tilted off the floor ever so slightly and it leaned stiffly back against the wall. He'd been guarding the stairwell and main elevator before my grenade played iceberg on his Titanic. From this angle, I could see that this suit hadn't been modified to allow for the agent's escape. The Nero was trapped. What a Calamity.

After thanking Him that the battlesuit had tipped backward rather than crashing to the floor, I kept straight on, crossing the corridor. Keeping away from the plexi-rail, I hoped to stay hidden from any wandering downstairs' guards. The left wall ended in a chest-level real wood counter-top that shone so Lemon Pledge, I could see my reflection. I peeked round the corner.

A frogman sat in the nurses' station keeping an eye on the prisoners' alarms. Reaching into my bag-'o-tricks, I produced a small tube, the size of a drinking straw. Pulling both ends, it silently telescoped to nearly a meter. A special little package fit snugly into the tube, and I set that end to my lips. Swinging my blowgun around the corner, I targeted the Nero and flicked a fingernail against the counter-top. He spun the leather chair and I blew into the tube.

A thousand tranq-wet slivers hit home. The few that found the flesh around his goggles were the only ones that mattered. He fell back to doze comfortably in his chair.

That was it. Three other agents rested in the nurses' quarters until the 11:30 floor check. We had twenty-seven minutes. "Target's struck," I whispered.

With providence, we'd be in another area code when they found the empty beds.

CHAPTER THIRTY-FIVE

I RETURNED TO THE MAINTENANCE room where e-girl knelt on the floor, her hand on a CV hard drive, eyelids fluttering over white orbs.

"How's it lookin', e-girl?" I whispered.

"Leave me alone," she said in a low flat tone. "FBT put in

electric eyes, metal detectors, and weight sensors. They . . ." She trailed off and I left her to her work.

The first saint reached the top of the ladder. I helped the Healer out of the elevator shaft. "Please get back to me as soon as you know they're ready to travel, Doc."

He nodded and headed for the hall. Four Movers came up and equipment began popping out of the shaft. The pods took up most of the space. They were why we needed two trucks. Plain and gray, my guess was this is what brontosaurus eggs looked like. These were the church's tickets out of here. Once sealed, oxygen masks would allow its passenger to breathe while packed in CO_2-insulative foam. What the pods lacked in leg-room, they made up for in safety. Their safety rating ranked virtually indestructible.

e-girl gave me an all-clear on alarms, and I began opening doors to our church members' rooms. Movers brought in the pods. I found Mom and Dad. Except for being in very deep sleeps, they were fine. Even drugged, Dad wore a frown. Mom's face was relaxed and peaceful. I placed a small gift-wrapped package in her escape pod. I'd done what I could to repair the *Flashpoint* bottle.

"Well Mom, we made it with an hour to spare. Happy Birthday," I whispered. Several emotions blew their cage doors off, and my tears swelled out of control. *This is neither the time nor place.*

I thanked Him for getting us this far and stepped back into the hall, wiping my face.

"There you are!" The Healer flustered toward me.

"Here I are."

"They're not drugged!" He peered from under bushy brows as though he'd explained something to me.

I glanced back at mom's room. "Everyone I've seen . . ."

He silenced me by waving palms in the air, then tried again. "They've been placed in comas."

Not knowing what to say, I gaped at him stupidly.

"They're on intravenous drips that keep them from slipping away. If we remove the tubes, they'll die."

Someone went upside my head with a two-by-four. Blood drained from my skull and walls bent. Had my mindware not kicked-in, I'd have have fainted like a black-'n-white-movie society-lady.

"How long does a full IV last?" I muttered.

"Ten to twelve hours. But unless we can replicate the serum, when we run out of IVs, these people will die."

My brain trudged on in tunnel-vision absolute facts. Drugging prisoners was the standard operating procedure, so we were dealing with a very cautious Nero boss.

This slagged our schedule bad. Escape just became very, very difficult.

But we were in too deep to come away skunked. "I'll get the Movers rigging the pods with IVs. Let's get as much of that serum as we can find."

He backed down the hall, "Right. Look in every refrigeration unit that you can find. The stuff's gotta be kept cold. Antidote too!"

We worked like lithium-greased lightning.

Well, everyone else did. I remained one cruise control away from a drooling mope.

We came up with liters of serum, but no antidote.

The pods were prepped and loaded in fourteen minutes. I knew from our practice-runs that we'd have the pods down the elevator shaft in another twelve minutes. By the timer counting down on my com-shades, we'd have to cut some corners.

My earphone crackled, "e-girl for Kid."

"Kid," I replied.

"Get in here!" I couldn't tell if the edge on her voice had been sharpened by panic, or excitement. Adrenaline sped me to the maintenance room, and jolted the shock out of me. The small room had filled with Movers.

"Whatcha got, Sis?"

"You gotta see these gumdrops! There's files in here that go all the way back to *before* Jeff's call to the hotline!"

"Before? That's not possible."

"Here, look. This was in a *sent messages* file." She took a chip from a slot on her tool belt, and held it in the air.

I plugged it into my com-shades and read:

Father's N.S. Log

The next mark is in the Chicago Metroplex. Go to
Chicago. Await further orders.

Spirit has processed an informer.

§ Informer called FBT hotline about Ward Six home church. Take over this case. The mark is connected.

§ Spirit found head of local FBT CV security to be a Symp traitor. Bait a trap with false data planted in FBT database. The mark's Hacks will look there. Set trap site at Chicago's Sunshine Chemicals plant. Await further orders.

§ This mark is key. Make all attempts to recruit. If these fail, terminate.

§ The mark's name is Calamity Kid.

§ Informant wants to work with us. Select trap site, give him trap data, then show him a second trap site. Let him believe second trap is real. Then release him. CK will take informer.

§ Spirit shadowed their Hack support covering Sunshine utility tunnel escape.

§ Spirit shadowed CK's Hacks to the sub-Ward where their base is located. Go to Ward Three. Spirit will contact you.

§ Informer2 called FBT hotline. Find CK at shelter called Terminal.

§ CK on the move. Wait until he settles for further orders.

end of file

Someone touched my shoulder. "Hey, Calamity." It was Schlep. "The treasure's buried."

The pods were in place.

I cleared my com-shades. "Through the trash chute?"

"Yep. Triggered the compactor myself." He poked at an imaginary mid-air button. The compactor-proof pods made the dumpster think it was very full. Very full dumpsters automatically signaled Waste Management for pick-up. Mammon's contracted garbage men would remove the church for us.

We'd done it. "Then rabid-ride the blip outta here. Fade fast-'n-hard."

"The team's spider-walkin' the duct as we speak."

A glance told me that Tinker had added his own touches. A foam tube lined the exhaust shaft to silence our escape. Of course it was probably filled with itching powder.

"Everyone packin' Greyhound snacks?"

He patted a bulge at his side and plastic crinkled. "We gots Kibbles."

"Great work guys. Thanks." I offered my hand.

He slapped it away with a grin, "No, to Him be the glory." He turned his attention to the team's getaway.

My thoughts switched back to the file notes. "e-girl, this all went down 'cause someone's after *me*?"

"Kid, someone's just opened another file in here. The password for that file was just entered on a CV in the room across the hall, through that wall!" She pointed.

According to blueprints, that room was the nurses' quarters. Off duty Neros would be using that as a base.

The blueprints!

In the blueprints I remembered that room having a refrigerator.

CHAPTER THIRTY-SIX

e-GIRL'S WEB-WORKIN' MONOTONE somehow sounded excited, "Now I'm spytappin' a Nero chat. The chatters go by the names spirit and jesus. spirit says: I can't chase them. They've ghosted the web. You gotta hear this, jesus says . . ."

I knew what had to be done and moved to the door. "e-girl, listen to me now. Your chatters are the guys behind that One-State-Brussels-money-trail that you chased. Copy what you can without gettin' snagged, then fade. Tell Grandpa everything. Gotta go

Sis, 'cause I know where the antidote is." I closed the door on her reply.

We were flat-out outta' time, and nappin' the next-door Neros was all I could come up with to buy our team some escape time. That would take brain waves. Breaking the BW blackout meant a game of smear-the-queer against Mammon's security goons, with yours truly in the role of *queer*. I keyed my band-aid microphone, "Kid for vader team."

Tink answered, "Vader team."

"Time to clear the hot zone. Grab Serene and fade. Not now, yesterday. Chase the Movers to the van."

"Hey, I probably oughta' tell you, since you're in charge here an'-all, that I used my taser-net gun on a naughty no-talent security squad."

"Razz. Like we need another new twist," I said to me. How long before these guards would be missed? I keyed my mic. "Where were they supposed to . . . just forget it. Where are they now?"

"I duct taped 'em together, and left 'em in the vader. And get this: I hung an out-of-order sign on 'em. Oh, and just so you know, we're waaayy out-a-time, Scrub."

Oh, this was news. "Yeah, so go! I'm not slaggin' my tail so you two can get bagged!"

"Kay, grumpy," He sniffled like I'd hurt his feelings. "We're at the vader shaft now."

Serene added, "Kid, don't do this. Come with us."

Luke 14:10 leapt to mind, ". . . take the lowest place, so that when your host comes, he will say to you, Friend, move up to a better place."

Concern weighted her words. "Then hang tough, 'n-kick rotten oozin' Nero tails. How are you gettin' out?"

"Haven't gotten that far. I'm hopin' Scottie'll beam me up or somethin'."

"Razz. His will Calamity Kid, His will."

She couldn't have wished me any better. "On earth as it is in Heaven, now go!"

One more person to clear. "Kid for e-girl."

Silence.

"e-girl?"

More silence.

"Follow vader team, e-girl."

Nothing.

She was too good to be outta touch. I had to scare her up. "Schlep, I'm not getting a response from e-girl. You'd better turn back and . . ."

Worked like a bowl of magically delicious frosted Lucky Charms, "Yeah, yeah. I heard you. No."

Kay, my Lucky Charms were soggy. I loaded my voice with a double-dose of hey-I'm-in-charge-here, "Hey, I'm in charge here!"

"Let me put it this way. No," she explained.

"Fade!"

"I'm killing my receiver now. Nags slag ace Hack support. Bye." A soft static pop told me that she hadn't bluffed.

I'd have dragged her out myself, but my com-shades now measured the time until the next floor check in seconds. No gum for Sis.

The Field Hack's recon chip showed that floor patrols always followed the same route, so I positioned myself down the hall and around a corner, directly in their path.

Forty-two seconds later, a door latch clicked. Hushed voices discussed the new Dakota Fanning flick. Footsteps approached. There was no way of knowing how sensitive their audio pickups might be so I only let them get halfway to me before I struck.

Blowgun tranq needles peppered faces—then I blurred. I dove headfirst, like a runner going for home. My duster protected me from carpet burn as I forced myself between Neros and floor. The bad-guys made no more noise than a dead-weight pat on my back, and I kept one from thumping his noggin on the wall. I collar-dragged them to an empty room.

According to all intel, a single slimy, stinkin', Hell-bound Nero stood between the antidote and me.

I twisted the door's unlocked knob. A bitter road-tar reek soured the air around me. The room held a three-high, four-wide stackhouse, the middle four compartments fitted with Egyptian cotton sheets. A copper cappuccino machine hissed on the kitchenette's counter. Three CV workstations sported suede recliners. The middle one tilted, occupied by the last Nero. Smoke obscured the figure so completely that I couldn't even discern the Nero's gender. Upon my entrance, as though I'd triggered some device, the cloud hissed softly and thinned.

After slight seconds, a man in a dark gray Yves St. Laurent suit with shade-subtle pinstripes, rubbed his eyes. The last wisps of smoke disappearing into his ears and nostrils.

Speak of the devil.

His recliner came up and with an eerie slowness, and he turned his head toward me. Fallen angels boiled and billowed in the whites of his eyes.

Unholy-smokes. Well, you know what they say: possession is nine-tenths of the law.

Father, in the name of your dear Son, deal with the fallen angels here as you see fit. Your will be done.

The Nero frowned at first, then a creeping cruel smile warped his lips. He pulled back his jacket's left sleeve and he spoke into a shirt-cuff flip-com. As his lips moved, many voices twisted horribly into one. Lions growled deep as claws screeched chalkboards. "We have guests."

"Indeed we do." I closed the door behind me.

Seconds passed without a response, and his smile darkened, but just a shade. I enjoyed those silent seconds, knowing that there'd be no reply.

Mastering the situation, he swiveled to face me, righted the chair, and crossed his legs. His smoke clouded eyes fixed on me, which made my own begin to water. I considered offering him my com-shades, just so I didn't have to see him.

His choir-club braid of voices said, "You play our game very well, Fundi. And you smell wonderfully fresh. You found this place, hopped a load of clean sheets and dispatched with my sentries. By my estimate, the church is on its way out, and you are here to buy time for their escape." He flicked the back of his hand in the air. "Have them then. They are enjoying their last hours of life."

While considering whether his choral speech or his marbled eyeballs were more disconcerting, I answered, "Why's that?"

His fingernails demanded immediate examination, which was fine by me. I got to escape those squidly eyeballs. "I have put you in checkmate. It is time our game has ended," he said.

"Not following you. Checkmate, Mr. Nero?"

He grinned a mouthful of un-naturally perfect teeth. "As much as I like that name, you may call me Jesus Christ."

Oh. The file e-girl gave me used the names spirit, jesus and father; the man before me was part of this unholy trinity. At his blasphemy I heard the blast of blood that flushed my face. "Why would I do that?"

My outrage swelled his grin to a choir of laughter. "The man that made me has a well-developed sense of satire. Sit down. There are things that you need to know." He patted the chair next to him with a grin that dared me.

I locked onto his swirling stare and sat. "I'm not afraid of you. Nothing happens that He doesn't allow, and I don't consider you to be 'happening.'"

Moving with ballet grace, he re-crossed his legs, and rested his elbows on the arms of his chair. In the manner of a lecturing professor, he steepled his fingertips together and sucked a loud breath through his nose. "I was once so like you. Ahh, to have all the answers. I remember that warm fuzzy feel-good experience. do they still call it being ablaze for Christ, or is there a new phrase this month? You look surprised. You are more like me than you would believe. It was very comfortable to be one of His chosen ones. To be a child of God.

"Alas, my parents would not hide it under a bushel. My family was placed in Rehabs. Long ago. When it first began. For months that seemed like years, I slaved in that Hell-hole. I prayed every waking moment of every day. Except when their CV procedures tore open my mind to feed on my fairy-tale beliefs. If god were really there, could he be bested by mere technology? It was not the brainwashing that made me doubt. My prayers fell upon deaf ears. Unanswered prayer cracked my faith.

"Then I met the father. What he showed me would have shattered even the real Christ's faith."

This man had a talent for turning my face red.

He noticed, and continued with a wan smile. "As he made me, I learned how the flock is controlled. I learned how kings and presidents used the religious leash to lead ignorant masses. The Christian leash. Catholic and Orthodox churches, the Protestant churches, and now the One Church, all tools used by leaders."

Sweet mother of squirrel, he was witnessing to me. Setting me up for unholy evangelism? What an optimist. I pointed out the obvious problem with his religion-is-a-tool-of-government theory. "Then why's it a crime to be a Fundamentalist?"

He answered as though he'd expected the question. "If only Fundis would follow Romans 13. When you defy authorities that He has authorized to govern, you become, in his own opinion, dangerous."

I squeezed the arms of my chair to keep my voice level in the face of his Scripture twisting. "When illegitimate oppressors outlaw His commands, you make yourselves false gods."

"A fine example!" Excitement lit his face and he leaned forward. "Thank you! You have sounded my point. When men decide what God has commanded, their actions become Holy. When extremists come together for God's purposes, people die and governments get overthrown.

"However, If people don't know what God wants, they can't go to war for Him. The One Church teaching the Bible to be myth and legend makes Christianity safe again."

"So you paint Fundamentalists as terrorists to make people afraid of Biblical ideas?" I asked.

His choir buzzed with pride, "You sound horrified, but I consider it an inspired strategic stroke. We have used the only group standing in our way as the excuse for our complete control. The masses have no reason to challenge our power. Their free-market greed shackles them. Which is funny because we use their credit cards and mortgages to keep them enslaved. For those realizing that there is more to life than toys, we offer lies. They can burn off their good intentions with fake elections or One Church rallies.

"You see, if nothing in reality is bigger than the One State, they have nothing with which to judge the One State. Between our distractions and their fear of you, the Body of Christ's holy war is the One State's greatest game. You are merely a pawn. An excuse."

He sat back, steepling his fingertips again. "You, Calamity Kid, are the reason that I am here. I came to offer you a way out of the game. Which is more than your Bible offers. A chance to rule with kings rather than hide in holes. The Fundis' mistake is that they try to save everyone. I only want to save the best. Like you. You, Calamity Kid, have evolved an intelligence that few possess. Few can see past themselves.

"Natural Selection gifts a few wolves to lead the pack. You are one of these. A king amongst peasants. Are you open-minded enough to let Nature make you the pack's alpha male? Or will you remain a lone wolf?"

I frowned, and crossed my arms. "Not sure I'm hearing your offer. You're telling me that the FBT runs the One State, and you want me in the FBT?"

He laughed. "By Darwin, no! The FBT is nothing. I am the second most powerful person in the world. The father sent me here for you." He lowered his voices as though someone might overhear. "Our beliefs make us every bit the Fundamentalists that you terrorists are. But instead of a dusty middle-eastern God, we believe in science. The difference is, our god is real.

"We have found a way to communicate with Natural Selection. People have always thought of it as a process, but it is really an intelligence. It guides the father in ruling the One State. It has shown him how to tap into mankind's psychic abilities using BW tech. It also tells him who has evolved the farthest. That's why I came for you, Calamity—to make you a Disciple—you really are a chosen one. You are slated for special training.

"When not traveling the world on assignment, you will live in your own One State apartment-mall condo. You will help bring the human race together. Think about it. World peace. The end of hunger. Medical care. Modern homes for all people—"

"And free steak dinners every night, right? In other words, you lead some kind of global secret police who protects the One State from revolution. What if I'm too closed-minded for such a dream?"

His chin came up. "Now we come to the part where I explain my checkmate. First, I had the church infected with a disease that made them comatose. Their IVs are keeping them alive. The only thing able to revive them is the anti-serum. Which is in my possession.

"Second, someone calling himself Junkman sold the FBT some information that proved quite helpful." He looked at his watch. "By now all your workers and orphans have been taken from Terminal. It is in my power to determine their future. I can see to it that these children are put at the top of the One State's adoption listing. On the other hand, One State researchers do need human subjects for much of their testing. You must agree that it would be 'a Calamity' if they ended up at one of these labs."

He leaned forward again, locking onto me with those swirling eyes. "I had to make sure that you'd join with us. Even if you are some kind of selfless Boy Scout, the future of one hundred Fundis and children depends upon your open-mindedness. I think you will do the right thing."

He just beat out e-girl for the number-one spot on my no gum list.

By a baker's kilometer.

CHAPTER THIRTY-SEVEN

I ROSE AND HEADED TOWARD THE room's kitchenette. "You seem to like chess Mr. Nero, so I'm sure you're familiar with the old saying about games: It ain't over till it's over. We brought a doctor with us. He discovered the church's comas, and we'll be paying Mammon for the extra IVs we took to keep them alive. As you guessed, I did come here to buy time."

I swung open the refrigerator door. On the second shelf sat a small foam carton of glass vials. I slipped it into my duster's pocket. "But I also came for the antidote."

I wore no watch, but looked at my wrist as though I were checking the time. "By now the agents you sent into our Terminal ambush are sleeping peacefully, and you've lost another dozen Goliath suits. A few hundred million in BW hardware may be pocket change for the One State, but your checkmate's flatter than day-old-soda."

Absolute-zero cool, Mr. Nero didn't even blink. "Everyone has a price; we just have to find yours. My offer remains on the table. I can make you a regular Boy Scout god of this life. Your resources and freedoms will allow you to do whatever you wish. Set up homeless shelters in Calcutta, orphanages in Bangkok, clinics in all of Africa. Our geneticists will make you immortal. They can stop your aging process. Father a thousand children from the hottest genetic stock. Unless you prefer men, of course."

I held my hands up defensively. "Kay, you're scaring me now. Thanks, but I'll pass. In dealing with Sandmen you must know that we've got skills. One of these is seeing the spiritual plane. I'd bet cash to candy-canes, that this Natural Selection force your father's been chattin' up is a hot-'n-heavy rabid notoriously fallen angel. You yourself have such an infestation that if I were you? Razz, I'd chase the Ex-Terminator crisis line."

What any normal person would have taken to be alarming news, he simply ignored. I couldn't tell if he already knew, didn't believe me, or if they controlled his mind so completely that what I said didn't matter.

Instead he spoke like a parent scolding a rebellious child, "Calamity, I came to Chicago to either recruit you, or stop you. Permanently. You can make this either good for you, or very . . . terminal."

Backing into the spot on the floor that I'd already chosen for a quick escape, I smiled and opened my arms. "Gotta go, but you'll be in my prayers. God bless. My God."

He rose.

There were few reasons for him to get up and I was betting he didn't need to use the restroom.

I jumped hard enough to crush myself against the ceiling, but my blueprint showed this to be a drop-ceiling, made of brittle square tiles. Crashing through one panel, I vaulted over the wall and crashed down through another panel. I landed softly on plush hallway carpet.

I'd gone three steps when he appeared at the doorway. "How dramatic! Do you realize this is a perfectly good door?" With a feral grin, he eased toward me. "I cannot allow you to leave."

"Not asking permission." I backed away, toward the dragon-atrium end of the hall.

"Then please believe me. I hate destroying you. You are a bright, likeable young man, and a competent adversary. I beg you to reconsider. You would make quite an ally."

"No—" was all I got out.

He dipped a hand into his suit-coat, reaching under his arm like a ganger.

My mindware squealed red alert and flicked out both nines.

His .357 revolver had a barrel the size . . . well, the size of a barrel.

Our shots sounded as one. My reformed senses slowed the world, yet he struck like a lithium-greased mongoose. Where Goliaths ran bulldozer graceless, his movements cut pure sonic.

Com-shades traced red lines right to my heart. Old-fashioned lead bullets plopped to the carpet.

His suit looked like silk, then again reformulated Yves St. Laurent Kevlar is supposed to, so I opened up on his forehead. Three shots from each of my pistols hit their mark. All six fell harmlessly to the floor.

When in doubt, empty the clip, so I fired till there were only four high explosive rounds left. I'd save those for a calamity.

He stood grinning too-perfect teeth.

Guess things could get worse than Goliaths. Opening his coat even wider than his smile, he holstered the big revolver in a shoulder rig, then closed the distance between us with eager strides.

"Jumping Jehoshaphat, what are you up against?" he said, echoing my thoughts. Reaching behind his back with both arms, twin short swords slid from inverted sheaths in his suit-coat's lining. "I am prepared to do this, you know. I have tracked you down, knowing your reputation as a Jesus freak . . . with skills."

I chuckled. "Though I walk through the valley of the shadow of death, I fear no evil, for He's made me the slickest Spirit-walkin' saint in the valley. You really don't want to try me."

He replied with a smile that belonged on a skull.

Dueling in this hallway would be tighter than Delisha Lix's wardrobe, but Nasty Nero gave me little choice. I advanced to gain maneuvering room.

That wasn't the only problem though. My leap over the wall gave a slight brainwave murmur that security probably overlooked, but my targeting system was a screamer. As if that wasn't enough, the shots from Nasty Nero's un-silenced revolver had sent Mammon security engraved invitations to a bring-your-own bang-bang Fundi hunt.

I had to nap this guy and fade. Fast.

His choir voiced warning "I know your capabilities. I know your limits. I've been tried by sandmen far more seasoned than you. Yet here I stand."

We met just my side of the hall's main intersection. My mindware must have judged him off-balance because in a single motion, I drew and lunged.

He tapped my blade, sending the attack wide, and sparks bounced across carpet. With shallow lunges and cautious jabs, I took the fight to him. His swords kept defensive positions, one pointing at the ceiling, the other toward the floor. He made zero offensive moves. My skill was being measured. Amidst spitting sparks, my poking won slow centimeters.

"Your confidence amuses me most. Though you are wondering about my abilities, you have faith in your reformation. In your toys and gadgets. You have yet to know defeat. And of course, being an ambassador from Heaven, you know it all anyway. Even when you're wrong, you're right. Right?" He handled himself with such poise that his chattering seemed to come from boredom.

Amazingly, he showed no hint of strain. Chatting while dueling a reformed Sandman came as naturally to him as breathing while chewing gum that I'd not offered.

"Even now, while you fear that you have met your match, there exists the hope that you might beat me. After all, I am possessed, right?"

Now he worked to create fear and doubt, but my focus was on being where He'd placed me, and my body moved of its own accord.

I faked toward his face with my right blade, then at his belly with my left. This stuttered his grace. Weight on the balls of my feet, I lunged, thrusting low with my right sword while arcing its tip upward.

He danced away. It forced him back two full steps, past the Goliath statue and into the intersection—my greatest single gain.

He arched brows and smiled. "Hey, very nice. Lightfast must be uploading an improved combat file these days. I never did discover whose skill he'd copied for the old one, but I have never met a Sandman capable of a finesse move like that."

His extra elbow-room in the intersection made my own Goliath-crowded corridor seem even narrower. He made good use of the extra space, and my poking got me nowhere.

And still the Jabberwok jabbered "I suppose you mistake your reformation skills to be proof that He is there. If that is true, my extra-sensory-perceptions stand as equal evidence of a different power: Natural Selection."

I tried the same move as before, but this time with a triple feint. He batted it away like Barry Bonds in a Little-League game.

"All that Lightfast has done, is awakened your natural ESP

abilities. He spins it in Christianese terms and rituals in order to make it seem spiritual, but your abilities are nothing more than senses and reasoning powers." He easily foiled a series of thrusts I hoped would gain me the intersection.

I'd thought his elbow-room and the Goliath bottleneck were my big problem.

I was wrong.

He exploded into attack mode. His blitz blew fast past rabid, to hot-'n-heavy. I lost quick meters.

Then for no apparent reason he slipped back into defense only. He turned it on and off like flipping a switch. His voices continued lecturing. "The Body is nothing new of course. Throughout history, extremists have pounded the Bible to justify murder. Your Lightfast is no different than those behind the Spanish Inquisition. Torturing people until they admit to anything. Or the Crusades' land grabs in the name of God. You write the modern chapter in a long, notorious tradition. Christianity's caused more suffering than anything else in history."

The hairs at the back of my neck tingled at the old lie.

I'd almost pushed him back to the intersection when he shifted back to turbo-sonic. His ferocity and speed flowed electric. Even with my reformed eyes his swords just blurred. How my mindware kept me from being diced, I could not guess. I gave ground at such a rate, that I simply walked backward.

His urban legends had lit my heart in an anger of truth. Until now I'd stayed in the Spirit, but anger had escaped its cage. He had me in full flight anyway. Who knows, maybe I'd sidetrack him with words. I tacked thoughts together between blocks. "As long as humans are Christians . . . sin will be found in churches, but don't . . . ignore unbelievers' history . . . Hitler's Germany, eight million killed . . . Stalin's Soviet Union, fifty million . . . Chairman Mao's China, eighty million . . . godless religion sets records, Nasty Nero."

Anger's whiff rippled from him. "I said my name is Jesus!"

I don't know how he pulled off his next move. Dueling with enough fury to drive back a reformed Sandman, while debating belief systems, he somehow found the focus to scorch me.

Not some half-hearted simmer either, but a spitting deep-fry. As his combat skills buried me, so went his overload attack. He scorched me so hot that it not only knocked me backward off my feet, but blew me clear over the meter-high third-floor safety railing.

Unfortunately I didn't lose my senses, like I had in Terminal's loft. That meant I would experience every vivid detail of my one-way express trip to the ground floor waiting area. To make things more interesting, his scorch convulsed my limbs. Ace.

But someone up there liked me. I landed atop the dragon, bounced once, and skidded into one of the cables that suspended it from the ceiling.

He appeared at the railing. Through a hazy tunnel, I heard, "Drat! I could not have done that had I had tried!"

CHAPTER THIRTY-EIGHT

READY OR NOT, HERE I COME."

I had to be in shock because his words echoed.

My clever response consisted of twitching limbs wrapped around cable.

Nasty Nero hopped atop the railing and leapt to the dragon with no more effort than a child skipping from one sidewalk square to the next. His velvet landing barely swayed the sculpture. He strolled toward me with the reckless abandon of a Bureau of Motor Vehicles employee returning from break.

Like he wanted me to recover. I finally got it. My confidence in reformation had blinded me. It finally sank in: I really wasn't a challenge to him. For the first time since my reformation, panic escaped my emotional dungeon. It squeezed my throat and forced short breaths.

The Spirit purred a reminder, *Do not be afraid of those who kill the body but cannot kill the soul. Matthew 10:28.*

Easy for Him to say, but I'd give it a shot. The mindware's healing centered on my woozy head and ordered my body to stand. That didn't make it very happy, but hey, duty before convulsions. The soles of my boots changed to something soft that gave better footing.

He paused a few meters away, one foot on a dragon's spine-plate, one elbow a-knee, like a climber who'd conquered Everest. "Well, ol' Lightfast hasn't changed his history file at all. If one wants to make Fundi murderers seem okay, just stand them next to history's famous monsters, eh? Just the sort of thing I expect from you, really. If you can ignore the Bible's command to obey authorities, I suppose that your mindware can think yourself into being right all of the time."

"Bad theology is what I expect from a Nero. The One State is no more legitimate a government than were the Philistines in Judges 15:11."

"Like I said, right all the time." He closed and attacked. The cables hung even closer together than the corridor's walls, so we were still poking at each other. Sparks scattered over the dragon's blue-green scales, spilled over the beast's ribs and rained three stories down to the waiting area. His attack blurred, yet he did not close in on me.

Why didn't he finish me off? Ahh, because he wanted to talk more. He cocked his head to one side, "Tell me what you think of this. It's fairly new."

Rabid toe-curling pain stabbed my every muscle. I collapsed in a heap before him. My joints tensed and threatened immediate explosion. My spine seemed bent on tearing itself loose from the muscles holding it in place. My rib-cage jailed my organs, agonizing them with angry fingernail pinches. My shoulders, neck, and head were either frozen or aflame, I couldn't tell. I realized the shrieking sound was my own scream.

From somewhere, a mad choir spoke, "Deep inside you, my brainwaves are taking a form not unlike sound waves. These vibrations are, cell by cell, cutting you cleanly apart." I was at his mercy but he just watched me writhe.

Through the pain, my mindware explored, analyzing this new thing. Then my body plunged into a bathtub of balm. The suffering became less than paralyzing, better with each passing second.

NN leaned against a support cable. "I think now might be a good time to remind you of my offer. As a Disciple, you would work directly under me. I cannot tell you how much money you would make because there is no set dollar amount. You get whatever you want.

"Like a home. Forget the condo mall suite if you would rather have a single-family home. Choose the mansion, and your name is on the title. The manor house on my own plantation was built in the nineteenth century.

"Your fossil fuel permit guarantees that your choice of cars will grace your driveway. My Corvette Stingray-Two has the Raptor-Skin paint job and a supercharged twelve cylinder double turbo. She does zero to 100 Km/h in three seconds flat . . . unless I use the nitrous oxide, of course.

"Find a woman and she will be yours. My gentleman's club membership has an STD warranty, but if you prefer a lady off the street, we literally have the technology for love potions.

"A peacekeeper class four license clears even surface-to-air-missiles for my personal firearms collections.

"As I've said, your wage has no set dollar amount. Now, am I really so skilled at torture that you prefer to experience the agony that I'm causing to all of that?"

I peered up at the boss of the disciples from under pain's brows. My voice rattled in my throat, "His will be done, not mine." I stood.

For the first time, the masterful smile eased from Nasty Nero's face. He spoke flatly. "Looks like I have to work on this new attack. Let me try something."

Again, my back arced in agony, but already, mindware handled his renewed attack. It shielded me immediately. Fighting an all-you-can-eat case of jelly-knees, I steadied myself on a cable and stood my ground. This time his mouth hung open.

Then, from behind, something poked me. Hard.

A gunshot sounded.

I shifted footing to keep from falling.

Poke, poke.

Two more rounds almost knocked me down, and I thanked Him for Tinker's Kevlar duster.

Foomp! Something that looked like a black tennis-ball canister coated with a greenish gel attached itself to the dragon's left wing, and a whitish gas shushed out its ends. I felt my breathing filter go to work, another mindware ability.

Nasty Nero looked annoyed. "Federal agent here! Cease fire!"

Even while speaking to Mammon's security agents, he opened fire with a new vibration attack that never stuttered. What he'd called his extra-sensory-perception multi-tasked mindware like an octopus.

Nasty Nero stepped closer. "I don't trust them. The amateurs will end up shooting you in the head before I'm done with you, and that would really disappoint me."

I was busy being amazed at his selfishness when he scorched me again.

CHAPTER THIRTY-NINE

MY SENSES FAILED ME. ALL OF them. For one merciful moment, I existed in a black muted void.

I re-entered the world through a terrifically jarring body blow. My ears came back online first. Crashing glass. Adrenaline rushed reality's return, triggered by the muscle-locking sensation of falling. My grapple had fired on its own and had bonded with something solid. Its cable reeled in at high speed. Wind rippled my hair, and I smelled outdoor air. My mindware protected me from a head-on collision by using the grapple to angle my impact with whatever surface toward which I sped. Blinking hard brought my vision back online. My mistake. From only meters away, a rock wall rocketed at me. My body dealt with this information by juicing muscles with enough power to win the Kentucky Derby, horse not included. I flinched so severely that my grapple released.

DONK.

The wall wasn't rock after all, but the façade exterior of the castle's Picture Window. Somehow, neither the window, nor yours truly, shattered. My boots and gloves bonded with the glass surface. Still recovering from my rude awakening, mostly wondering how Nasty Nero had scorched me hard enough to send me through the very thick window, my body instinctively launched itself into a bug walk up the glass.

Reaching the top, I clambered over a brief rampart, fell to the gravel rooftop, and lay blinking like a beached fish. Surely the team had escaped by now. I checked my pocket, feeling the boxy package holding the antidote. I feared it would be wet with anti-dote. Nope. I hoped that meant it was surviving my beating better than I.

Time for e-girl and I to make our exit. This rescue was skunked unless we came through with the antidote. It had become a pass-fail, all or nothing performance. And for starters, I had to get off this roof!

Stupid mindware.

A steel door clanged against cinder block wall somewhere close.

Too late. If He were placing me into another duel with Nasty Nero, at least we'd have room to swing up here. The rooftop was the perfect arena for a sword fight. Temperature-conditioning units, a ventilation intake penthouse, and a few dozen exhaust vents broke up this wide-open space.

Ignoring all the evidence presented by my sensory perception about the superiority of having a nap right here on the gravel, I stood up and explored discomfort's limits. I forced my legs to get me away from the roof's edge, stashed the carton of antidote under a pipe, and texted e-girl its location.

Distancing myself from our church's only hope, I waited for him near the penthouse. The man I refused to call Jesus crunched across the gravel toward me.

"There you are!" he called in that choral voice.

His cheerful tone triggered my desire to egg his Stingray's rap-tor-skin paint job. "The devil himself."

"I understand why Natural Selection marked you for service. You are very good. As a physical specimen, you have remarkable endurance. A high threshold of pain as well. Forgive my delay, but I never dreamt that you managed to grapple to the building, yet alone climb to the roof. Perhaps Lightfast has stumbled upon something by reforming kids."

"Wrong on two counts. I'm not a kid, and it's His will I'm still around."

He ignored me, and drew his swords. I figured he wouldn't go away, even if I said pretty-please, so I drew mine. It occurred to me that before grappling to the castle wall, my mindware had first sheathed my swords. Remarkable.

I assumed my position, left arm bent back, blade over my head in a scorpion's sting, knees slightly bent. I targeted my opponent down my right shoulder, arm, and sword. Wondering how I was going to slag this guy, yet alone get away from him long enough to escape, I Spirit-walked, and left the Boss to worry about it.

Bladed fist a-hip, Nasty Nero stood his weight on one leg and hissed a long dramatic sigh. "Now where were we before you so thoroughly penetrated that Picture Window? Ahh yes, Fundi hypocrisy." He lifted his sword.

My body surprised me by leaping at him. Thought I was fresh outta leap. Lunging with my forward blade, my stinger sang through the air, slicing a shoulder-to-hip slash.

He twisted sharply, parried my blow, and countered.

I blocked, and made use of my elbowroom, returned with a wide scissors' move. We blazed the rooftop in sparks.

Nasty Nero story-time. "My favorite Fundi-bust happened during an IRS audit."

"Here we go again." Thrust.

Parry. "Had he not cheated on his taxes, the investigating team never would have been sent. They found a closet full of Bibles. Had he read even one of them, he would have known about giving unto Caesar what is Caesar's."

"A human sinner. How unique." Once again I gained slow centimeters while he enjoyed hearing himself speak. My mindware tried moves designed to get me around his side, where I'd face only one sword, but he excelled at keeping me in front of him.

"Unless one lives in a Rehab, a Fundi in the One State must live a lying life. The alternative is to sneak around and locate and join the terrorist underground. All Fundis ignore the Bible verses that address your own personal sins, but gossip about the sins of others. You are living proof. How does one love an enemy with a sword?"

"Do not suppose that I have come to bring peace to the earth. I did not come to bring peace, but a sword. Matthew 10: 34."

"Pardon-me, I forgot that you are a know-it-all. The only part of the Bible upon which every Fundi agrees, is the part where you get into Heaven. Do you people honestly think unbelievers are blind to your ugliness? Why would anyone be interested in being a Fundi?" After dropping the question he switched back to turbo-sonic.

My overdrive cranked up its own RPM. He still forced me back, but now at a crawl. I even snuck a couple counter-strokes into the blurring of blades.

"Because what you say is true." The words came from my lips, but my brain hadn't ordered them to speak. I'd walked so deeply in the Spirit so that my mindware had me speaking! "If humans could live by the rules, Christ wouldn't have had to come."

I'd retreated to a temperature conditioning unit. Slashing a reverse backhand scissors variant, I leapt a backward somersault, stuck an Olympic gymnast landing atop the unit, and struck my scorpion pose.

Three meters below, he held out his arms to stress his point. "You're a slave to this Savior of yours. Can you not see that is why your Bible is such a great tool? You all live under the idea of helpless guilt." He leapt over the unit, turning in the air to face me.

I parried eight blows as he flew past.

"Doing wrong beats you down, devils beat you down." He sprang a second dueling arc, this time sailing right over me, turning upside down at his leap's apex.

Sparks bounced off my com-shades.

"Science has explained the things for which primitive men wrote the Bible," he said.

On his third pass, I leapt with him. We dueled down to the rooftop.

"Yet a herd of losers unable to think for themselves cling to this outdated book. Since Fundis refuse to lead, you insist upon being led."

I rolled a few meters back before striking my scorpion stance. "Unquestionably . . . by Him." My lips walked the talk, and I rewarded them with a smile.

Waves of dry laughter lapped at me. "Ah, yes. The all-seeing, all-knowing, all-powerful, all-good perfect being. Your one god, who is sometimes three, protects you from all the little evil spirits that he made, and then sent to torture you. Using magic called miracles, all the nice frogs turn into princes, and live in paradise. Us *bad* people will live in a lake of fire, where we will be endlessly poked by pitchfork toting elves. Am I forgetting anything? I hope you see how some might detect a bit of fairy tale in your thinking."

His swordplay worked far better than his logic. Again, my lips moved on their own. "So pretty much the same as the Natural Selection god turning Earth into paradise?"

His mouth opened, then closed, beneath a frown. For the first time, he was at a loss for words.

I heard the rocket coming, but only had time to cover up with my duster. My senses showed it streaking straight at me. Bullet-proof, yes. Rocketproof?

Pray the Lord my soul to take.

Mindware muted my ears. Shockwave and a gravel wall blast-ed me over. The missile had detonated much too soon. In my free time I'd contemplate the mystery, 'cause right now I was about done. My eyeballs rolled, but I managed to fight them back to focus.

I struggled to my feet. Nasty Nero watched a gray saucer the size of a garbage can lid cruise toward us, hovering a hand's-breadth above the rooftop. A security drone.

It jerked a few meters straight up, then dove. It leveled-off, banked left sharp, and a fully-automatic 300 Win-Mag turret chat-tered, kicking up gravel all over the rooftop. The drone's search-light winked on and off, waving wildly in the night sky. In a final act of madness it slammed into a temperature conditioning unit.

Nasty Nero spoke into his wrist flip-com, "One more shot from you people, and rehabbing Mammon's entire security group will be my top priority." He closed his marbled eyes and pointed at the drone. The crash had rendered the drone's motor a smoking doorstop, yet the thing floated straight up before sailing off into the dark, in the direction that NN had pointed.

e-girl sounded in my ear. "Now aren't you glad I hung around? I spytapped security's communications and hacked the drone's signal immediately after launch.

I keyed my throat mic and croaked, "Could tell from its flight you had to be driving,"

She huffed quite satisfactorily. "Just thank me. You'da been crosshair toast."

"Thanks. Please get the antidote and fade."

"Got your text message. I'll get the package. Security should be— Oh! Gotta go!" Static pop.

Nasty Nero had opened his eyes and strode toward me. "Well. I'd hoped for one so young that your beliefs would be more flex-ible. I must ask, if there is so little difference between our supersti-tions, what keeps you from switching teams?"

I gathered my thoughts and spoke slowly. "Truth. Just because your faith's in what you can see and hear, that doesn't make it more reasonable than mine. You and I have very different ideas about what the universe is. Our beliefs end at very different places."

For an instant, my bones became white-hot irons.

The world went black—for a second's fraction.

I found myself on all fours.

"Quite different ends. And this is the end at which you keep arriving. It does not have to be this way,"

"So you've said," I grunted through clenched teeth.

"Since I am unable to use the filthy little urchins at Terminal, I will make sure that the next *two* hundred orphans freed from Fundi shelters will become lab rats. You are in the position to save them from such a fate. I'm guessing that your opinions are more important."

I pushed back to my feet, and adjusted my com-shades. His expression said this was impossible.

We faced each other within a sword strike's distance, yet Nasty Nero's arms hung limp. His sword tips pointed at the rooftop. Shaking his head like a disappointed dad, he raised his right sword fist in a motion improper for swordplay, so this time I was ready when he tried to scorch me.

He swatted toward me with the back of his hand. I even had time to wink before the air between us blurred. I resisted better than I'd expected, but it was like a crane lowering a bus onto a weight lifter. Although my veins pulsed, the outcome was never in doubt.

I crashed backward and clattered through gravel.

Guess my ears still worked.

He replaced his blades in suitcoat sheaths while crunching toward me.

Eyes were workin' too.

Boss, in the name of the Son, I need strength. How's NN doing this?

The Spirit surprised me with an answer. *When He arrived at the other side in the region of the Gadarenes, two demon-possessed men coming from the tombs met Him. They were so violent that no one could pass that way. Matthew 8:28 . . . One day the evil spirit answered them, "Jesus I know, and I know about Paul, but who are you?" Then the man who had the evil spirit jumped on them and overpowered them all. He gave them such a beating that they ran out of the house naked and bleed-ing. Acts 19:15,16.*

I can be really stupid at times, and this was one of 'em. That cloud back in the nurses' quarters explained so much. Like his multitasking ability. His voices.

NN took hold of the back of my collar and dragged me. The scorch had scrambled my nervous system. My arms moved when they were told to, but couldn't follow directions.

At the roof's edge, my mindware tried to over-ride muscle control. I flailed about faster than any human's ever thrashed.

He just stood back and waited.

After it had passed, he said, "Time to feed the hounds." Nasty Nero picked me up by my coat's lapels, and held me at arm's length. "What a Calamity. Here's your truth."

He chest-passed me like I was a basketball. I marveled at the upper body strength required to throw me that far.

CHAPTER FORTY

MY LIMBS STILL OUT OF ORDER, the mindware fired my grap-ple when an arm happened to be pointing in a useful direction. Even as I tumbled in mid-air, targets began blipping on my com-shades. I pitched head over heels until a grapple fired, bonded, and reeled. As it angled me into the window earlier, it now angled me at the ground four-stories below.

My shades lit-up five targets, all 50–200 meters away, and closing. Guess which sandman left his butcher scrap back in his shoulder duffel.

Time for my appointment with gravity. I bounced hard on thick turf, then sprawled like a baseball doin' a line-drive. Thank God for manicured lawns.

I kept my arms and legs wrapped around me to keep them from being torn off. Oh, NOW my muscles worked. The flinch response did the rest. Lotsa' pain, nothing broken.

Once at a stop I came up in a crouch only because I had to.

Part of a Greyhound's beauty is its streamlined design. When the first two came close, their mutations horrified me. Compared to bodies, their heads were huge, widened to contain ridiculous jaw muscles and oversized teeth. These poor creatures' necks twitched at the strain of keeping their heads up. Their forelegs had been grossly thickened to allow for claw-flexing muscles, and I sensed the damage this caused to their normal-sized paws.

Despite my pity, these two circled like wolves awaiting the rest of their pack. The wait took only moments and together they closed in.

I decided against tranq rounds, because whoever engineered the animals could have built them to be resistant. When they sprang, I leapt straight into the air with everything my legs had left. I had to get all the dogs together. The pack's huge white and tan Alpha leapt in full stride, missing my legs by only centimeters. Had his claws struck, I'd have been hauled to earth and dissected.

I winked and sent my cone-shaped scorch straight down. By the time I landed, they lay scattered across the lawn. I couldn't resist rubbing the toe of my boot against the nearest animal. Its fur came away, leaving a bald spot. I thought of Legacy and forced a laugh.

Well, I was down from the roof. I couldn't see Nasty Nero up there. He didn't seem to be the kind of guy to bet on mutts over a Sandman, so I assumed he was on his way. Which reminded me: I was awfully lonely considering the rep of Mammon's best-of-the-best security. I headed for the building's rear.

Kid to e-girl.

She responded immediately. *I've got the antidote.*

Spiff. Nice work. Question though. Why am I not surrounded by security goons?

They're all in the utility tunnels holding a few dozen Sparky Techs until the PKs can get here. Sparky's boys claim they got some kind of massive emergency call from Mammon's automated system. Funny thing though. Their Sparky badges don't seem to check out. I bet they're terrorists.

I chuckled. *Not bad at all. And I bet they can't see me on their sec cams either.*

What sec-cams?

'At's what I thought. I'm circling around back.

Who am I, Helen Keller? Leave the CV stuff to me. Now, dust this Nero or I'll leave ya' here, then she hung up on me. Freakin' sister manners.

I headed for the reflection pool outside the basement service entrance. I walked until the still glass water reflected tonight's large orange moon a-top the castle wall. I stood amidst perfect evergreens and plush lawn while crickets sang to twin moons. Awed by creation, it reminded me of Someone.

Boss in the name of your Son, I hate to be a nag but it's me again. A buncha saints need our help. If it were up to me, I'd get it to them, but for the good of us all, Your will be done. I'm fightin' the good fight, but runnin' on empty. Please stay with me. If I'm gonna fall to Nasty Nero and his legion of demons, I ask that you welcome me home. So be it.

He answered immediately. *Jesus knew their thoughts and said to them, Every kingdom divided against itself will be ruined, and every city or household divided against itself will not stand. Matthew 12:25. For our struggle is not against flesh and blood, but against the rulers, against the authorities, against the powers of this dark world and against the spiritual forces of evil in the heavenly realms. Ephesians 6:12.*

That was it! Question was, how?

Footsteps crushed in the grass behind me. That familiar shrieking-roaring-grunting chorus spoke "You are a hopeless insomniac. What a Calamity indeed." I turned to face him, just in time to see a smoke gather around his head. He bugged ugly mottled eyeballs and lit up a 300-watt predatory smile. "Your sister is here!"

"Your mother wears boxers."

"The Bible values children . . . but you ignore even that part of your holy book."

The harsh whine of a powerful electric motor spoiled the setting, and made him pause. A Waste Management truck strained away from the service entrance. It carried a dumpster. He waited patiently for quiet to return while joy bounced around my emotional dungeon. They were out.

Ask and it shall be given.

Thanks, Boss! Joy juiced the last of my adrenaline and I got my fourth wind.

When the crickets drowned out the truck's motor, NN resumed his thought. "If the idea of lab rat orphans fails to sway you, burning holes in your Hack sister might do the trick."

"Sounds like you've got a millstone round your neck."

"Every time a terrorist survives another round, I repeat my offer. This is it. e-girl's last chance, Fundi brother."

I wasn't sure if he'd be able to hear my thought speech, but I had to try. *And they call us terrorists.*

He jerked and gave me a frown.

Time to try something beyond my *Peacekeeper* experience. *So, you can hear this. Good, because I want to show you something.*

Like changing channels, my senses switched from the material to the spirit plane. The first thing that struck me was his size. Immense. My com-shades measured him at three-hundred-thirty meters across, and rising some thirty-five meters at his center. His . . . well, his body, defied reason. A hideously twisted mass of tentacles, talons and limbs tangled together with sinew and membrane. Two large tentacles ensnared the most fantastic swords I'd ever seen. Engraved with strange symbols all down hot-orange blades, three gilded spokes formed their hand guards. Each guard ended in a dagger for slash-punching when locked with a foe. Braided silver wire wrapped their hilts, and the pommel ended in claws clutching large red gemstones. They hung poised to strike.

Razz. I'd been dueling demons armed with . . . those.

Let's do it, Boss. I knew this might kill me, but in faith's service, I opened my being to this doomed man, and prepared something like a mind-fax. Hoping that I'd properly understood the Spirit's remarks, I sent a replication of my spirit half.

My message rose in the form of a crackling blue electric softball. Parts of me, ideas, thoughts, beliefs, sparked across its surface. The idea that all men are glorious, but twisted: that a human being is greatest when attending to others: that loving your enemies isn't fuzzy silliness, but caring for them as humans in the face of their hatred: that evil and hate are not opposites of good and love, but corruptions of them.

The ball floated toward him like a fat firefly. Boneless limbs seized the package, and stuffed it deep into his center.

A great shudder ran through his bulk. An inhuman moan turned to a shriek which blew light-years past human hearing. The stench of tar grew so thick that I gagged and retched before I could offline my sense of smell. Pieces of darkness shot away, howling black smears smoking from a greasy cannon.

When darkness' fireworks had finished, a small pale mousy thing lay before me, trembling.

My eyes blurred back to the material world. I fell across the grass. My com-shades flashed the word "exhaustion," and jellied legs couldn't support my body. Without a few moments to compose myself, all I had were my four high explosive rounds. All I could do was sit and watch him finish me.

The horrible shriek had crossed into the material plane, and I caught its echo fading off Mammon's walls.

The man I refused to call Jesus looked . . . afraid. He failed to keep panic from his voice. His own single human voice. "How? What . . . What did you do!"

I could have talked trash. Instead, I replied soft. "I let you know real love. You took it into yourself. It drove out your fallen angels."

Squinting at me, his head bobbed. He smelled of concentration. He was trying to attack me. A shallow empty sigh hissed and his shoulders drooped in defeat.

My com-shades cleared. I struggled to my feet and drew my swords.

"Let's wrap this."

Looking around, then to himself, his gaze fell upon his own swords. He let them tumble from open hands as though they were meaningless. Fumbling inside his suit-coat, he found the revolver. His eyes took on a lunatic gleam.

That triggered the flinch response, and my arm shielded my head.

It turned out to be a waste of energy. He planted all six shots in the sod around me. After he was empty, his pistol's hammer kept clicking.

I pointed a blade to his swords on the lawn. "Pick them up and show me your big finish."

Wide eyed, he shook his head, trying to clear it.

"This is the part where you put me out of my misery, right? So let's go." He glared like I'd run a shopping cart into his fancy Corvette. "You little punk. You find a way to cripple my ESP abilities and then demand a duel? Your sportsmanship . . ." He posed like a courtroom attorney in righteous spin.

I cut him off like a hangin' judge, "Present arms or I bat you into the center of that pool." I closed on him.

CHAPTER FORTY-ONE

YOU'LL NEVER DO IT," SAID NASTY Nero. He turned to walk away.

The flat of my blade scorched the seat of his trousers, and NN splashed down dead center in the reflection pool, spoiling the mirror image moon. He drifted face down in the silvery water.

I picked up a quiet hum from my left. My com-shades pegged the hum as a 2028 Ducatti Requiem. The motorcycle was Grandpa's idea. He arranged for a Symp to leave it in Mammon's lot earlier in the day. "Just in case," he'd said. e-girl ignored the keep-off-the-grass signs, and stopped the bike in front of me. "Wow. You look all rode-hard-'n-put-up-wet."

"Not as wet as him." I eyed NN's impression of an air mattress. "Oh, just a minute."

I rolled my eyes, sighed exasperation, and stepped into the shallow pool. "If Nasty Nero drowns, guess where he goes."

e-girl giggled at his nickname.

Wishing my pants were made of smart material that could become waders, I slogged out to the middle of the pool. I fished out the waterlogged mope and hung him over the edge to drip dry.

"Awww, da bad ow' puddy tat awww wet," said e-girl as I mounted up.

"That's good, but I'm too tired to even laugh. Home, Sis."

The old Requiem had both electric and bio-fuel power plants. Its running lights disabled, e-girl hummed the electric motor down the drive by torchlight until we sighted the guardhouse.

"They know we're comin'? Never mind, I see 'em." I zoomed in my vision. "I count eight sec-men lying prone in firing positions."

"What?"

"I'll take care of them. You just worry 'bout drivin' this thing."

"You worry 'bout hangin' on," she warned.

"You've had your license one whole month and you've never driven a bike. I'm very worried about hanging on."

Thumbing a button on her left handgrip, she switched to bio-fuel, and 900 CCs of roar shredded the darkness.

I flicked out a pistol, loaded a fresh clip, and grabbed the panic strap. Our velocity screamed; wind blurred my targeting system.

It took me five shots to nap three of the sec-men on the ridge. Armed with shotguns and SMGs, they'd been waiting for a closer shot before firing. It tends to spoil your aim, however, when the guy next to you slouches with a forehead welt. I put a high explosive round right and left of the drive just to discourage any overachievers.

The bike's roar easily covered my spitting pistol, and my com-shades had us at 80 meters away, so it was unthinkable for them that the shots came from us. Being the safety-minded employees that they were, they fled for cover.

"Don't forget about the tire spikes!" I yelled into the wind.

At the last second, e-girl left the drive and powered up the grassy ridge.

I white-knuckled the panic strap as we flew longer than anything without wings had any airborne business. Empty moonlit road stretched out below like a runway.

I screamed like a little girl.

CHAPTER FORTY-TWO

I FELT ALL RECHARGED. I OPENED my eyes, stretched, and smiled at the beige plastic of my mission stackhouse ceiling.

I remember holding on to e-girl, wondering if she was *trying* to break every Illinois traffic law, or if it was just that new driver thing. We shot down Lower Wacker, the concrete underground half of Chicago's famous double-decker street, home to the homeless. This was in the escape plan. It got us away from sky-cams. On one side of the street flowed a mass of thick brown sludge known as the Chicago River. On the other lay basement entrances

to highrises. At some point we parked the Requiem, and handed the keys to a man slumped next to a three-wheeled shopping
cart.

I remember e-girl leading me through downtown's escalators
and moving sidewalk tubes. I'd mapped this route to lose us in
pedestrian traffic, with the Body Surfers running hack support
on street cams, but my mindware hibernated on me. Last thing
I remembered was climbing into the back of a delivery van and
passing out.

I reached all-the-way-awake and realized something was
wrong with the back of my right hand. A CV chip had been taped
there. I found my com-shades on a ledge near my feet and lay
back, loading the chip.

It started with a text file:

```
Bro,

    We  did  it!  Lightfast  delivered  the
    antidote  and  says  everyone  woke  up!
    He uploaded everyone's mindware before
    coming  back  here.  Can't  wait  to  see
    Mom-'n-Dad with gold eyes!

    I just chased the web for Legacy. Still
    nothing.

    Grandpa needs me, hold on . . .

    He  just  had  me  transfer  three  million
    to a Mammon account to cover damages.
    He says the Body always cleans up after
    itself.  Like  they  need  that.  With  all
    the Webwire time they're nettin', their
    stock's up 6%!

    I just finished a Disciple/ evil-Trinity
    mindware file to be spread throughout the
    Body. I chatted with FairFax too. While
    we  were  away,  she  crashed  the  hardware
    that spirit was using to shadow us in
    the Web. He's offline for awhile. And,
```

```
hold  on  to  something  before  reading
further, she said you do good work!

Also, I got some news off the Terrorist
Webwire. Scan this drama:
```

e-girl's text faded out, and Delisha Lix's pretty pout filled my vision.

"As you all know the new Kid on the block got away. HOW-EV-ER . . ." She closed her baby blues and smiled a big comfortable sigh. ". . . Calamity Kid's as solved as yesterday's crossword."

"Double up that price tag. You heard right, two days after his subsidized scalp was first tagged, Kid's made the FBT-top-ten-list!" She super-pouted her bottom lip, batted sad-eyes, and went baby-talk, "At 20 miw-yin dowers dis punk's mo wanted dan I yam!

"NOW, my grandmother used to say that calamity is the test of a brave mind. So don't go short bus on me people. The One State don't just hand out ritz. This kid's earned his price tag. He's slick as oil and burns twice as hot, so call the hotline and let the FBT choke his grease fire." Sitting on a CV workstation's desktop, Delisha crossed her long legs, pulled out a compact, and checked her makeup.

The e-strump faded and e-girl's text popped up:

```
Nice  to  know  you're  wanted,  huh Bro?
Well a girl's gotta sleep sometime ya
know?
Night.
```

```
end of file
```

Between good work, good sleep, and good news, I felt great.

My com-shades said I'd slept for 21 hours and 53 minutes.

I slid out of my bunk. Somebody needed to check in on Terminal, and I had to find out when we could see Mom-'n-Dad. I shrugged into my duster as the stackhouse door opened. My back was to the door, but my senses told me a small crowd of people were there.

Then I caught a whiff of *Flashpoint*.

I froze.

"I thought a Sandman would have'ta be bigger!"

It was Dad's voice.

Reaching into the foot of my bunk, I grabbed the only things I kept there. The family Bible and picture frame.

I never even tried to lock cell doors when my soul's dungeon went rabid.

A Sample from . . .

WAR OF ATTRITION:
BOOK TWO OF THE UNDERGROUND

Frank Creed

A Lost Genre Guild Book

The Writers' Café Press

PART ONE: WAR OF ATTRITION

at·tri·tion (ə-trĭsh'ən) *n.*
1.   A rubbing away or wearing down by friction.
2.   A gradual diminution in number or strength because of constant stress.
3.   A gradual, natural reduction in membership or personnel, as through retirement, resignation, or death.
4.   Repentance for sin motivated by fear of punishment rather than by love of God.

An alarm sounded but only I could hear it. I pictured myself shattering an antique alarm clock with a twenty-pound sledge. The brain-wave reader-chip in my com-shades got the idea, and the speakers mounted on their earpieces stopped chirping.

Sleeping propped-up in a concrete basement's doorless closet had me all fresh-'n-frosty. I raised my head from crossed arms and neck muscles cried no-fair. I cracked one red-eye. The heads-up display projected 5:57 p.m. on my com-shades lenses. *Augh.* Not even close to thirty winks. Getting dressed-up on Sunday mornings was so much easier than underground life.

With a thought I called-up feeds from the six micro-cams I'd planted on my way into this century-old, four-story cobwebbed corpse of a building that woulda looked better in a 9-11 rubble heap than standing upright. Even the homeless considered this place too dangerous.

I rolled my neck and blinked at images of gutter-punks closing on my position. If these were the best Ward Three's Capone could send into my trap, the crime lords were either Christmas-cashier-busy or permanent-welfare-lazy. I consoled myself with the fact that pulling a good ambush ranked on my favorites' list—right between napping peacekeepers and finding my own time for sleep. *Good ambush* is a pretty relative term. A bad ambush would be micro-cam footage of me walking that long-hall with feeds playin' across Neros' com-shades lenses.

After an hour's squatting in this concrete-basement-closet-corner-shadow, my Kevlar duster wore a web cocoon. Web strands tickled my face. I removed the com-shades, waved my arms around then rubbed my face and head. More spiders lurked within arms-reach than inside my grandma's garage and back-yard storage-shed combined.

Man, I feel like slag. I never thought one could awake feeling this way with re-formed mindware. *Gotta get caught-up on sleep.*

Big-red-bold-italic flashing numbers. My com-shades took the liberty of rating my get-up-'n-go at a sickly sixty-seven percent.

Yeah, Thanks.

They sensed the sarcasm on my brainwaves and the display faded.

I slothed around to lie on my side so my head peeked from the closet, and I waited. Shadow cast my doorless closet in a shade of midnight, while the room's far-end featured a string of 60 watt bulbs hung from a long stretch of cable tray that had once been hidden by drop-ceiling tiles. It ran the length of the basement's main hall and extended through the distant well-lit doorways. For some reason most bulbs were burned or missing. Only the convenient spots were lit. What an ambush coincidence.

My reformed senses kicked-in and I noted twelve different shoe-scuffs belonging to six separate individuals, all of whom were doing a really bad job of sneaking between this room's doorways. Their clothing bulged in the most dangerous places: hip-pockets, and waistbands. After they'd passed, I grunted to my hands and knees and shook my head hard to inspire a little more get-up-'n-go.

Their footfalls faded down the hall. I ordered the Smart-Soles of my boots into a soft powdery surface and haunted after the six gunslinging gangers. The seven of us moved down the short end of the hallway toward organ sounds of a Biblical Fundamentalist wedding.

I, however, knew the *wedding* to be mere noise, piping from a remote speaker sitting on a tore-up card-table that I'd left in a bare concrete room at the hall's end. The digitally recorded decoy rang absolutely blissful.

A few weeks ago the Terrorist Webwire reported that Ward Three's crime-boss, Alphonse Virago, had rounded up eight Fundamentalists from corners of the our Lost Ward, and handed them over to the Office of Homeland Security. So that you understand the hugeness of this event and appreciate Virago's lithium-grease moves, images of grey-haired-gangers-in-suits shaking hands with One State peacekeepers and Federal Bureau of Terrorism agents *still* accounted for half of the breaking-news links on the Terrorist Webwire. Chicagoans are quite used to mixing politics and organized-crime. It's the local definition of *government.* But Virago's method was historically slick on a much bigger scale.

This was the first-time-ever that any North American governmental body *officially* recognized a criminal organization as a law-keeping force. You got it—Virago's goons had been deputized to clean house in our Lost Ward. The Capone army advanced atomic-clock steady. At the rate they swallowed whole blocks of Chicago's Ward Three, Mission would be overrun in days. Our base was wedged so deep underground that the temperature stayed root-cellar steady. Al Capone's *real* vault would be unearthed before they'd find Mission. I saw this as an opportunity.

So here I slunk. Instead of Teflon Capone foot-soldiers, a handful of dirt gutter-punks blundered the passage ahead of me, and now peered into the dead-end rectangle speaker-room. The com-shades said I paused five-point-three meters behind them.

"What the slag?" said the short one.

"You gotta' be razzin' me" said the ugly one.

They dropped their sorry attempt at stealth and entered the speaker-room, the same room where my new partner, Barren, lay a-top a narrow air duct just over the remote speaker. Have I mentioned that I love pulling ambushes?

I moved to lean against the doorway and crossed my arms. These guys still had no idea I was behind them. Were they mice, this would have been the cheese-moment when the steel spring-loaded arm snapped down.

They addled up to tore-up card-table. After uttering expletives involving unmarried mothers and a variety of animal species, they dove into the finer points of investigating a mystery.

"This some kinda freakin' joke?" said the clever one.

"Dat's a remote speaker," said the less-than-clever one.

"*Duh!*" said the ugly one.

"So now whadda we do?" said the clever one.

"I dunno," said I.

Should'a been there. One by one, expressions of hey-wait-just-a-freakin'-minute-here warped their faces. They looked around. The clever one actually looked up. The fact that he missed Barren lying on that narrow duct says more than I ever could.

Finally it settled on them all that the stranger-in-the-door must have been the source of the unfamiliar voice. I kept a straight face only by biting the inside of my cheeks. Hard.

"Beat it, *scrub!*" ordered the clever one.

"Um—no," I replied, cocking my head and hipping hands inside my open duster.

Any Lost-Ward resident with the IQ of a sewer-rat would recognize my posture as easy access to a concealed weapon, and my position blocked the room's only exit. I'd keep that to myself though. Didn't need sewer rats goin'-all Geico Caveman on me and filing a class action defamation suit.

The Crud Crew looked at each other, then hauled-out more non-lethal weapons than bowling shoes have colors.

Gangers without lethals? The Capones were taking this peacekeeper-wannabe thing a little too seriously.

Being twenty years-old, full-grown, and a full head shorter than your average male, I'm accustomed to this degree of disrespect. That Grandma with all the spiders used to say, "The size of the dog in the fight doesn't matter. The important thing is the size of the fight in the dog." When people learn that I am the notorious-FBT-multi-million-dollar-price-tag-wearin' Calamity Kid, that kind'a rep can be handy. But these guys weren't exactly your typical Terrorist-Webwire demographic. We'd have'ta play this out the fun way.

With gangers' attention on me, Barren dropped to the floor, right behind them. I coughed as he hit the ground. He was *supposed* to be my surprise cross-fire cover, but using surprise on this crud-crew would have been like shelling nuts with the Jaws-of-Life.

Only Ugly had heard my partner's landing. He made the capital BAD of swinging an elbow.

Barren slapped it down and pepper-sprayed Ugly's face, then touched two more Cruddies with each of his Electrocutioner shock gloves. They went down like cheap carpet.

The remaining three spun and gaped at their downed friends. Two on three left us *mathematically* outnumbered, but Barren just put-down half their crew faster than you could say *sewer rat*.

The cruddies puffed-up to look intimidating, but their shade-of-pale screamed terror.

I waited for Ugly pepper-boy to quit his shrieking before I spoke. "Razz, I told'ja to just shoot these guys. Even if they're smart enough to know anything, they're not gonna be spillin' goods to us *sandmen*!"

The three standing gangers all spoke at once. I chinned my right collarbone and peered from under I'm-a-waitin' brows. They felt my threat and shushed. Barren just shrugged his extra-large flannel-over-T-shirt shoulders. He's not a tall man but his arms and dead-eye expression just fume intimidation. The Cruddies were so busy eyeing myself, Barren, and pepper-weepin' Ugly, they nearly tripped over their shock-gloved friends who lay moaning softly on the floor. The three edged into a corner. As they moved the clever one spoke, "We don't want no trouble, we're . . ."

I cut him with a word, "Any."

Clever's eyes wandered thoughtfully.

I explained. "You don't want *any* trouble. Which is pretty hard to believe considering you came here with pockets full of trouble." I stepped toward their corner. "Wanna try using the tazer-net gun trouble in your hands, and see what happens to you?" Thought I'd keep him rattled and see what shook out.

Clever dropped his gun and showed his hands' palms.

"Look, we work for Virago. Junkman's a vapor and Lost Ward Three's up for grabs. We're stakin' Virago's claim." He locked stares with Barren and slowly extracted a flip-com from his T-shirt pocket, and flicked it open. "So 'less y'all wanna' see what Virago's bad side looks like . . ." He hovered a thumb over the auto-connect key, left the threat to hang, and pointed at the door.

I first met my new partner only days ago, but Barren's rep had run explosive through the underground, and a few word-of-mouths had even echoed through Ward Three. Barren and the Kid—clear the sidewalks. We were nitro-glycerin—extremely un-stable whether shaken *or* stirred.

Very quietly Barren said, "Oh, I think we're just-now dea-lin' with Virago's baddest side."

Clever turned red and thumbed auto-connect.

Barren snapped both arms straight-out toward the ganger. Quick-Draw holsters popped two IMI 9mm Desert Eagles with built-in flash-suppressor-silencers down the wide sleeves of his flannel-shirt, and into his waiting hands. Soft thumps sounded and three tranq rounds took clever-boy high in his forehead. He fell like a tree-farm evergreen in late November, and his head *donked* against the concrete floor. I winced. Tranq rounds are with reformulated box-jellyfish toxin, and instantly affect the nervous system. Even one round is a guaranteed migraine—this poor kid needed a fist-full of Excedrin.

The last two standing gangers panicked, and raised tazer-dart pistols.

Barren went *thump-thump*.

Gutterpunk tazers clattered across dusty cement and gang-ers sprawled boneless. Barren's Baby Eagles vanished back up his sleeves before his targets had even kissed concrete.

The pair who'd been informally introduced to Barren's Elec-trocutioners began to stir, and tears had mostly cleared Ugly's eyes of pepper-juice. I turned off the wedding-bait speaker but turned-up the tough-guy song-'n-dance. "Shoot the other three and were done."

"No, Wait!" cried the short one, rising to his knees.

"Don't wait, Barren, shoot."

Through Shorty's eyes I watched survival's instinct tweak his brain-matter into action, perhaps for the first time ever. By the frenzied pace with which he rose and moved toward me, I realized that Shorty really was in fear of his life. He beckoned Barren closer, removed a pair of earplug microphones, dropped them on the floor and ground them under his heel. He whispered, "We're wired. Backup's on the way."

"And you'd rather play hostage than feed worms?" growled Barren.

I switched my com-shades back to the micro-cam feeds and watched four men wearing designer suits on cameras one and two. Here came the respect we deserved.

"From your sleeve-guns I'm guessin' you guys are Fundi terrorists?" asked Shorty.

The kinda people who once called African-Americans the N word now called Fundamentalist Christians, Fundis. "I'm sorry? What kind'a terrorists?" I prompted.

Realization tweaked his eyes fearfully wide. "Hey, I didn't mean to insult. You religious people . . ."

Barren's tone lost its threat, and he helped Shorty with a genuine smile. "We're just Christians. It ain't a dirty word."

Shorty nodded stress. "Got it. Sorry. Let me live and I'll wise-you-up to tonight's bust on a Lost Ward Three Fund . . . Christian-run orphanage."

Mindware kept my face poker by clamping-down on panic's cage in my emotional dungeon. There was only one orphanage in Ward Three. Terminal was also a homeless shelter. Terminal's security was my job.

The suits reached cam-three. I counted five of them.

I nodded at Barren and took a step toward Shorty. "What's your name?"

"Shorty."

I coughed once. My jaws clenched and my breathing steadied. It was a lot like swallowing a big air bubble. "I did think a Capone would be bigger. Talk about this orphanage, and talk fast." I keyed my hearing to *record*.

"It use'ta be a dance-club called Terminal, and a Capone called 'Junkman' ran biz outta the second floor. The raid's at ten tonight. Lots of us will be around the place . . ."

"Who's *us*?"

"Virago's men. But we're not workin' the raid, we're just perimeter guard. Virago's bringin' in a special team."

"Ace kid, thanks. Your backup's here. We gotta move."

Then I spoke loud and pointed at the conscious gangers. "You three, drag these nappin' speed-bumps into the next room."

When I said *nappin'*, pale flickered across Shorty's face. He just realized we were never a danger, but now he was in-it.

I thought-speeched Barren. *You see the cams?*

Yep.

We'll face 'em in the next room and fall back here if we need retreat space.

Copy that.

We followed the gangers as they dragged their tranqed buddies back into my cobwebbed-closet room.

Shorty struggled last with his load and I walked with him. "Don't believe everything you see on the Com Vision kid, sandmen only use tranq rounds. We're not enemies, and I know you're just survivin' in this Hell-hole as best ya can."

"Hey. What if someone wanted to join your gang?"

"We'll need to talk, but I gotta couple things to take care of first. Can you look me up at Terminal late tonight?"

"Naw, busy. How 'bout three or four tomorrow afternoon?"

"Sounds au-ight."

He gave me a crooked grin and a nod, but fear never left his eyes. This kid was a beaten dog. I helped him drag his napped friend into the room. "Now pile 'em in front of the far door and just stand there," I ordered.

The suits squeezed into the room, knotting just behind the barrier of bodies. Each Capone held an Arazzi nine millimeter machine-pistol.

A dark haired man in an olive topcoat smiled hard, "We're here for da weddin'."

You wanna play? Fine, let's play. "Friends of the bride or groom?"

Squint-creases deepened around his eyes. "We're da ushers."

"Look more like pallbearers to me," Barren mumbled.

A redhead in a tan overcoat glowered at the gangers before him. "Dat works, 'cause we'll be buryin' our dead and gutless. But all Fundis are under citizen's arrest."

I'd expected better than the gangers, and these guys were it: well-dressed egos disguised as humans. But even the best Capone hitters wouldn't brave this. Facing down a pair of sandmen with nothing more than mere firearms for confidence, was either cross-eyed stupid or askin' to wake-up with a tranq-headache. Something was off, so I went fishing. "Our feelings were hurt when we thought that these," I gestured at our speed-bumps, "were the best Virago could offer. Glad to see we rate the *special* team."

"Don't flatter yourselves. We got bored," answered a grim-voiced Capone with a suit so navy that it looked black.

These fish weren't biting.

I thought-speeched Barren. *Naw, something's wrong here. These guys are too relaxed. There's gotta be a reason for their confidence and that worries me.*

Don't ask me, you're the strategy expert.

"So it's jus you two?" asked Navy-Suit. "Dis won't take long." He smirked.

Long as they felt chatty, I'd play this out. I smirked back. "We make up in quality what we lack in quantity."

Before I'd finished speaking, Olive-Topcoat roared at the three gutter-punks "Attack!"

Yeah, right. Round-eyed gangers looked ready to wet themselves.

"Scram, guys," I suggested.

Gangers rushed past their Capone backups, who were too busy covering Barren and I to point their Arazzis anywhere else.

"Well, it *woulda* been eight on two, but," I nodded at the hundred-meter dash deserters, "even *they're* smart enough to know that's bad odds."

"Dose guys missed tird-grade math," answered Navy-suit as he pulled plastic zip-straps from a jacket pocket and stepped carefully over the speed-bumps. "Le'sse how you guys come along. Dead or alive."

"So, Virago's now declarin' war on Liberator?" I asked.

Their licked lips, shared glances, and raised brows told me two things. They weren't positive that Barren and I were members of the Body of Christ, and they thought we might be working for a different Capone. One who, according to our own planted rumors, ran Ward Three. Liberator was our code-name for God.

"You sayin' dat Liberator ordered a trap for Fundi weddin' crashers?" asked Olive-topcoat.

Barren, this has been real, but we now know all we're gonna get out of these guys. Time to get LARGE.

Copy that.

I'll take the three who've spoken, you've got the two silent-types.

Game on.

I spread my hands. "Liberator just wants a little love, so how 'bout you go mind Virago's business? Thanks for stoppin' by. Nice talkin' to ya."

Didn't give 'em a chance to even think. My mindware hit overdrive mode. I let my body do its own re-formed walkin'-in-the-Spirit thing. Fast as thought and not in control, I leapt straight up and pushed sideways off of the cable tray with both legs. Overdrive meant I was moving at least five times quicker than normal humans. My senses told me I was the normal one, and the Capones had slipped into slow-motion. My Quick-Draw sleeve-holsters palmed my twin Baby-Eagles. Mindware's targeting-system meshed my muscular and nervous systems. The targets I called marked on my com-shades.

In the second's fraction that it took, Barren's two pistols had fired seven rounds: four tranqs and three steel-tipped. Arrazis clattered across concrete, their hair triggers spraying a few random rounds.

Look for

WAR OF ATTRITION:
Book Two of THE UNDERGROUND

In bookstores May 2008
For Advance Orders visit www.thewriterscafe.com

Want to keep up-to-date with
THE UNDERGROUND
Go to Frank Creed's website and sign up for
THE UNDERGROUND newsletter:
new release information
articles, artwork, fan fiction, contests and more
www.frankcreed.com

WAR of ATTRITION:
Book Two of THE UNDERGROUND
Frank Creed
ISBN: 978-1-934284-06-3
300 pg; paperback; May 2008
The Writers' Café Press
Indiana

Chicago: 2036

The one-world government has outlawed
belief in the Word of God.

You have the choice between
Godless patriotism and
living your faith underground.

The Body of Christ saints living in the underground
take you in and reform your fallen body
in line with your soul:

stronger
faster
senses of a predator

But—the agape-code only allows use of
non-lethal weapons.

Are you up for it?

Take a street name, get your body and soul re-formed,
survive against peacekeepers, gangers,
fallen angels and One-State agents
like FLASHPOINT's Disciples.

Ours is a spiritual battle so love your enemy
in the darkest of times, and walk in the spirit.

This is your only advantage.

FLASHPOINT:
the RPG

a "game" of
evangelism and discipleship

Windwalker is sure to be a hit. Its elements of romance and jeopardy will charm enthusiasts of fantasy, romance and adventure. It's an enjoyable, enticing read that will want you to pick up the next Sundblad novel. —*D K Gaston, author*

The beauty of this story is its very human humility. You'll enjoy this read, and the prophetic "Tellings" of the Windwalkers. —*Frank Creed, author and reviewer*

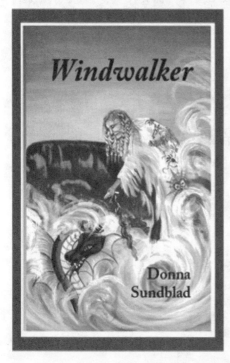

Hundreds of years ago, the Stygian race welcomed diseased riddled Jonnick to their shores despite prophetic warnings. Concealed powers of darkness disembark with the refugees.

Manelin, a social outcast, and Jalil, a lame Jonnick girl find themselves thrust into the midst of unfolding ancient prophecies and a world on the verge of annihilation.

$14.99 print–$5.00 ebook
Publisher: epress-online
Publication Date: September 2006
ISBN: 0977222489
Available at epress-online's bookstore www.epress-online.com

INFINITE SPACE
INFINITE GOD

Karina & Robert Fabian, Editors

Infinite Space Infinite God

EPPIE
2007
Winner

Karina and Robert Fabian, Editors

SF collection
$18.95 trade paperback
ISBN 1-933353-62-7
available August 2007
from
Twilight Times Books
http://twilighttimesbooks.com/

"...an excellent collection of science fiction short stories. These authors' imaginations are astounding, pulling me into each and every story from the first paragraph... The characters come alive in vivid detail making each story's uniqueness stand on their own merit. Highly recommended, not only to devoted sci-fi readers, but to those who have never read the genre before." ~ *Reviewed by PJ for Scottieluvr's "Chewing the Bone" reviews.*

Come explore the worlds of "Infinite Space, Infinite God." Meet genetically engineered chimeras and aliens who wonder what a human religion holds for them. Share the doubts, trials and triumphs of humans who find their journeys in time and space are also journeys in faith.

Experience spine-tingling adventure. Marvel at technological miracles—and miracles that transcend technology—and meet the writers who made a leap of faith and dared to incorporate familiar religion with fantastic universes.

Copies can be ordered through your favorite bookstore, Baker & Taylor, Ingram, or the publisher, Twilight Times Books, P. O. Box 3340, Kingsport, TN 37664.

"It was Allen's sister Clarice who found the
genie that turned the Mad Scientists
into superheroes."

League of Superheroes
Stephen L. Rice
ISBN 978-1-934284-05-6
Late Spring 2008

The
Writers' Café Press
Indiana

A
LOST GENRE GUILD
BOOK

A Novel by Stephen Rice

Four teenage boys and one little sister
discover someone in a chat room
who claims to be a little girl named Genie,
but whose scientific knowledge and technology
are a few centuries ahead of anyone else.

Who or what is Genie?

The most intelligent mortal in history—an
integral part of the most powerful force
mankind has ever unleashed.

And she does not consider herself subject
to the laws of God.

Born in Chicago, Frank Creed now resides in Indiana with his wife Cyn, writing partner Mavis A. and six other "masters" (cat owners know what this is all about!). Although FLASHPOINT: Book One of the UNDERGROUND is his debut novel, Frank has had a novella and several short stories published in anthologies and ezines. Visit www.frankcreed.com to learn more about Mr. Creed and the UNDERGROUND.

Frank is founder of the Lost Genre Guild, an organization of Christian artists whose mission is to increase the visibility of Biblical speculative fiction and glorify Him as they do so. Visit www.lostgenreguild.com for more information.

Date Due
